One Indian Summer

Books by Wayne Curtis

Currents in the Stream
One Indian Summer

One Indian Summer
a novel

Wayne Curtis

GOOSE LANE

©Wayne Curtis, 1994.
No part of this publication may be reproduced, stored in a retrieval system or transmitted, in any form or by any means, without the prior written permission of the publisher or, in case of photocopying or other reprographic copying, a licence from the Canadian Reprography Collective.

Originally published by Wild East Publishing, 1993, ISBN 0-9694147-5-7. This edition published by Goose Lane Editions with the assistance of the New Brunswick Department of Municipalities, Culture and Housing, and the Canada Council, 1994.

The author thanks the following people for their support and input while writing this book: Sheree Anderson, Phil Cassidy, Winston Curtis, Fred Cogswell, Blain Gillis, Jill Hovey, Rebecca Leaman, Jack Manderville, Clarence and Gail McKibbon, Alistair MacLeod, David Adams Richards, Doug Underhill, Evelyn Weller and Maggie.

The characters in this book are fictitious and a product of the author's imagination. Any similarity to those living or dead is purely coincidental.

Edited by Margaret McLeod.
Book design by Joe Blades.
Cover photograph by Eric Bagnell.
Guide pin illustration by Brad Morrison.
Printed and bound in Canada by Kromar Priting, Winnipeg.
10 9 8 7 6 5 4 3 2

Canadian Cataloguing in Publication Data

Curtis, Wayne, 1945-

    One Indian Summer
    ISBN 0-86492-151-9

I. Title.

PS8555.U77O64 1994   C813'.54   C94-950132-8
PR9199.3.C87O64 1994

Goose Lane Editions
469 King Street
Fredericton, New Brunswick
Canada E3B 1E5

Acknowledgements

Portions of this novel have been published in *The Cormorant, Eastern Woods & Waters, The Maritime Sportsman, Miramichi Leader,* and in the book, *Currents in the Stream: Miramichi People and Places,* Goose Lane Editions, © Copyright 1988 Wayne Curtis.

"Bouquet of Roses" Words and music by Steve Nelson and Bob Hilliard
© Copyright 1948 by Hill & Range Songs, Inc.
Copyright renewed. Assigned to Chappell & Co. (Intersong Music, Publisher) and Better-Half Music Co. for the U.S.A. only.
All rights outside the U.S.A. controlled by Chappell & Co.
International copyright secured. All rights reserved.

"The Green Door" by Marvin Moore and Bob Davie
© Copyright 1956 Alley Music Corp. and Trio Music Co., Inc. Copyright renewed.
Used by permission. All rights reserved.

"Indian Summer" written by Wilfred Campbell.

"The Waste Land" written by T.S. Eliot
from *Collected Poems, 1909-1962*
© Copyright 1963 T.S. Eliot.
Used by permission of Gilles Delamore,
Faber and Faber Limited, London, England.

"Why Don't You Love Me" written by Hank Williams, Sr.
© Copyright 1950, renewed 1977.
Acuff-Rose Music, Inc.
All rights reserved.

No part of this publication may be reproduced, sorted in a retrieval system or transmitted, in any form or by any means, without the prior written permission of the publisher or, in the case of photocopying or other reprographic copying, a licence from the Canadian Reprography Collective (CAN©OPY), 214 King Street West, Suite 312, Toronto, ON M5H 3S6. Ph (416) 971-5633.

For John and Brycie

CHAPTER 1

"It's that ol' St. Patrick kickin' up a storm," Tom says, looking out the window. "He's waited 'til All Fool's Day to drop a bundle on us."

Snow and ice pellets drift in wavering sheets across the fields and frozen river. They cling to tree branches and the shingles of the buildings around the dooryard. The burdened trees snap with a twist of the wind and power lines drop, leaving the community in darkness. The blizzard goes on for days and we strain within ourselves, waiting relentlessly for the wind to dim and the snowing to stop, until we have a newfound strength of endurance. We press our faces to the frosted window, breathing small melting circles, glimpsing a different landscape each time, each more barren and desolate than the last. The fields become a frozen ocean: long winding snakes of snow twist over the waves of drift, adding blue pockets and crystal peaks. Only a charcoal abbreviation of shrubbery is visible in the swamp, a single strand of pasture fence across the flat.

"It's the line gales come with it," Katie says. "The sun's crossed the lines."

Katie sits in the rocking chair, one of Tom's sweaters thrown over her knees to cover her feet. She knits hurriedly, even forcefully, an uneasiness in her strained face. Her grey-streaked hair is up in a net, and beneath the spectacles her eyes are the same faded grey. On her dress she wears a brooch, a brass spider with blue eyes, and above her on the wall is a plate with a map and letters that read "Come to P.E.I."

There is no school and Danny's Grade Four reader, *Up, Up and Away*, has not been opened through the storm. Instead, he stays upstairs by the warm smoke pipe reading my comic books: *Matt Dillon*, *Ringo Kid*, and *Kid Colt Outlaw*. Danny looks like a young Kid Colt, skinny with blond hair combed in a wave, his cap gun in a holster on his hip.

"Oh, dear God, it's an awful night, surely to the Lord!" Katie exclaims, putting a stick in the stove. "Steve, get dressed and bring in the night's wood so your father won't have to."

"Okay, just as soon as I finish this chapter," I say. It's my correspondence course, this month's lesson. "Eustacia's got Wildeve under her spell now."

"And bring in some blocks for the furnacette."

"Put the damned ol' book away fer a spell," Tom says. "You'll ruin yer eyes readin' in the dim that way."

When the woodboxes are full, I go upstairs to my room. Here, only twilight and storm cast a dull grey light through sheer curtains. I look at myself in the bureau's mirror and shave awkwardly in cold soapy water with Tom's safety razor. Then I wet my hair and comb it forward and then back, like Tom's, and finally I part it on the side. God, I need a haircut. I put on the new spring shirt and the Cuban-heel boots that make me one inch taller, and lie down on the bed. Blocking out the storm, I remember Cindy Long from last summer. I can almost smell the water and sand on her curved body after she comes out of the swimming hole to lie beside me on the grass. A vision of Cindy and spring. I take off the new shirt and boots, muss up my hair, and go downstairs.

Tom sits by the furnacette, asleep in his rocking chair. He sleeps upright like a tired old workhorse, his big square hands resting on the arms of the rocker. I think that his thin grey hair and stubbled beard add years to the weathered face that must have looked much like mine once. He snores and his mouth drops open. Waking, he looks around the room, his piercing eyes squinting beneath the bushy eyebrows.

The kettle simmers on the polished stove, the clock ticks loud in the silence. Tom's thirty-thirty Winchester hangs on a nail behind the stove, with his long belt with the guide pins. The grey felt hat with orange feathers in its band hangs on the door.

Before dark, he gets dressed and snowshoes out to the barn to feed the animals. Katie watches at the window, edgy in his absence. When he returns, he stomps snow on the kitchen floor.

"She's an ol' nor'east son-of-a-whore," he says, brushing himself off with the broom. "A bad night for fires." We all listen to the logs shifting in the stove and check the stovepipe's warmth with the back of a hand. The wind forces a draft that moves like an invisible blade around the kitchen door, and the lamplight flickers across the brown wallpaper. Katie puts Tom's wool coat against the bottom of the door and shoves a knife through the jamb to hold it secure.

After dark we go to the window and look out for chimney sparks. Only the apple tree is visible, a frozen corpse in the dooryard, its arms white against the night. Further off in the storm, the buildings huddle around the dooryard, creaking and snapping in the cold the way river ice settles and snaps before a storm. Hydro lines hum and we huddle in our beds, our breaths clouds of vapour. I throw Tom's old army coat over the blankets and sleep, but not soundly.

The following midday, the sun breaks through the dark clouds like a blinding lamp. The dooryard is white frosting, its layers furrowed into drifts by the knife of the wind. We dress and venture outside, cautious as mice released from a box trap. There are a few stinging pellets of hail in the wind as we shovel battlefield trenches to the woodshed and barn.

CHAPTER 2

"Heavy ice," Tom says. "She could go tonight as well as not if the water keeps on raisin'." He turns his back on the river and talks to us over his shoulder while he urinates into the rotting snow. "I hope there ain't much damage done."

Yellow water covers the ice; the shores are open, black. The river looks to me like a giant snake, twisting between the hills, waiting to erupt in anger and shed its cover at any minute.

"Boy, oh boy," Danny says, "I hope it goes today. Once the ice is gone, it's really spring then."

Raindrops cling to the stunted cedar on the river bank. The tall juniper sway, dropping showers on the dirty snow. Insects crawl beneath the trees — sap flies. There is a scent of woodsmoke that mixes with the sour dampness.

"Boys, I tell ya, one spring she jammed in here on the flat. What a mess."

"Way up here?"

"Oh hell, yes, right where we're standin'. Took out every bridge on the Jesus river. What a son-of-a-whore-of-a-jam that was."

"How long ago was that?" I ask.

"Now let me think. It was twenty years ago, before the war. Around '35, I guess it was. I had logs piled here on the bank and the ice took 'em. Lost everything that year. A whole winter's cuttin' down the goddam river."

Tom turns and faces the river once more, lights his pipe with a wooden match scraped on the seam of his wool pants, cups the flame in his palms and draws it into the bowl. Grey hair on the back of his hands covers the freckled veins. He puts his thumb over the pipe bowl and puffs, talking now without taking his eyes off the river.

"Boy! I can't wait 'til it starts," Danny says in his high young voice. "I hope it goes before dark so we can see it." He makes snowballs with his bare pink hands and hurls them out onto the ice.

A wooden bench sits upright on the ice near the shore: bench, ashes and a coil of rusted wire. I think of a January night and the game of hockey, two-on-a-side, boots for goal markers. It seems like years ago already. Back then, the ice was a playground and the communities facing each other across it were one. Now, it's a different ice, angry and suffering, worn thin by the currents. The horse and sled tracks on the ice have moved so that the road up the hill and the one on the river are separate. The manured sled tracks on the ice are like a railway switched toward open water. There is no way across except for the cable bridge down below the next farm.

Unlike the rain that comes in winter and brings a cold dampness, this has warmth, and a light hollowness that makes thin sounds echo beyond where we can see. We reassure ourselves that this is not a winter's thaw. We check for spring signs. The shingles on the south side of the shed are blackened with rain. We listen for crows hollering, higher pitched than the raven. We check the willows and find tiny rabbit paws of hope, white along the black stems. And there are tunnels from the manure-stained brooks that zigzag beneath the pathway. Visible beneath the ponds on the flat is spongy grass: dirty blond hair waving under glass. The yellow stubble that emerges on the flat is a contrast to the baring furrows on the plowed land and while the snow remains deep in the woods, the swamp shows visible kinks of alder like the claws of ravens. We watch the signs strengthen with each warm day.

Tom coughs and clears his throat with a long deep snort, spitting into the snow. "Yessir, boys, a long cold son-of-a-whore," he murmurs.

Down on the highway, a car grinds past, its fender rattling. It splashes muddy water over decaying snowbanks. I can see Cindy Long, who is walking, stepping off to the side to let the car pass. She lives across the river and has crossed the wire bridge. She turns in our driveway up ahead and goes into the house.

A dark cloud blows low over the tree tops and the rain drifts slanting across the shabby fields and river. The large drops are cool against our faces as they hammer like kernels of grain upon the steel roof of the barn. We're getting soaked through, but we don't hurry. Getting wet in the April shower is a small price to pay for spring, a pleasant discomfort.

Tom begins to sing. Catching the words in his shaky voice, he murmurs bits and pieces of his favourite song. Some of the words are shrill, others are lost altogether in the slump of a footstep or a cough from his tobacco smoke. It's like someone singing in his sleep. "Ka-ka-ka-Katie, beautiful . . . You're the only one that I aaddooorrrhhh . . ."

Danny and I poke along behind, quiet. The song brings our three souls together, I think. As we reach the dooryard, Cindy slips out of the house and when Danny sees her he lifts his thin chest and joins Tom in the song. "I'll be waitin' at the ka-ka-ka-kitchen doooorrrhh . . ." They go into the house, singing.

Cindy's blonde ponytail spills over the short winter jacket that doesn't cover her tight blue jeans. She smiles when she speaks, her forehead furrowing. "So how's it lookin', anyway, the ice?" she asks.

"Oh, it's all open at the shores," I say. "Tom thinks it could go today if the rain keeps up."

"Let's go down, Stevie. I wanna see it," she says. But she has just come across the bridge. I say nothing and nod okay.

One Indian Summer

We walk over the plowed field toward the river. Culverts bubble and chuckle beneath the pathway as flooding swamp brooks boil yellow in deep brown ponds that flood our footsteps. We're balancing each other around ponds, and she clings to my jacket to keep her balance. Nearer the river, Cindy slows, losing interest in the ice.

"D'you have any tobacco?" she asks. "I'd give anything for a smoke."

"I have two tailor-mades," I say, "hidden there in the millshed."

We walk in that direction. I'm taking short steps, packing them firmly so she can follow in my tracks. Edges of furrows are now showing through the hail and we make greasy footprints, slumping through in places, tracking mud onto the snow.

The day is all soft and fresh with dampness. It is the kind of dampness that you can smell and taste everywhere. My jeans are clinging wet, my wool coat is steaming from the rain, and I'm uncomfortably sweaty beneath it.

The old millshed haunts the upriver corner of the plowed field. Black and rain-soaked, it has a forlorn magic around it that pulls me in if I am anywhere near. I lift the latch and the sagging door falls open. A gust of wind against the shed lashes us gently forward. Inside it is dark, the only light from the empty windows and the wide horizontal cracks. There is a strong musty smell of cat urine, old clothes and wet sawdust floor. Two cats scamper out past us, moaning and snarling as they run. We sit on an old car seat and light the cigarettes.

Cindy has her eyes closed, enjoying the smoke, not talking. I ease myself back beside her, stretching my legs upward to reach an old metal trunk. I inhale the smoke, holding it deep in my chest before blowing it toward the wavering rows of rusted nails that splinter the board roof. My secret from the family; I am sharing it with Cindy. It gives me a feeling of independence. I relax, enjoying each dizzy puff to the fullest, watching the grey smoke curl upward in streams. Cindy unfolds beside me, her eyes still closed. She has a pretty dimpled face, one which I haven't really looked at much before. She used to have freckles. I can smell something sweet and fresh in her hair. She's become very attractive, I think.

"Steve, gimme a kiss," she says without opening her eyes.

The smoke catches in my throat. "Huh?" Her eyelashes flicker. One pale hand moves toward me across the old vinyl seat.

"I wanna kiss. Kiss me?"

I kiss her cheek, then drag roughly on my dying cigarette and grind it out on the damp sawdust floor.

"No, a real kiss," she says. This time she turns her head, and I kiss her on the lips. "Gimme a hug," she says.

I put my arm around her, I kiss her again, and we're holding each other tightly, her leg draping over me as if she suddenly can't get close enough. Beneath the open jacket, her snug red sweater has lifted from her jeans; I ease my hand under it and touch her smooth back. She presses down now with hot kisses and my cold fingers work stiffly on the alien hooks of her bra.

"I never done this before," Cindy whispers. "Stevie, you gotta stop it." But she wriggles closer with more of those kisses, her bra opens beneath the sweater. All I can hear is our breathing. My hands move down her back, down to the small waist of her jeans. "This feels so good, Stevie, you make me feel so good."

"Cindy, you're beautiful," I stammer.

"Oh, Stevie, Stevie, stop it. You're so bad."

Are either of us listening to our own words? "I've been thinking about you," I say. "I'm glad you're here."

"D'you always do this with your girlfriends?"

"Just the special ones."

"You're sweet, Stevie, very special." Cindy's hands tighten across my shoulders. "I really like you a lot."

"You do?"

"Oh yes, I like you so much."

Suddenly from behind the shed there is a hollow crack like the sound of a rifle, then a rumble that makes the millshed tremble the way a siding house is jarred by a passing train.

"Ha whooo, hu hu," someone far across the river whoops. A voice on this side echoes, louder, "Ha whooo, hu hu!" The world is deafening; churning, crashing, cracking. I pull away from Cindy and look out the window. Tom and Danny are half-running, half-slumping across the field to the river.

The ice is running.

"Oh, my God, I gotta go! I gotta get across! The bridge might go!" Cindy scrambles to her feet and pulls at her clothes. We hurry out the back way, and Cindy hurtles over the field to the highway.

The ice has broken into wide zigzags across the river. As I watch, the water is piling thick chunks into house-high heaps. Above, in the bend, it has broken up in smaller ice slabs upending and bucking, dirty water spilling ahead of the jam. Heavy triangles crowd the banks, scraping the bark from trees and lodging high in the bushes. The constant rumble is like a summer night's storm, like Niagara Falls.

"Stand back!" Tom shouts a warning. "Stand well back. She's a wild ol' bitch today, boys."

A tall spruce snaps beneath a sliding cake of ice and falls full length into the jam, leaving a splintered stump in front of us. Tom's eyes sparkle with excitement. He clenches his fists and shouts as though the angry river is challenging a new kind of spirit in his old body. "Lord God Almighty, what a jam! God be praised!"

Danny and I stand safely back on the hillside above the bank, drawn close together by the crash and thunder of the river. Danny points to things adrift in the current, a few boards scattered on the ice. "Look! Look, there, it's an old shack goin'," he says. "Lookit out there!"

"Boys, there goes Harrison's Road," Tom says, the tension leaving him now. "Poor ol' Maggie grounded now agin fer the summer. Good God." He sighs and turns toward the house, the excitement ended.

As the ice breaks up, it moves along more freely, more quickly. And behind the jam there's black water.

"Look up there," Danny points. "It's all open."

We leave the river. In our minds the ice has gone, though the floes will be running for days. Tom has already made his way up the hill, and I think I can hear him playing "Katie" on his homemade flute. Danny and I follow, glancing back at the open river as we walk.

Cindy waves to us from the other side; with her brother, Nick, she'd climbing the hill to their house.

In the evening, the rain stops and the clouds scatter and drift away, letting the sun cast a sudden warmth against the far shore and its hillside. The breeze carries a false scent of summer as it catches the new water, making patches that sparkle like jewels. In the dooryard I can hear the tiny jingle of the wind chimes, little glass birds hanging behind a web of Virginia Creeper. And beneath the hill, in the alder swamp, the season's first robin begins to warble and chirp above the sounds of the freshet.

CHAPTER 3

The Easter lily on the table bows its head as the organ music filters from the radio. "What a Friend We Have in Jesus." Katie's favourite hymn. Tom and Katie sit quietly, gathering in every word. Tom has his necktie neat over his flannel shirt; Katie's in her black Sunday dress. A roasting chicken sends savoury odours from the kitchen. On the dining room table there are purple Easter eggs in a bowl, and lime juice in a glass pitcher. The radio preacher speaks in a slow positive manner, and there is coughing in his congregation. Tom has trouble hearing so he moves nearer the radio and cups his hand behind his ear. The volume is turned up so it can be heard outside, where the dooryard is tranquil in the sun, its dead grass raked in heaps. Tom nods his head, approving the preacher. He stares out through the window. The outbuildings around the yard have a Sunday air, solemn but friendly. The old apple tree becomes the tree in the Garden of Eden, the hydro poles along the road are crosses, the animals huddling by the barn are Noah's own. Even the broad river that laps restlessly in the cold breeze is from the Bible: the River of Jordan. We stay by the radio until the service is over. It's part of the Sunday.

The past days have smelled of new oil cloth, whitewash, and wallpaper paste, as Katie did her housecleaning. We have made long ribbons from the wallpaper ends and tossed them about the house. We have listened from the yard for the sounds of motor boats and hurried to the river to watch them pass. We have collected eggs from nests of straw and crayoned them in deep purples and blues. Our spring jackets have come from the Eaton's catalogue order, and new green fishing lines from the five-and-dime in town.

Nobody has crossed the bridge since the freshet, the river having risen into the spans. Danny and I have gone down to watch it tossing and slapping in the water. Even from our beds we hear the water churning and the bridge squeaking drearily in the night. We pray for its survival. There is always more to do on the other side of the river, I think. The water has dropped slowly so that the bridge is hanging free again. Grey cribwork piers on each bank hold the cables that have stretched lopsided, and the page wire railings are a blanket of dead grass and sticks, ragged and brown just inches above the water. The snow has gone from the fields but there is still plenty left in the woods.

"That's a cold bastard of a day," Tom announced when he came in from the barn in the early morning. "That upriver wind can ruin a whole spring. If it blows on Good Friday and Easter Sunday, she'll blow that way now for forty days, mark my words."

We are too much into spring to listen, Danny and I, and as restless as young animals. After dinner, we get dressed in winter coats to go to the river. Tom comes with us to see if the logs are running. We wave at passing motor boats and watch them fish on the other side. We are not allowed to fish on Sunday.

"I must go over and see Howard," I say. "Visit and watch them fish. Just watch."

"What's that?" Tom swings his eyes from the river to my face. "Yer goin' ta visit?"

"Yes, to see Howard. Watch him fish."

"Better not cross 'er, lad. She's not safe. Keep off 'er 'til it's fixed. And it's Sunday, Easter Sunday. Ya know what happened at Moose River."

"But they're crossing it all the time."

"I don't care. It's dangerous. It'll throw ya in the river, that upriver wind blowin' that way."

Tom goes back to the house and I walk down along the bank to the bridge. It sways in the wind like an empty hammock. Across the river, in the warm dead grass, chunks of grey ice melt near the bank. The houses seem bright and warm, each with its own weathered shed that contains a few scraps of winter wood and the winter's garbage. The big open river has set the farms farther away, I think, yearning. Fringed with forest, they are a Grandma Moses painting and their grey wood fences bask softly in the sun.

From a grove near the opposite abutment, a line of smoke rises between the trees. There are voices and the sounds of a tapping hammer. Howard's board boat lies belly-up on the grass. He and Nick move about it, hammering at its caulking. I gaze across, my need to be there growing. With Howard, there are always good times. He quit school four years ago, in Grade Seven; he's got some experiences to share. He knows about boats, fish, and women.

"Better not cross 'er, lad." I climb the abutment steps, Tom's words playing again in my mind. His voice has been my law; but the spring sun is bright and the wind is fitful, and I'm not a kid any more, and our Sunday silence doesn't seem to touch the far shore. I know the bridge's strength; I have watched it struggle in the high water.

It sways now, the grass-filled page wire tossing with the icy breeze, and the brown water rolls below, lapping the lower strands. I walk slowly, holding tightly to the furled top cables, trying to keep my eyes on the opposite shore. The lure of the river draws my attention; with a glance at the water inches below, the writhing bridge seems to move upstream. I look up again quickly, freeze to the railings, close my eyes for a moment to get my balance. As the abutment nears, the spans tighten and the bridge becomes strong.

Across! I sag against the railing and shift my strained eyes to the solid ground. The dizziness clears. The wind pushes me now, flapping my jacket, and brings tears. From this side, the hills look larger, the flat broader, the houses less quaint. It is a different landscape, colder than its distant illusion. I can see the smoke low across the flat and smell hot tar, so I hurry up the shore.

Howard and Nick are huddled in a gully in the shelter of a large pile of driftwood. They are using the hood of an old car for a fire box, and it looks like a half canoe, fire snapping in the bow end. A pail of tar bubbles above the blaze, suspended on a green alder branch. The long boat lies on the grass, its corduroy bottom bleached, and Howard pounds caulking into the cracks with a stick and hammer. Nick carries to the fire.

"Ya made 'er across did ya?" Howard wipes his face on his sleeve, concentrating on his work. "I wouldn't a crossed 'er today. Not in that wind and all the grass hangin' in the wire."

"It wasn't too bad, really."

"It'd be too bad if a tree or a cake of ice came down an' tipped 'er over with ya out there."

"I could see up the river, nothing was coming." I want to forget the bridge. I busy myself and become one of them, stirring the tar. Behind us, two ravens cry and cackle in the elm skeletons. They chase each other low over the brown field and mate in the trees beyond. The sun goes into a sudden cloud.

"The only way I could get up the nerve ta cross that bridge on a day like this and it lopsided," Howard muses, "is if Amanda Reid was on the other side in a bikini, beck'nin' me ta come across. Then, by Jesus, I'd cross 'er, if I hadda get down and crawl." Howard saw Amanda Reid once in a restaurant in town. He talks about her like he knows her.

"An' what if ya made 'er across? What could ya do?" leers Nick.

"Oh, I'd find some way ta entertain 'er. We'd think a somethin'." He speaks still without looking up from his hammering. "How 'bout you, Steve?"

"I'd run away with her tomorrow."

"Ah, she wouldn't go with you anyway, lads," Howard says. "One like that, she needs a man, not no boy."

The clouds blow low and a slanted upriver squall bounces hailstones off the boat. They lodge in the grass and hop on the pathway, and hiss in the river like coarse salt sifting into a water barrel. The fields fade to grey and then whiten, the dead grass bending beneath the weight of ice, looking like sugar over Shredded Wheat. Nearby, the wire bridge rattles and squeaks, its grassy railings blowing ragged. Smoke drifts in circles, eyes sting. For a while it is a winter's day, a blizzard. It stops as suddenly as it came.

"Yessir, boys, Amanda Reid, the prettiest thing on the river," Howard goes on. "What'd a man give, though, just ta have 'er fer a night!" And he launches into tuneless song: "Horny in the mornin', horny in the evenin', horny at suppertime, Come an' be my baby, I'm horny all the time."

He ends his song with a whoop and leaps on top of the boat, dancing, clumsy and awkward, staggering on one foot like a circus bear. He whoops and laughs, looking at the sky and pulling his cap down into place above his ears, tilting its peak upward.

This is a good day for Howard. He doesn't get out much and so he enjoys our company. He swears more than normal, acting. Since he quit school, he's been cutting pulpwood with his father, Charlie. But he has not changed for as long as I can remember. He wears the same loose gum rubbers, soiled grey coat, and a peaked cap with his dirty blonde hair curling out below it. He still walks with a nod, grinning and squinting, homely, with beaver teeth.

Now he sits down on one end of the boat and gazes across the water, strangely innocent, wiping his nose on his sleeve, grinning at the river, talking almost to himself. "Sex machine, that Reid girl. She'll be takin' more men than the Mounties 'fore she's done. But Steve, a man should be married, though, shouldn't he?"

"Yes, I suppose so."

"But ya know, boys, she'd make a good wife fer some lad, some lucky bastard." He takes the pack of Player's tobacco from his shirt pocket, rolls himself a smoke, and passes the makings to Nick. We each roll a cigarette and huddle together in the wind, sharing a match. I spit out the loose strands of tobacco. It tastes sharp and hot.

"Jesus, what I'd give though, ta be able to see like you lads in the dark," Howard says suddenly. "I'd give anything, d'ya know that, Steve?"

Howard is night-blind. He never goes anywhere after dark without Charlie and a lantern — to the post office, or the store. Sometimes he goes to the barn alone, always with the lantern, to feed the horses. He's never been to a dance.

When I am with Howard alone, we are best friends. When there are three of us, when Nick is here, I'm his second-best friend. They're from the same side of the river. But this isn't important today. Today we are equal. We share Howard's tobacco, fishing rod, and work.

Howard pours the bucket of hot tar over the boat and quickly paints it with a short-handled mop. The rank tar sticks between our fingers; sometimes it burns our faces, spattering in the wind and stinging our eyes. The tar smell is strong enough to taste.

"That's good 'nuff, boys," Howard says. "Piss on 'er." He throws the mop into the trees and stomps over to the fire, rolling a cigarette with one hand and spitting the ends into the blaze. He stands there, warming his red fingers, then kicks the tar pail into the trees, grinning, the dry cigarette sticking to his moist lower lip.

The boat gleams, its new coat steaming against the quick breeze. Nick and I take turns with the fishing rod, waiting for the tar to dry. There are no fish.

Suddenly Howard picks up one side of the boat and flops it over. He spins it, end to the river. We rush to lay poles on the ground for it to roll on before grabbing the gunwales to push. Afloat, it sways with the breeze for one long promising moment; then kidney-shaped pools form on the bottom, and within seconds it's covered, the water seeping in from everywhere. Howard throws up his hands, paces the shore, swearing magnificently as his boat fills.

"Bollocks!" he yells. "She's leakin' like a fuckin' basket! Haul, boys, haul 'er out quick, 'fore she sinks on us!"

We lean on the rope, bracing our feet into the slippery shore and putting our weight against the boat in short tugs until it is moored on the skids. Much of the soft tar has scraped off on the grass and the poles. We prop the boat upright against some bushes and shelter behind it from the wind. The fire smoulders. Howard fishes.

In the distance we see a fan of spray, a grey motorboat coming at top speed around the bend with its bow sitting high above the water. As it nears, we can make out the peaked caps and gold badges of three men sitting straight as Russian soldiers. The fish wardens. Howard flips the rod into the bushes as the boat swings to our side of the river. We stand and smile and wave, and the wardens look us over and lift their hands in perfunctory greeting, passing close to the shore without slowing. The swells from their boat wash in the grass and muddy the water's edge.

When they've passed, Howard sticks up his finger and shouts: "Go it, ya sons-a-whores — like ta' take me rod, wouldn't ya!" Nick and I stand and give them the finger, too, as they disappear.

"It's no use," Howard complains. "It's no use in fishin' now. Not with a big motorboat goin' through the hole like that."

This is a good day. I expected no more. But Tom's words about the bridge come again and again to haunt me through the afternoon, and an edge of guilt takes something away from my day. Howard's jokes become boring, and at times I fake a laugh to please him. I'd go home, but the wind's still too strong to risk the bridge.

"Just takin' a little walk up the shore," I say.

"What? Don't like our company?"

"No, no —"

"Wanna 'nother smoke, Steve?"

"Later, when I get back," I call over my shoulder.

The wind muffles the sounds of distant motorboats that buzz at intervals like houseflies caught in a hanger. Water laps the shore. Away from the fire, there is a more obvious smell of river, the wind-dried fields and the budding willows. Cindy's house, up ahead, makes me think of what happened in the millshed, the day the ice went out. I haven't seen her since: the high water and the damaged bridge, no way across the river. In the millshed, her bold warmth filled an emptiness in me, yet Cindy was the one pleading to be touched, to be loved. Maybe she's more honest with herself than I am.

I climb the hill to her house.

The Longs live in a grey-shingled old place with a barn and a few smaller sheds around it. In front are a couple of giant elms. The water pump is on a small platform in the back year, where a board-walk runs to the woodshed. I rap on the kitchen door, and two voices call me in to the warm, food-smelling kitchen.

"Oh, it's little Steve, is it, from over the river? Grown up sa much I wouldn't know ya!" Cindy's mother greets me. She is tall and skinny, pale, with wire-framed glasses and several chins.

"Happy Easter," I say.

"I'm an awful sight. I shoulda put on a clean dress, Easter an' all."

"Oh, Mom, it's only Steve," Cindy says. "Ya don't mind Steven Moar."

I sit on a cot behind the stove. Several cats stretch around me, and there are coats and wool socks strung up to dry. Mrs. Long washes dishes; Cindy dries, and I watch her. Her jeans are too short and too tight in the waist, the top button undone. When she reaches for the top shelves of the cupboard, her ankles and lower legs are bared. Her small bare feet are black on the bottom.

"Now tell us all the news from over the river," Mrs. Long says.

"There isn't any news. High water this year, wasn't it?"

"Have they fixed the bridge?"

"No."

Cindy's father, Will, comes in from the barn, smelling of cows and carrying a half pail of milk which he sets on the kitchen table. He nods to me and goes into the parlour.

"D'you have a girlfriend yet, Steve?" asks Mrs. Long.

"No."

"There's a lady here who can't seem ta find a lad, either."

"Mom, I told ya I don't wanna boyfriend," Cindy says, blushing.

"I'd better get back and help with the boat," I say. "We're tarring the boat today, down at Charlie's shore."

"Oh, good time, good time," Mrs. Long laughs. "What's yer hurry?"

"I have to get back over. Get home for supper. They'll be wondering where I've got to."

"Cindy, why don't ya sing yer piece fer Steve, 'fore he goes? Steve, you'd like ta hear her sing, wouldn't ya?"

"Ya wanna hear me sing?" asks Cindy. "Can ya stay fer a song?"

"Sure."

I drop back down on the cot and Cindy picks up her guitar from the corner. She sits beside me, close, and starts to strum "Your Cheatin' Heart," like on the radio. But she doesn't play well, and her voice strains for the notes. It's almost embarrassing to listen. They don't seem to notice.

I cover up with a compliment when the song ends, and Cindy and her mother both seem pleased.

On the shore, I find Howard and Nick have dragged the old car hood to the water's edge. They have piled its fire with dry sticks that burn freely, smoke billowing across the water. Howard shoves the hood adrift with a long pole, and it floats away, a burning battleship on a rough sea. It bobs with the waves, rocking into the spray, drifts upstream in the eddy then catches the wind and swings out into the current.

Howard wears a broad grin, pleased with his idea. He puffs on his cigarette, straining to see through his own smoke, tobacco smoke and the smoke from the fire. "Heh-haaaah, bollocks, lookit 'er go, boys! Just a boggin' 'er down the Jesus river!"

Then he drops to his knees, grappling in the clay to find rocks which he throws at the barge, making it hiss in puffs of steam. It drifts off toward the bridge, fire bright. I have a vision of the bridge burning, the barge setting its dry grass on fire. But it catches on the bridge, twists under, and goes to the bottom; tiny black bits of debris scatter in the current.

In the late afternoon, the wind dies. I hurry across the bridge, thinking of nothing but getting home. Tom and Katie are busy, dressing for church, and my absence has escaped notice. Tom calls to me to tidy the cab of the old half-ton before they leave: he's still fighting with the knot of his tie.

CHAPTER 4

We have grown into spring, hurrying the season, wearing our spring clothes while the days are still cool. Sometimes the wind grabs us at the corner of a shed or in the shade of the barn, and we hurry into the lee of the sun to stand against the warm-smelling shingles. It's a kind of game. It is always coldest at the river, which has dropped now enough for the bridge to be repaired. There are logs and pulpwood adrift. In the evenings children huddle at the eddies, chub fishing. Across the river, Nick burns black map-shaped patches in the dead grass on the side hill. As the sun sets over the swamp, sprouting alders turn a deep purple.

There is a new calf fenced with its mother in one end of the cow stable. We can smell the Royal Purple disinfectant from the dooryard. We hear Tom milking, the singing sprays of milk against the empty strainer pail, its frothing as it falls. While the sunlight lingers, I work in the barnyard, dismantling the bobsleds and repairing the harrows for Tom.

Before dark, Howard and his father, Charlie, come. Howard carries the lantern. Old Charlie, short and frail with grey eyes set in deep sockets, smiles piteously and constantly. In a bran bag slung over his shoulder, something grunts and jabs.

"Ya made 'er back okay Sunday," Howard calls to me, and I grin and nod.

"Here, lad, take this inside and turn the separator for Katie," says Tom, passing me the strainer pail of milk and crossing the yard with Danny to meet our visitors. "I'll see what he wants." I take the pail and go in. I don't have to stand in the yard to follow the conversation; Charlie and Tom have the same exchange every spring.

"Ah-huh. Ya brought me another pig," Tom says without looking at Charlie. "I wasn't gonna bother this year, d'ya know it."

"Eh, ya'll be glad ta have 'im come fall. I'll kill 'im fer ya."

Danny and Howard go to the river; Charlie follows Tom to the pigpen. He release the squirming white piglet into a pile of straw and almost in the same motion pulls a flask from his jumper to treat.

"A little drink, Tom?"

"God bless ya, don't mind if I do." They each take a bulging mouthful, then light up their pipes to talk.

In the kitchen, Katie has the cream separator assembled and I pour the fresh milk into its wide bowl. The two metal arms extend to twin pails, one for the cream and one for the blue-casted skim milk. When I turn the crank, a tiny bell rings on its handle.

"Crank faster," warns Katie. "Yer bell's still ringin' there."

The separator purrs, building speed until the warning bell fades to silence and the handle turns almost by itself.

Charlie and Tom stand talking in the centre of the dooryard, looking like twins in the same mackinaw coats and grey wool trousers, ceramic figures. But Tom is cut from a different cloth than Charlie.

It's strange. "Charlie brings me a pig for one reason," Tom says each spring, "so he can come back in the fall and kill it." We know how Charlie likes to kill; he butchers for all the neighbours. According to Tom, Charlie once threw gasoline on a porcupine and set fire to it, because it destroyed a tree of his. And Tom raked him one thrashing day for throwing a cat into a barrel with two rats to watch them fight. Still, tonight, Tom is obliging to old Charlie, showing him the same respect he would give the minister or anyone else who visits our place. I think Tom is almost overly nice, bordering on the phoney.

They talk their way to the house, and Tom brings the flask to the kitchen for Katie to mix them more drinks. She serves the brandy with hot water and sugar, in her best tumblers. The two men set in the parlour, their hats in their hands, chatting. A dense cloud of tobacco smoke drifts waist-high through the softly lit room, smells like medicated ointment.

Outside, sunset leaves a purple land. The farm seems vulnerable now, under the stained sky. A bird drums its wings, high out of sight as though it were meant to be heard and not seen. The air is damp, the sounds of the river audible now from the dooryard. Howard and Danny come in from the river, red-faced from the cold, the smell of fish and angle worms on their hands. Howard sits in the hallway watching Tom and Charlie, as if he must catch up on the missed part of the visit.

Now the warm house shuts out the night, and the brandy makes the two men good companions, trading bits and pieces of old songs.

Charlie launches into the long ballad of a lumber camp murder. He forgets many of the words and stammers, repeating the same lines. Then he whoops and laughs, the same ghostly laugh. In the kitchen Katie doubles over with laughter, wiping tears from beneath her glasses with a ball of Kleenex.

"D'ya mind "The Spree at Somers Hill?" asks Tom. "I knew it all one time, every word."

"I remember the spree," Charlie says, "but I don't remember the song."

Tom sits on the edge of his chair, staring at the opposite wall. Suddenly the words come to him:

> *"Two by three they march in the dinin' hall,*
> *Old men, young men, women that wasn't men a'tall,*
> *Some come on bicycles, because they have no fare ta pay,*
> *And them that didn't come a'tall*
> *Made up their minds ta stay away."*

When he finishes, he sits back and drains his glass. "Here, lad," he says, "have Katie fetch us another drink."

"Like a good boy," Charlie adds. "'Nother little drink wouldn't do us no harm, eh, Tom?"

Then, with a gust of night air behind them, Nick and Cindy come in; they've been fishing, and Nick has a black salmon which he leaves on the veranda floor. Cindy takes off her jacket. She's wearing the same tight red sweater, her blond hair falling over her shoulders, and the same tight-fitting blue jeans. She smiles when she catches me looking. How many times have I pulled the petals from a daisy to end in her favour? *She loves me, she loves me not, she loves me.* She has brought a kind of magic, an excitement that preoccupies me and undermines my thinking. I go to her, breathing the perfume that scented her hair in the millshed: "Unforgettable," like Katie sometimes wears.

"So, how's school?" I ask.

"I dunno, I quit."

Something like a chill runs through me. "But, you'll go back in the fall?"

"Nah, I'm gettin' a job in town, at the Delux Grill."

"But you could be a teacher, or a nurse, or even a social worker."

"No way. I have more school now than I'll use. 'Sides, I'm gonna marry a man with lotsa money and have a big family and live in a big house in town. Ya don't need education, if ya marry someone with a bundle."

"I suppose that's one way of looking at life."

"Yerself, Steve?"

"Me? Oh, I'd sort of like to go to university," I say. How is it that we never talked about this before, I wonder? But then, we've never talked much, never looked far ahead.

"Well, I guess it's kinda different fer a lad," she says, considering it, her head titled back. "But don't go ta that college fer too long. It'll make a sissy outa ya, so ya don't wanna work hard."

"College wouldn't do that to me."

"I sure wouldn't wanna see ya turn wimp like that ol' teacher, what's-'is-name, Dinnie Brown. Walks just like a girl, didja know that, and he talks somethin' like a girl. Daddy says he got that way from too much education."

"But how could knowledge change him physically?"

"Dunno. But 'fore he went to college he was a good worker, helped 'is father in the woods all the time, Then he got over-educated, ruined 'imself."

"Somehow, I could never picture Dinnie Brown working in the woods."

"I'd hate ta see that happen ta you. Turn soft when yer father needs a good worker."

"Well, you don't have to worry about me," I say. "I'll never be over-educated, that's for sure."

The music is sweet and mellow, and I've heard these tunes all my life. Family portraits hang around the parlour, coy in their oval frames: Tom's mother and father, Katie's mother and sister, Edith, taken when she was a girl, and the King and Queen taken in 1939. Across the corner is the old black pump-organ, not played since mice ate its levers twenty years ago.

Tom is in the middle of another song, and Charlie is humming along off-key.

> *"Oh, Dan ya know and Mario,*
> *Perhaps they'll go with so-and-so,*
> *And all the boys from here below,*
> *We're 'sembled at the spree."*

> *"There was Mike and Dan,*
> *Mary-Ann and Pat MacKann,*
> *And all that ol' upriver clan*
> *As drunk as drunk could be."*

They whoop and laugh and raise their glasses.

As Cindy sits beside me on the folding cot, I feel the weight and warmth of her body. I think of the day in the millshed and I wish we were alone now. Is it right to want someone's body and not their soul? Certainly we're on different roads. But my hands remember the softness of her very well.

Tom and Charlie cannot recall any more songs, so Tom takes his mouth organ from his sweater pocket and starts to play "Home Sweet Home" in all the variations. He cups the mouth organ, his big square hands trembling against the reeds. His white-stubbled cheeks puff in and out as he strains to keep the music going, keeping time with his feet. He hammers the instrument against a pant leg to dry it, before starting another tune. He plays, "The Irish Washer Woman" and "The Fishers Hornpipe," and Charlie claps his hands.

"Drive 'er, Tom!"

Suddenly Cindy springs onto the floor, pulling me to my feet. We swing to the music, bobbing around the room, and she flashes her wonderful smile. I'm warm with embarrassment but happy to have her in my arms. And when Tom runs out of breath, pulling out his handkerchief to mop his brow, Cindy and I drop together onto the cot, still holding hands.

A train whistle blows in the sudden silence; the express passes, its windows a string of yellow lights twisting across the farm. Sparks scatter from its wheels.

"C'mon, Howard, we have ta go, it's near 'leven," Charlie says, jumping to his feet. "Thanks fer the sing, Tom."

He puts on his mackinaw, lights a wooden match with his thumbnail, and tilts the globe of his lantern. It flickers, darkens, then gives a steady yellow light. The smell of kerosene is strong through the house. Howard follows along behind Charlie, nodding in the light, his hands in his coat pockets. They pass through the front gate and onto the mud-packed highway, lantern swinging.

The evening is over. Nick and Cindy leave too, calling good-byes down the dark driveway. I feel an emptiness when Cindy is gone, and the house is quiet again. I'm glad I danced.

Sometime in the night, she comes back to me in a dream, and my evening's strongest desires emerge. I am helpless. She clings to me, hot and breathless, with her angel-blond hair falling over bare shoulders. Her breasts are firm and yielding both, her inner legs silk smooth. The hidden freedom surfaces and races. Then the eyes of conscience, church, and family close in; suddenly Cindy is mocking, wicked, shameful, in a pose that only minutes ago was inviting. It's like I've exploited a single part of someone's universe to satisfy my selfish desires. But the warmth of this dream lingers into the days ahead.

CHAPTER 5

Early May carries the smell of grass fires as farmers burn dead meadows and dried-out swamp land, a thin haze settling over the river. Along the railroad, the stunted blueberry bushes form purple patches that project like rug hooking beneath the smoke as trolley men torch piles of rotting ties. In a field, between the tracks and the wire bridge, a tractor has dug a cellar for David Cain's new house. He is moving home from Ontario after two years away.

The strengthening sun has brought new life to the river. We no longer stop what we're doing to look at a robin or a blackbird, and swallows squeak in the eves of the barn. The rooster chases clucking hens in the dooryard and the limbs of the juniper have tiny yellow brushes, the pasture patches of green. There are mayflowers on the top-hill and logs and pulpwood adrift in the river, which has dropped so its gravel shores and clearing water pull us to its edge to peer mesmerized toward the amber bottom and shadows of moving fish. The sun penetrates the crisp air even at the river, and the wind, which according to Tom "still has a bit of a rake in it," is both warm and cold, without being either warm or cold. Clothes flap on Katie's propped-up clothesline and the pile of split firewood by the shed has turned from its honey colour to bleached bones.

By now the storm windows and doors have been replaced by screens, and the slapping of the wooden screen door, slammed shut by its coil spring, sounds around the dooryard. From George Cooper's place, the hollow *clong* of a cowbell carries above the shrill singing of toads and, in the evenings, the din of the peeping frog pond.

Tom has commenced to harrow the flat, turning the faded soil a dark orange and carrying the armfuls of tangled switch grass and root to the sod ground to burn. Tomorrow morning, before the wind comes up, he will sow the oats. "Farmin' time," Tom calls it, "when the alder leaf's a mouse's ear." I will carry the buckets of seed to him while he paces, ankle deep, broadcasting the seed. He does this with an even stride, arms swinging like a Russian soldier. But today, Nick Long and I are going to town.

As we stand on the siding waiting for the express, our anticipation has an undercurrent of unease, because we are going for the first time without an adult. We watch the long grade for a first glimpse of the train and listen for its snapping on the rails, Finally we hear it and then see the engine in a radiance of brown dust coming around the bend, its headlight beaming high against the forest. A kind of panic hits me as I step between the ties and wave a white handkerchief tied to a broom handle. There is a shrill whistle, the engine's response, and soon the baggage cars are rumbling past. The wheels of the lone passenger car squeal to a grinding halt beside us.

Every day, old Henry Cain comes to the siding to see the train pass and pick up the mail bag. Today, as always, he wears a long black sweater, wrongly buttoned, and chews tobacco, bits of juice running down his chin. He is hard of hearing, but fond of talking.

"Goin' ta town, boys? Eh? Goin' town?" He tugs at my sleeve.

"Yessir, that's where we're headin'."

"Would ya be goin' ta town?" he shouts.

"YES, SIR!" Nick bellows in his ear.

"Ah hell," old Henry says, "I thought ya was goin' ta town."

The conductor tosses a stool onto the platform and, smiling, helps us climb into the coach. Inside, the train smells of new metal paint, stale beer, and cigarette smoke. Nick and I sink into seats facing each other and watch as the small siding house and shimshack disappear. In the distance, Henry Cain is walking across the field to his place, carrying the mail bag.

After slamming a trap door, closing out the railway sounds, the conductor comes down the half-empty coach.

"Town?" he asks, hunching down on the seat's arm.

"Yes, return tickets."

He gives us each a ticket and continues up the aisle chatting here and there with the passengers.

There is quiet when he is gone. We watch the scenery pass, tinted by the glass. We're travelling fast and high and I feel sophisticated, like the coach has given us dignity. I wave to the people who look up at the passing train. Nick is wearing his new western shirt, jeans and boots: a cowboy without the hat. On his first trip to town without his parents, he's depending on me. A false security. Hands beneath his chin, he stares out the window, looking beyond the scenery, deep in thought. The train pauses at a small siding and some people get on and sit near us. The conductor sways back through. Nick faces out the window, keeping a distance between the new passengers and us.

Nick spends too much time alone, I think, his only company on his side of the river being Howard. He seems nervous even when there are only the three of us. I realize for the first time how far away from town we all live.

To the faint rumble of the engine and the constant click-click of the wheels, steel against steel, the long coach rocks and sways as it sweeps around bends and follows the river. At times we can see the engine and its stream of smoke drifting across the water. We pass ledges of black rock, hills of forest, open fields and deep trestled ravines where turbulent water runs beneath the tracks.

Soon we pass over tinkling roadways and the train begins to slow. Its whistle sounds; the houses become closer together, the road crossings more frequent; then, over the long river bridge, we see the hazy jumble of roofs up ahead.

"There she is, the Big City," says Nick, coming out of his reverie.

"Yes, it won't be the same town after today," I answer, grinning, overtaken by sudden anxiety.

The train moves slowly over a network of rails and everyone jumps to their feet, crowding the aisle to the end door. Soon it grinds to a stop beside a long crowded platform and everyone files into the sunshine, scattering like ants in all directions. Nick is close behind me.

We stand under the awning of the stationhouse, watching as the many strange people hustle about. A hunchback man in worn shoes pulls a wooden cart loaded with luggage. Groups of women and children hurry here and there and taxi drivers shout to the crowd. A thin man approaches us, smiling with recognition, and tells us he's a little short on cash. Nick quickly digs out a dollar for him when he says that he's a downriver relative we've never met. Then we hear him repeat his story to another fellow, and another. A professional bum. I should have caught it.

Checking first with the station agent for a departure time, we start to walk downtown. A lingering scent of burning coal and blistering tar drifts from the long sleepers beneath the tracks. On a nearby street corner, there is a store front on a private home, and we go in for two bottles of pop and a package of Matinee cigarettes. Lighting the cigarettes in the wind of passing cars, we stroll down the town hill. Our half-Wellington boots, with their half-moon metal heel protectors, are loud on the cement and our downhill strides lengthen as we near the business section.

At a long stone fence beside the sidewalk, we stop to rest and look around and finish our smokes. The flat top of the fence leads to an iron gate, and behind it a lawn stretches up to a big white house. There's a cedar hedge, and the grass is tall and green, higher than the grass at home and in need of mowing. Nick slips behind the hedge to have a leak, and I keep watch to warn him if someone comes. When he finishes, I take my turn behind the hedge. The house really is big, with dark green wood shutters that sag from upstairs windows and make a backdrop for the pale green leaves of a budding elm on the lawn. A wooden sign with scrolled lettering reads:

Elm Inn
Rooms — Restaurant
Joseph Reid
Innkeeper

A white convertible, its top down and radio playing music, sweeps suddenly into the yard and stops behind the house. There is a honk from the horn, then laughter, and a girl screams as she is chased around the car and across the lawn toward us. She stops quickly when she sees us, a little embarrassed, and curious.

"Hi, guys," she says, flashing a wonderful smile.

"Howdy," Nick says.

"Hello." I think that Nick is reading too many western comic books.

She turns and runs back to the house, graceful as a dancer, her long dark hair waving. She is the Spanish girl on the cigar package, I think, but without the sombrero and boots. We walk along downtown but she stays in my mind. She is the kind of girl that you meet and know at once that knowing her will have its price.

"Nice, eh?" Nick says.

"Beautiful, but out of your class."

"Whatta ya mean, outta my class?"

"You wouldn't get to first base with her."

"Bullshit!" Nick says. "She's just another girl, nothin' special."

On the main street, where all the stores are, the white convertible passes us with the same girl behind the wheel. She's dressed in white now, with a red bandanna over her hair. It seems that she hasn't tried to look attractive, but does anyway; a kind of built-in class, like town girls sometimes have, the ones whose fathers have money. In my mind, I see us driving on and on together in her car.

The business district is old, with slanted false-fronted buildings propped along the crest of the hill overlooking the river. The sidewalks and curbs and even the manhole covers lend us their awkward support. The buildings watch our every move and the sidewalks are busy with clusters of young people. Many are wearing crested school jackets. The girls are pretty. Everyone has that look of town, I think: open, almost to a boldness. The town people are different. They even dress different, with T-shirts and shorts this early in the season. In my blue jeans, plaid shirt, and Wellington boots, to be wanting someone like the girl at the Inn seems hopeless.

But Nick and I try to fit in. We pick up street names and use them as we talk to each other; we use the names of town people we've heard of, saying them loudly when we pass those other kids. We try to act sophisticated, using "sir" and "guy" instead of "lad" and correcting each other when we forget and slip back to our own ways. The town people are exciting; right now, I wish I were one of them, part of the crowd and the hum of the traffic and the jingle of bells as shop doors open and close.

In the barbershop, the air is thick with smoke and the strong scent of hair tonic. There are two young barbers and an old one, all in white, mumbling in the ears of the satin-caped customers before them. Sometimes the barbers chuckle when their customers make comment. But they snip on unceasingly, leaning and turning the chairs to and from the mirrored wall, occasionally dusting powder in choking clouds. We wait our turn. I pick up *The Boxing News* and try to read, glancing at Nick who watches for his place in the rotation as people move in and out of the chairs and shop. I look at the boxing photos. But all I can see is the girl at the Elm Inn, running across the lawn, her hair blowing in the wind like a model in a Kotex magazine ad.

"Next!" the old barber says. I want to wait for one of the young barbers, so I keep my eyes glued to the magazine, hoping someone else will respond. "You're next, young man, make it snappy!" He is nodding at me.

I spring to my feet, self-conscious; as I get into the chair I smile at the barber, but he doesn't smile back. He chokes me slightly with the cloth and nudges the chair upward with a lever at the back. I can't tell this man how I want to look, the stylish haircut I have in mind. I try to keep my face emotionless as he cuts my hair high on the sides with the clippers and snips it short on top. The piss-pot haircut, I think, like Tom used to give Danny and me.

When he finishes, the barber greases my hair with cream and combs it over one eye so I look like Adolph Hitler without the mustache. Then he shakes the cloth and nods to the next victim.

Nick is just getting up, equally greased and shorn, and looks down at the clumps of hair on the worn linoleum floor. A shiny silver dollar lies among the dust and snippings, and Nick stoops to pick it up. It's glued to the floor. All the men in the shop glance at each other and I can read the lifts of eyebrows, the small smiles. Embarrassed, we hurry outside.

On the sidewalk, the smell of tonic lingers and we scratch bits of hair from under our collars, the breeze cool around our open necks.

At the clothing stores we try to buy new jeans and shirts on credit, but we're too young and don't have steady jobs. Nick wants a new suit for the prom, so we pick another store and he says he is George Cooper. George is also refused credit. At the mercantile store I buy a bag of spikes and a set of gate hinges for Tom. Then we go to the shoemaker's, where Nick leaves his Wellington boots for new soles. The old cobbler gives Nick an ancient pair of gum rubbers with no laces to wear around town while his boots are being worked on. Nick is embarrassed, but he wears them.

In the Delux Grill, we play the jukebox and stand around smoking. I watch for the girl from the Inn.

By late afternoon the town in growing thin around us, its offerings fewer and simpler. There is a sadness in the dying sun and the streets fade grey and damp. We feel empty and hollow and we long for warmth, comfort and steady friends. We feel something less than our true selves, shadows of whoever it is we are trying to be, and so hungry that our heads ache. I'm wishing for one of Katie's home-cooked meals. We'll have supper at the Elm Inn, I think. It's on our way to the train station.

The Inn is shaded from the last of the sun by the huge elm beside it, and the yard is damp. The white convertible sits behind the house, top up.

We go into the lobby slowly, made uneasy by the winding staircase and the red carpet everywhere. An old man in a grey shirt, who wrings his hands as if he doesn't know he's doing it, shows us to the dining room. A waitress gives us a leather-covered menu and is gone. There are only two other people eating here, in an aroma of roast beef, coffee and cigar smoke. Nick and I have never before eaten where the tables are draped in white linen and each has a silver candlestick. Around the room are dark sideboards, and the mantle of the fireplace is decorated with ancient dishes.

"Do ya have any money left?" Nick asks.

"Some."

"How much?"

"Five dollars."

"I've got one dollar left," says Nick.

We order hot sandwiches and sit with our hands under the table, trying to look comfortable. Piano music comes to us from across the hall, soft and perfected, classical music. A magic comes with it, the kind captured in the stained glass windows at the church when the sun sets against them. I can hear symbols in the music, refined like a parlour tapestry or an old poem from the books in the school library. It lifts me to an inner world, mystical and free, playing on the senses like a dream, a state of unreality. My mind drifts with the moods of the music.

When the music stops, brief applause is followed by a silence, and when the piano is heard again a woman is singing. The words of her song are poetry put to music, her voice tender as apple blossoms. I think of the rough sing-songs that Tom and Charlie have — raspy folk singing, their feet tramping out the music. Tom has an ear for music, I think, but it seems to me that his talent is like a seed not cultivated, buried in the grass roots of the land.

"Let's go listen," I tell Nick, "just while we're waiting for the food." And we go across the hall.

The singer is the girl of the white convertible. Only now she's dressed like a movie star, in a pink evening gown and high-heeled shoes; her long dark hair is done up in a confection of ringlets and curls. She smiles at us, over the heads of people I hardly see. I think of heroines and sirens in books; I think of Eustacia Vye. This is a new kind of desire, greater than any I've had. The love of this girl could bring me the ultimate happiness, I know it, but to get to know her is to fight insurmountable odds. And a rejection could bring a new kind of despair. Suddenly I know that this is Amanda Reid. I wish I'd never seen her.

Later in this long day, in the passenger coach, the music is still in my ears. When the train moves slowly beyond the town perimeter and into the darkness of the wooded countryside, my thoughts are of town. The dreary whistle sounds as we cross the bridge. I wonder why Tom chose to live so far out into the country, so far from society. Out here we are all loners, I think. Moody, deep-thinking survivors of the land, alien to the finer things.

"What are you thinking about?" I ask Nick.

"I'm feelin' happy, happy to be goin' home. You?"

"Oh, nothing, really," I answer. "I might live in town someday. I think I could get used to it."

"Not me," says Nick. "I'm stayin' in the country. People are nicer to me in the country."

As we lapse into silence, staring into the dark beyond the windows, someone in a group at the front of the coach begins to play a fiddle. Another plays a guitar. They sing in French and play jigs and reels. The conductor says they're on their way upriver, heading into the woods to work for the summer. They play and sing, laughing, whooping at the end of each song as they drink from a pocket flask.

CHAPTER 6

Everything has been planted: oats, potatoes, and the vegetable garden, which was left to last because of the possibility of frost. On our last fine day, which was over a week ago now, Danny and I helped as Tom made the drills with a bench marker and we sprinkled the fertilizer before he dragged a chain along each, giving it a salt-and-pepper look. When we dropped the seed, he nudged the thin layers of soil over them and tapped the rake's heel firmly on top. No one else could do it to suit him. The next day it was raining softly and when Tom saw the hens outside feeding — according to him, the sign of a long wet spell — he went to the swamp to fix up his fencing, from the railroad around to the Coopers' place. Danny and I put on our rubber boots and winter coats and went to help him. During the winter, the barbed wire had fallen and was buried among ponds of bog and dead weeds. We lifted it and fastened it to the insulators that look like grooved peppermints glued to the grey stakes. Tom wanted to get this done so the cows could be turned out if the rain lasted.

It is Sunday and I stay in bed until late morning. All night, I dreamed of Amanda Reid. In the dream, I was living at the Elm Inn, a talent scout from Columbia Pictures, driving around with Amanda in her white convertible. Later we sat in the big parlour and I wore a new grey suit and smoked a cigar; I was listening as she sang classical pieces which I pretended to know. Then we were down on the red carpet, snuggling together, her eyes looking into mine as if I were the most important person in her life. I am aroused. When the sun beams into the room, warming the bedclothes, a vague disappointment follows the surfacing of reality. I do not have breakfast, but go outside and behind the binder shed, smoke a secret cigarette.

The grass is both warm and damp as the sun cuts through the last tangible coolness in the mellowing east wind and begins to dry the dandelioned dooryard and the rain-dimpled garden. This morning, the fields are yielding, offering themselves with kindness. Everyone is outside, even Katie who stoops over a flower bed in front of the house. Danny appears quietly beside me as I walk toward the garden, where Tom stands, hands on his hips, his long pipe between his teeth. He moves so slowly he could pass for a scarecrow.

"Now, boys, be careful, don't ya step on the drills," he says. "They're just breakin' through — Jesus! Be careful!"

The clay has begun to crack and the plants are peeking through. There are green knuckles in the bean row, tiny pale strings of webbed grass in the carrot row, purple sprouts in the beet row and the cucumber hills have pairs of dark green rubber leaves, furred and positive among the tall open strands of switch grass. Already the garden needs hoeing, I think.

"And get something on yer feet, lad. Ya'll be laid up with consumption. That ground's still cold," he says, lighting his pipe.

"Let's trade in the old half-ton," I say. I've thought about this. Spring is the right time to ask. "Get a car."

"Yes, we could, I guess," Tom answers. "But how would we get me cows ta bull and the like a that?"

"Hire Howard or Charlie, their truck."

"It'd be nice alright, a car, ta go ta church in and all."

"And I'd work hard, help with the payments," I offer.

"Ah, we'll see, Stevie. Sunday plans, you know."

"We could go downtown tomorrow if it rains and we can't work, look around."

"We'll talk about it tomorrow," he says, and walks toward the front yard to meet Katie. I let myself feel hopeful. It looks good.

Upstairs, in my bedroom, I flex my muscles in the mirror, comb my hair back, forward, and then sideways. I put on my new shirt for the Sunday, go back out and drive the truck in tight circles around the yard, then down the wagon road to the brook. A blue '50 Chevy, rickety, with a cattle rack on the back. I take a bucket and rags, and I wash and polish its cab, scrape manure from the box. The truck shines while it's wet, but when it dries it fades like powder.

Sunday is a day of moving from one string of thoughts to another. The day is breezy now, the sun hot, a clearing day after the rain. We have more things to do than there is time for, things we share, to get the most out of this rare day. Danny and I walk to the river with Tom and Katie. We look at the pickets Tom has driven to set his gaspereau net and stare into the water to see if the gaspereaux are really running. We walk about the fields, lean on line fences, and look at the neighbours fields — Cains' on one side and the Coopers' on the other. Each parcel of land carries the spirit of its owner. On the top-hill, Danny picks a bouquet of violets and dandelions and brings it home, where Katie puts it in a vase in the centre of the dining room table. These are tiny pockets of happiness that draw us close.

Tom takes his hammock to the front garden, where Danny and I untangle its tiny end ropes and hook the rings to the rusted hooks set in a pair of heavy elms. He lies down, pulls his hat low on his forehead, and opens the Bible. Barely settled, he looks up suddenly.

"Aaah huh, hear that?" Tom raises to his elbows.

"Church bell ringing," I say.

"Boys, we shoulda gone ta church. We'd have better luck next week if we did." A gust of wind blows hard up the river now, and rattles high in the elm trees. "That goddamned east wind. Too early ta lay out yet."

He swings out of the hammock, unhooks it from the trees, gathers it in his arms, and goes into the house. He'll be listening to the radio, to *The Brotherhood*, a hymn sing. Danny follows him, but I go down to the river to have a smoke.

On the other side, at the Longs' shore, Cindy is lying in the boat moored high and dry above the water. Her jeans are rolled up to above her knees and she has her sweater pulled up under her breasts, baring her whole midsection. She faces the sun. Probably has her eyes closed.

I ease our boat into the water and paddle silently across, When the bow hits the shore near where she sunbathes, she sits up and wipes her eyes.

"Oh, it's you, Steve," she says. "What brings ya way over here?"

"I came over to see you."

"That's nice of ya. Here, I've got cigarettes." She tosses me the package of Export.

"I could get there beside you in the boat," I say. "It'd be warmer out of the wind."

A breeze is on the river now, contrasting gusts of coolness that wrinkle the water.

"Sure, if ya want to. There might be room." She shifts herself slightly; I take one of her cigarettes and lie down beside her. I light my smoke from the end of hers, roll up my pant legs, and toss my shirt onto the shore.

"How did you get tanned so dark with all the rain?" I ask.

"Iodine mix. I'm rubbing it on. Like it?"

"Yes, you're very handsome and lovely. The tan makes your hair seem even more blonde."

"I'm gettin' ready fer a talent contest in town."

"Doing what? Singing?"

"Play the guitar and sing. Do ya like my singin', Steve?"

"Sure."

"I'm singing 'Cheatin' Heart'."

"You do it well." The lie seems inevitable, and kind.

"Thanks, Steve. Hey, I'm glad you came on over."

"So am I."

"We're always happy together, though, ain't we?"

In answer, I kiss her cheek and lay my hand on her leg. "You have nice legs," I say. She pulls my hands away.

Her legs are close together, and look fatter than when she is standing. I close my eyes now, content just to lie here and hear her breathing. Then she leans on me and puts her lips on mine. I kiss her, long and hard.

"You're moochin' with me, Steven Moar!"

"I know."

I kiss her forehead, her nose, her cheeks, her mouth again. Her breath is warm against my ear. She's really very lovely; I tell her so.

"Let's go to sleep here together," she says.

"OK, let's sleep then."

We lie quietly for a moment, but I am electrified, vividly aware of the gentle rise of her ribs with each soft breath. Then I feel her shiver in my arms, and I pull her against me and kiss her again.

"Oh, you're so nice. I'm afraid of myself when I'm with you, d'ya know that, Steve?"

"Let's sleep. Try to sleep."

"OK, I'll try." But Cindy sits up, bats her hair away from her face and lights two cigarettes, passing one to me. "Will ya really go back ta school like ya said? Why would ya bother with that?" She's propped on one elbow, wanting to talk now.

"I want to. It's a dream I've had."

"I was hopin' you'd stay around. Work around here. There's good money in ownin' a truck, ya know. Haulin' lumber."

"I don't think it's me. Not my kind of thing."

"You're strange. D'ya know that?"

"I suppose I am. Let's not talk about jobs today, though. Let's not be serious. It's Sunday. Sunday plans never stand, Tom says."

We lie back, tossing our cigarette butts toward the water.

"What kinda girl would ya want when yer educated? Different, maybe?"

"I don't know. Who cares?"

"Someone might."

"I doubt it."

"Could I — could a girl change ta be that type? I wonder if I could change."

"Don't change, Cindy. I like you the way you are."

"Do ya?"

"Sure."

We're close now and I hold her tight and kiss her and touch the bare skin of her back, and the sun shines into the warm beached boat, and I can smell the iodine on her skin and feel her chest moving quickly. Her arms twine around my neck like a frightened child clinging to its mother. I force my eyes open to reassure myself that this is not another dream.

"Cindy! Cindy! Where are you?" Someone calls from up the hill. "Cindy, yer supper's ready. Are you at the shore?"

"It's Daddy!" She stands up and tugs her clothing straight, and strokes her hair over her shoulder. "Come an' see me," she calls back to me, hurrying away.

I get into my own boat, push it adrift, and paddle quietly back across the river, home.

Tom is listening to the radio. Allen Mills sings folk songs and tells stories, then it's the Salvation Army broadcast with the brass band playing. Later in the

One Indian Summer

evening, it's Charlie Fuller's ministry. And when the church services are over, Danny turns the dial as he does every Sunday night and listens to *Gunsmoke*, starring William Conrad, brought to us by the makers of L&M Cigarettes. Spurs jingle, dogs bark, and gunshots roar from the radio as I sit at the kitchen table, doing an assignment for my correspondence course.

CHAPTER 7

The wind has dropped, the morning calm promising a fair day. The sky holds only the occasional small white cloud and the sun beams through the young-leafed elm and the old apple tree, making broken shadows in the dooryard. Houseflies buzz against the warm side of the house, and the sour-smelling back door. The cattle have been turned out to pasture, but we hear that there are still patches of snow in the thick woods. This is a preliminary warm spell before the river warms enough to swim in. The trout fishing is still excellent, a run coming in with the gaspereaux.

I pass Tom the twine mesh as he sims the gaspereaux net, stationing the brunt cedar blocks at two-foot intervals along the top line. Then he weights the bottom rope with strips of sheet lead. Later in the morning, we take the net to the river and I hold the boat while Tom strings it off the outside pickets. Then we return to help Katie as she prepares to move the centre of our life to one of the grey rambling sheds on the back of the house: the summer kitchen.

As she sweeps its floor, clouds of sand and cobwebs belch out the back door. She sweeps off the doorstep, the sand-baked yard around the step, the woodshed floor, and the outhouse. She goes back inside and scrubs, kneeling and scouring the boards until they are bleached the colour of split wood. Danny and I carry empty pork barrels, creamers and bits of winter clothing further into the woodshed. As we bring dishes from the main house and fill the corner shelves, Katie mends the feather mattress on the cot behind the stove. Then she strings a curtain around the washstand to hide the slop pail and polishes the piece of mirror hanging above it.

Tom swears and beats the stovepipes in the yard, leaving piles of rusty ashes in the grass. We wire the joints together, elbowing them around a beam and through the roof. After he polishes the stove top and shines the chrome roosters on the warming closet and oven door, he puts on a fire. The range sputters as smoke leaks around its top covers and fills the kitchen. We open the door. Outside, smoke from the low chimney settles in the yard. It smells sour, like burning popple. With the fire on in the summer kitchen, we have officially moved out for the season.

Danny brings the old radio from the main house, sets it on the end of the table, and plugs it in: Don Messer is playing "The High Level Hornpipe." Tom turns up the volume and makes a few fancy steps in front of the radio. Then he gives a bellowing "Haa whoo hu hu" that makes the old summer kitchen shake and the dishes rattle on the shelves. "Face me, stranger," he calls, grabbing Katie's arm to pull her into his dance. "I'll play the fiddle with ya, Kate."

"Tom, please! Go and set down!" She scolds, pulling away from him. "The boys are watchin'. They'll think yer crazy."

But Katie, too, is pleased to be moved out. She steps lightly as she prepares the first meal, slicing a loaf of her home-cooked bread and stacking the slices on a saucer. Then she makes the tea and warms up the beans. As she wipes clean the shiny new tablecloth and puts the dishes on the table, a light breeze whispers in the screens and houseflies butt against the screen door.

The outside kitchen is cosy, decorated with Katie's personal touch. The rocking chair has been brought from the main house to set beside the stove. The curtains are new, patterned with little teapots tipping forward. The corner shelf that holds the dishes is covered with wax paper, its edges scalloped in Vs like the blade of a mowing machine. Inside, with the stove taken down, the house itself is cool and smelling of varnish. New linoleum covers the stovepipe hole.

The first meal outside is a novelty, but as silent as any. Danny and I sit on the long bench behind the table; Tom and Katie sit at the front on chairs carried from inside. Tom holds himself very straight, elbows on the table, hat beside him. He eats a large helping of beans and molasses, folding thick moist slices of bread and mopping up his plate. When he finishes, he puts on his hat and goes out to the woodshed to work.

I go inside to the dining room to work on an essay for my course. When it's done, I put it in an envelope to mail. I've run out of writing paper, but there's a storyline bubbling in my mind, and I'm desperate to put my ideas down before they're lost. So I write on the back of a big calendar, and then on another; there are many calendars, advertising seed suppliers and the hardware store in town.

My story is a western. I use the imaginary town from *Gunsmoke* for my setting, where a young gunslinger is destined to die on the street in a shoot-out with the marshall. Danny's quietly mischievous personality slips onto this main character, and seems to fit. Writing furiously, I work on my story well into the night.

In the morning I wake late, feeling hollow and drained. I rest the story, but keep it turning in my mind. As I work with Tom at odd jobs, sometimes I'm not paying enough attention to what I'm doing; I know already that I'll get writing paper from Katie and print out my story as neatly as I can, and I'll send it off to the *Star Weekly* and wait.

"C'mere and gimme a hand here, lad!" Tom shouts, irritated now that he has to ask me. "Jesus Christ, that boy's dead from the arse up." He mutters to himself as he kicks things about the woodshed, looking for his axe and saw. "Get a wiggle on," he snaps. "No wonder yer played out, yer up all night readin'. Well, well, well, what's the country comin' to, it's a terra ta hell, a grown man layin' up with 'is head in a Jesus book. Shame us all yet."

We go behind the binder shed and I turn the grindstone as he sharpens the axe.

"You'll not amount ta row a beans, if ya don't learn ta work and make a man a yerself," he says, moving the axe blade in circles, upright against the stone. I say nothing, but crank continuously and pour on water. "You'll end up pickin' shit with the hens. When I grew up there wasn't no books ta read. We couldn't afford 'em."

When the axe is sharp, he grinds the hoe and the scythe. Then he takes the bucksaw and sets it on the wheelbarrow, rests its frame across the staves. He squints and files. "It must be great fun fer George Cooper," he says, spitting in the general direction of the neighbours, "me raisin' an office-type man."

"Good God, Tom, leave the boy alone!" Katie, at the clothesline, has overheard. "The boy never stops helpin' out."

Danny brings me a coupon he has cut from the back of a *Kid Colt* comic book. It advertises a Union Cavalry saddle, available by mail order from New York for ten dollars. I fill out the coupon, in Danny's name. Tom says that Danny will have to cut pulp to pay for it.

A black car drives into the dooryard, and Katie goes into the summer kitchen, wiping her damp red hands on her apron, to put on the tea kettle.

"Now who ta hell's that, comin' around ta bother people?" Tom asks, without looking up from his work.

"Looks like Mr. Cunningham, the minister," I say.

"God damnit, yer right. It is him, too."

The minister goes into the house by the front door.

When Tom finishes his filing, he hangs the saw over a peg in the woodshed. "Well done," he says. "Now we're ready fer the woods. Tomarra we'll head back bright an' early if she's fine. The preacher, eh?" He brushes off his shirt with his hands and goes reluctantly inside.

I wander off to the river. The day is warm now, and I take my shirt off to splash myself in the cold shallows. Then I lie down in the bottom of our canoe to let the sun bake me dry. I think about the essay and the short story and flip through the current issue of the *Family Herald*, reading the comic strips "Juniper Junction" and "Red Ryder."

Across the river, Cindy and her father work in the garden. Cindy is in shorts, on her knees between the drills. Will stands, resting on the hoe. I close my eyes and listen to the faint east breeze and to the water as it bubbles around the pickets, and I drift to the edge of sleep.

Then I am dreaming, and Cindy Long is chasing me in a field of daisies. I can hear her screaming my name. Then her voice gets louder, lifting me out of the dream, and I sit up in boat. Someone is in the river, swimming hard for our

One Indian Summer

shore. It's Cindy, her blonde hair dark and wet, her head held awkwardly above the water. She puffs and coughs my name, and keeps dog-paddling. But she's losing her direction against the current, drifting downstream, losing ground.

I slide the boat into the water and pole it towards her. She is gasping when I get to her, and I push the pole between her clutching hands, pull her to the side, and grab her arm to pull her into the boat.

She is cold and trembling, blue-skinned and goose-pimpled, and she gasps for her breath, gagging and vomiting over the side of the boat. Her teeth chatter when she tries to talk, laughing and crying both.

"Don't talk," I tell her, and pole the boat to shore. Mopping her off with my shirt, thinking of the wide river and the current, I can't help scolding her. "You could have drowned out there, taken a cramp and drowned!"

"Oh, please, Steve, please don't tell Daddy." She coughs between words. "He'd shoot me if he knew."

"I can keep a secret."

"Steve, I can't hear ya. Me ears are poppin'. Oh, me head's achin', what a Jesus headache!"

I throw my shirt over her shoulders and pass her a lighted cigarette. She sits smoking and shivering, her legs and feet pale and her nipples erect against the cold wet blouse. For a long time she says nothing, but sits with her knees tucked up, smokes, and stares across the river. Then she talks.

"I s'pose yer mad at me now, are ya? Tryin' ta swim the river ta see ya an' near drownin' meself. I thought me lungs would bust. D'ya know, me whole life flashed before me."

"I'm not mad. But, yeah, that was stupid. The river's still high and it's cold, too cold."

"But it was so Jesus hot over in the garden. I just had to cool off. Now I'm played out, weak as a rag and fuckin' well freezin'. Look at me!"

"Just lay there in the sun."

The boat is warm and, not unpleasantly, fish-smelling. There's something about lying side by side with Cindy Long, having a cigarette and feeling the sun soaking in. I reach out for her.

"Jesus! Don't touch me! I'm cold an' tired." Then her voice softens. "But thank you for helpin' me across, Steve."

As the sun shines into our hideaway, and we smell the tar and oakum from the boat's cracks and the scents of gaspereaux and mudsuckers from the end where the net was overhauled, Cindy recovers and relaxes and becomes herself again.

"Now you're looking better," I say. "You're getting some colour back. You always look so nice."

"So do you."

I kiss her on the cheek, testing her mood, and then just touch her lips with mine.

"You're moochin' with me, Steven Moar," she laughs gently. "Bad boy. Bad horny boy."

"I know, I suppose I am."

"But don't tell Daddy, will ya, about the other? I wanted ta see ya, that's all."

We lie together, looking at the sky. There is no breeze and the sun is hot, but Cindy's mind keeps returning to her fight with the river. I try to shake her preoccupation, distract her.

"How did you make out at the talent contest?" I ask, suddenly remembering her song, but knowing the answer.

"Lost. A Jesus fix, that's what it was! Someone from town won 'er all."

Someone from town? In my mind I hear again Amanda Reid's sweet voice; I see the dark wood and red carpets of the Elm Inn, but the picture won't come clear. I turn back quickly to Cindy.

"Why do you swear all the time like you do?" I ask her.

"They're doin' it everywhere nowadays. It's a general thing to do. In town an' society they talk like that."

"They do?"

"You should get out more, get around," Cindy says seriously. "Learn the 'in' words."

"I'll get out more when Tom trades the half-ton."

"You wouldn't say 'shit' if ya were up ta yer arse in it, would ya? I s'pose ya talk sa proper an' clean from readin' all the time. Readin', and all the preachin' church services the Moars listen to."

"Shit, yes," I say, feeling foolish.

"Writin' too, I s'pose, are ya?"

"Some."

"That's why yer sleepin' in the boat in the days? Not sleepin' nights, with yer books?"

"I guess so."

"But ya won't tell, though, will ya? Ya won't tell anyone."

"No."

"Daddy says ol' Tom Moar is swearin' one minute and preachin' the next, and he likes a drink every now an' then, everyone knows." Cindy reaches over me for my package of cigarettes and lights up again, waves her cigarette in the air while she talks. And I watch the smoke rise slowly in the still air.

"Tom's a bit of a hypocrite, I guess," I answer, "but he's got a lot of good points."

"But how could anyone read on a day like this?"

"What's the difference? Some people play darts or cards or music."

"Yer strange." There's an edge creeping into her voice.

"I know it."

"I always thought books an' poetry was fer girls, not men."

"It's for whoever likes it."

"Well, ya don't see men doin' it around here."

"This is a small place."

"Not that small."

"I'm not afraid of books. I'll be myself, strange or not, that's all."

"Oh, fuck off, will ya. Nobody could talk ta you. Ya know it all."

"I wouldn't say that. But I know what I want."

"Well, there's no money in the way yer headin'. Readin' an' writin', all that foolishness. An I wouldn't wanna see ya teachin'."

"I'll probably never teach."

"Well, Daddy says there's money in truckin' an' if he was a young lad that's what he'd do. Ya wouldn't have ta leave home neither."

"Yes, but I wouldn't like driving a truck."

"But the money, the money, damnit. The money's good. Ya don't have ta like it, do ya?"

"I'm not sure yet what I'll do," I say, sorry now that I've been drawn into this, wishing we could just lie in the sun, and touch, and leave the words alone.

"For someone who has 'is head in a book all the time, yer not sure of much."

"I'll decide what I want to do in my own good time."

" 'I'll decide what I want to do in my own good time'," she mimics.

"Now you're not being nice."

"I don't give a shit. I just don't feel nice."

"I could have been naughty myself and let you drown."

"Oh, Steve, ya won't tell Daddy or nobody about that, will ya?"

"I can keep a secret."

"I'm sorry. I just hate ta see a nice lad turn girlish an' soft from books. I'm sorry, Steve."

"C'mon, I'll put you over."

I push the boat into the current and paddle toward her shore. Cindy lies in the bow, smoking. Her feet resting on the gunwales are wrinkled and white from the water. She acts like an overtired child, I think, staring away, ignoring me and blowing smoke to the side. When we reach the far side and grate up on the gravel, she jumps out and runs up the hill without speaking. I know this will be the start of not telling.

CHAPTER 8

Tom has traded the old truck for a '53 Chev. Two years old, but in good condition, and a car. It's robin's egg blue with white top and a lot of chrome, curved and shining. When he brought it home, he parked it in the front yard beneath the elms, and now folks stop to see what kind of a deal he made.

"Is she brand new, Tom?"

"She's in good shape fer a '53."

"Boys, it must be nice ta have money!"

And Tom says, "Yeah, thought I'd spend some of that ol' rusty stuff at the bottom of the barrel."

Danny and I spend all afternoon cleaning the already clean car. We Simonize and buff and coax the deep shine out where, here and there, the paint had faded. On the inside we polish the chrome ring on the steering wheel, the clock, the speedometer gauge, the windows. The doors stay open and the radio plays; we look under the hood at the Six, nodding knowledgeably, and check the never-used spare whitewall tire. I drive the car around the yard, holding my breath. And in the evening Tom gives us permission to drive down the wagon road to the river. We feel rich.

The river has been full of pulpwood and logs, and because of that we took up the gaspereaux net, but Tom has salted down nearly a half-barrel. He says, "There are still plenty of the little blue-backs in the river yet."

But the drifting logs meant the drive was coming and we kept an eye out, hoping to see "the corporation" go past. When it came, we rushed to the river to watch: men and horses walked the shores and there were scows and a cookhouse-boat at mid-stream, with a white-aproned man standing on the deck under a plume of white smoke from the cabin's slanting stovepipe. The whole crew whooped and sang and called out dirty rhymes as they snake in the logs and pulpwood caught in the bushes since the high water. The shores are left clean and greening.

With the net up and the drive gone and the cattle put to pasture, Tom is eager to go to the woods. He has taken the truck wagon from its shed, greased the hubs and put on the plank box. "Now boys, we have ta work t'gether ta pay fer that new car," he says. "We don't wanna lose 'er." Danny and I have a new ambition: we want to share in the new car.

Until now I have never thought of the trees as money. And there are so many *ifs* in turning it into dollars — *if* the mill's buying, *if* the weather holds — not until I see the cheque from the lumber company will I be sure. But we are all committed to this proud new cause, and find a new zest for woodswork.

It's a hot sunny morning. We leave the new car gleaming beneath the elm trees; our old horse pulls us to the woods with our bucksaw, axes, peeler, and lunch box packed in the back of the truck wagon. A rough ride, it grinds on the rocks going up the hill and bumps with a numbing jar over the railway tracks. The wagon hubs *cluck* on their greased axles. We cross the top-hill, Danny jumping off to open the bars of the pole-fenced pasture. Danny stands on the back, bracing his feet and clutching our clothes for support, while Tom and I sit up front, a sack of hay beneath us. Tom rests one foot on the box; he hums and slaps the reins up and down on Prince's rump. He has soaked his handkerchief in fly dope and wears it around his neck, like a plainsman.

The road is two mossy grooves, sunken among the young breaks. Limbs brush the wheels and plank box as Prince follows the track.

"Make 'im gallop!" shouts Danny, as we approach the sandy stretch through a stand of princess pines, "Give 'im the whip — haah, haah! Get up! Get up!" His shirttail flaps loose and he waves the old felt hat of Tom's that he seems to wear constantly, making it a cowboy's hat, an outlaw's.

Prince labours on, steadily. The wagon wheels grind deep and the fine sand spills through the spokes. Tom is stern-faced, and he hums without changing his expression.

When we reach the brook we leave our lunch and black boiling pail, and cross a small bridge of poles, driving on into a thick stand of var where we will work.

Tom stops the horse. Danny jumps down, brandishing a cap-gun pulled suddenly from his pocket. "OK, *hombres*, git down off the wagon, nice an' easy, hands in the air so no one gits hurt."

I jump from the wagon, wrestle him down and twist the toy gun away.

"Boys, boys! Stop actin' the fool. Let's get ta work," Tom says, setting his big leather top boot on the hub and swinging himself to the ground. I toss Danny's gun into the wagon, and we help take Prince out of the staves. Tom loosens the harness collar, gives the old horse some hay, and ties him to a tree.

It is early, but already getting hot. While there's dampness in the sally bushes, the trees are dry and warm. They sigh in the rising heat, shade each other from the sun, block out any hint of breeze. Only the poplar moves; it rattles restlessly without a breath of wind. But the woods are alive with birds — not farm birds, like the swallow or robin, but birds of the woods. A woodpecker screams from a pine stub. Young crows cackle and rasp. Other voices we hear are unfamiliar: tree spirits. There are locust, and the warm damp moss whispers with beetles. Flies swarm in tangled clouds, blackflies, mosquitoes, and a few horseflies.

Tom carefully picks the trees we'll be cutting. He leans back and looks up the trunk, his hat in his hand. Then he grabs the axe and chops the undercut with strong, certain strokes. I help with the bucksaw, kneeling in the moss, straddling the roots. The thin blade works in unison with my strength and Tom's, and we inch our way through.

"Don't bear on, lad," Tom puffs, "let the saw do the work in 'er own time."

As our blade bites into the undercut, the tree twists from its stump — "Watch she don't kick ya now," Tom shouts — and drops limbs and dirt, coming to rest on the skids that hold it for peeling.

"What time is it now?" asks Danny. "Near lunchtime?"

"Good God, now listen to 'im. We just got here. Ya can't be hungry already."

When the branches are trimmed, we pry the bark loose. It falls, hollow and greasy and cool, and I can taste the smell of the pitch, like ointment, sharp and bitter. The trunk gleams in the breaks, white and naked, like a giant snake shedding. The pitch attracts more flies; they seem to come out of the wood itself. Our hands stick to the axe handles. The broken skin on my palm stiffens in the pitch as we saw the tree into four-foot blocks and toss them into loose heaps to dry.

The sun gleams through gaps in the trees and we strip off our shirts as the day warms. We're greasy with sweat, peppered with dead needles and flies, smelling of the bitter 6-12 fly dope, and wanting for a cold drink. We look for a pool or trickle of water among the damp clumps of moss but there is none. Only tea berries and hard-rooted knolls and rotting stumps. The drying pitch forms scabs, and the sun climbs the sky.

Through the day we find our routine. As my body works, I think of other things: the new car, driving it to town, Amanda Reid, taking her parking, the new-car smell, playing the radio softly in the dark. There could be dates with Cindy — but somehow she doesn't fit into this special car dream. I see her in an old shed, a boat by the shore, always there under my outstretched hand, there for the taking.

I look forward to lunch as much as Danny does, for a break from the work and the heat as much as for the meal. Smoke from the boiling fire will chase off the flies, I think. I pray for wind, to cool the air, and I pray for rain, so we can get out of the woods.

But nothing changes. The day remains hot and sticky. We taste our own sweat as it drops from the tips of our noses. We wipe our eyes with pitchy hands, gumming eyelashes closed, and the pitch-caked axe handles cling to our burning hands. Prince stands with his head down, harness hanging loose. He gives a chuckle and stomps his feet, switching his long tail at the clouds of flies. A breath of wind stirs briefly in the boughs. It's the same wind that swirls in the dooryard, picking up chips and sawdust.

"A twister," Tom says, "the sign of a dry spell."

When the horse yawns not much later in the day, Tom says, just as firmly, "Ahuh, the horse's yawnin', sign of a wet spell." I'm too tired to smile, and at last he gives the word: "Boys, when ya finish that tree, we'll lunch."

Danny and I finish quickly and hurry gratefully back to the stream, more hungry now than hot. I fill the pail and lower myself to drink. The stream has a white sandy bottom and its water is so cold it makes my jaws ache. I lie for a minute with my face in the water, the nutty taste of moss and wood everywhere, green slime adrift on the water's edge.

Tom starts the fire with birch bark. We cough and wipe our eyes as the rankness of its smoke fills our lungs. Like a tea berry leaf or a blueberry blossom, it's not meant for tasting. Danny carries dry sticks to the fire while I bring the water, and Tom finds pitchwood which he carves out with the toe of his axe. In the fire it blackens the smoke and drives away the flies. A green sapling holds the pail over the fire, and Tom throws a handful of tea into the bouncing water. We hold slices of bologna over the fire and wolf them down with Katie's fresh bread.

Moose birds chirp in the trees and glide down fearlessly not far from us. They carry off and hide the crusts we toss them, and swoop back for more, closer each time. Their dark eyes are deep, like jewels. Ancestors? Tom claims they are. He has names for each one.

"They come outta nowhere when ya light a fire ta boil," Tom says, seriously. "Spirits of the ol' woodsmen." The birds crowd closer and eat from our hands, and one pulls at the wax paper wrapping our sandwiches. "That must be ol' George Cooper. He's sa greedy."

The tea is hot and strong, and we drink it slowly, but already the work of the afternoon is reaching out to us.

"Boys, we'll take a tree here and there," Tom says. "The Cains ruined their place, didn't leave a tree. They cut 'er all, living from hand ta mouth, cut 'er clean with the big buzz saw."

He stretches, and goes into the woods, cruising for a chance for the afternoon. While he's gone I roll a cigarette. Danny puts green boughs on the fire, making it crackle, sending smoke signals he says. We wait for Tom to return, and when I see him walking toward us, buttoning his fly, I put my cigarette quickly into the blaze.

"Boys! Don't put brush on that fire. Let it go out!"

He squats down, putting his gloves under him, hands on his knees. Under the thick grey hair on the back of his hands, the skin is freckled. He pushes his hat back and wipes his brow, and lights his pipe.

"This here woods will be yers someday, boys. Now if ya take care of it, ya can make a livin' right here, an' ya don't have ta leave home. It's a good life. Now, y'know, that is, if the woods is looked after an' not abused. She'll support a family."

"Just take the biggest trees, here and there, you mean?"

"That's it, Steve. Then yer woods is never cut. Harvest it right, boys. Someday, when I'm dead an' gone, she'll all be yers."

"Mine too?" Danny pipes up.

"Yes, yers too, lad. A woods is money in the bank if ya take care of it, she'll do ya a turn."

After lunch, we load the wagon box with dried sleeper chips to take home for kindling.

"Whoaa! Settle down there, ya buckin' bronco," Tom says to Prince, standing heavily asleep under the trees. Then he winks at me, sharing his joke.

Working together, we cover almost an acre of woods, cutting a tree here and there. And finally, at four o'clock, Tom thumbs the face of his pocket watch and straightens his back. "That's good 'nuff fer today, boys. Let's get ta hell outta here."

CHAPTER 9

After the first day of woodswork, we are sore and tired. Our muscles ache, and scabs of pitch pull the skin on our arms and hands. On the way out, we use our shirts to swat flies, and Tom is in his flannel undershirt, the wide sweat-stained braces hanging around his hips like a harness. His hat and soaked handkerchief are on the floor of the wagon. As he drives, he hums an old tune around the stem of his fragrant pipe, and the tobacco smoke is sweet in the heavy heat of this fading day.

Tom's pleasure reaches me and Danny, as if our exhaustion is a measure of time well spent, as if earning money with muscles and sweat has made us better people, men to be respected. But our minds are free of the woods while Prince still drags the wagon down the rutted road between the trees. I see the house, the new car shining in the dooryard, I taste the river in the savory smell of fish frying in the summer kitchen. Danny and I jump awkwardly from the wagon, muscles already stiffening and protesting, and go to the river to wash up.

The water seems shallow as it flows over the pebbles, inviting us out of the hot sun. But it's breathtakingly cold, and we go in only to our knees. We splash each other and shiver and scrub with the sand-caked soap, struggling to catch breath between clenched teeth, then wade with huge hurried strides to the warm shore. The shadows are lengthening quickly, but the sun is still strong enough to dry us. Danny combs his hair into a cow-lick, his freckles standing out against his pale cold skin. He's very tired, just a kid. We lie on our damp towels, smoking, listening to the hammering down at David Cain's new house. One hammer rings out, and then two and then three together, and their echoes answer across the river like an army of discharging guns. The new house is going up.

In the outside kitchen, Katie mops Tom's back with alcohol, rubbing and then towelling it dry. He puts his braces back over his shoulders and hobbles to the cupboard for a flask of brandy.

"A little alcohol rub from the inside," he says to himself, taking a liberal drink and putting the bottle back. "Good fer what ails ya." He stretches out on the couch and falls immediately to sleep. Danny pretends to catch a fly and goes through an elaborate act of dropping it into Tom's open mouth, giggling to himself and trying to make me laugh. Katie gives us one of her looks, and we settle down — Danny goes off to play cowboys in his room, and I open my lesson books in at the dining room table.

Supper is frying and the fish smells drift outside, mixing with the wood smoke and teasing the house flies that buzz against the screen door. Long shadows of elm and apple tree fall across the dooryard and onto the woodpile. At a knock on the front door, sudden in the near-silence, Katie hurries through the main house to answer.

"Good evening, Mrs. Moar, is it?" The visitor is a slim-built man, balding and softspoken, in a dark suit and dark-rimmed glasses. "My name is Brooks — Dale Brooks — your new minister from St. Peter's."

"Oh my goodness, yes, come in! Have a seat, sir."

Katie leads him to the parlour and bustles back to the outside kitchen to wake Tom. On her way past the cupboard, she pulls a clean apron from a drawer and ties it around her to cover the stain on her dress.

"Tom! Tom, wake up! Wake up, the preacher's here."

"Who?" He comes out of sleep like a cranky old man, slowly.

"The preacher. Mr. Somebody, I dunno."

"A teacher?"

"No, the preacher. Yer goin' deaf!"

"What the hell does he want now?"

"He come ta visit. Ta meet us, I suppose, that's all. Good God, can't ya come in and talk ta the man?"

"Now what the hell's that man doin' here again? He was just here the other day," Tom says. "Is he got nothin' better ta do than ta bother people?"

"That was Mr. Cunningham. He's moved away. This is the new preacher, another man."

"Good fer him. That's lovely altogether. All right." Tom grumbles as he gets up from the couch. "That's what this river needs, another preacher."

He limps to the parlour, pale, like a man rising from a long illness. Curious, I follow, and lean in the doorway near Katie. "Well, sir," Tom says, giving the minister his hand.

"Mr. Moar, how do you do, sir? I'm Dale Brooks." Mr. Brooks is small beside Tom. His handshake is as soft as his voice. "You have a nice place here, Mr. Moar. I've always liked the farm. I was born in the country myself, the west, Alberta."

"How's that?" Tom says, cupping a hand behind his ear.

"I like a farm!" The young minister raises his voice. "It's nice and peaceful out here."

"Oh, hell, yes, sure thing," Tom says. "Alberta, eh? Why'd ya leave it?"

"I left to go to university in Toronto. So I rode the rails east, came most of the way on a boxcar — couldn't afford train fare."

Mr. Brooks has struck the right note with the old man.

"Hell, I used ta travel the boxcars meself in the old days," Tom says, warming. He settles into his chair and signs the minister to sit down nearby. "I loved it. Once I got on a train, even on the side ladder, and she started ta move across the country, I didn't give a damn if she ever stopped an' I cared fer nobody an' wanted nothin' more. Funny how a thing like that will get in yer blood, though. I just loved it."

"Is that a fact, sir? I'll bet you have a few stories to tell — the old days and the trains. But riding the rails is a risky business. You have to know what you're doing, isn't that right, Mr. Moar?"

"Tom, call me Tom. Oh yes, I knew what ta do alright. We'd steal aboard a freight in town, steal on in the dark just when she was movin' out, hang on the ladder, get up on top and lay flat. We'd jump 'er back here on the grade when she slowed down, jump 'er back there in the rock cut."

"Is that a fact, Tom."

"Yes, an' I'd hang on between the cars on a cold winter night, jump off back here in the snow an' roll down the hill. But she'd be movin' slow in that grade, ya know."

The minister nods.

"Well, sir," Tom says, "what did ya say yer name was?"

"Dale Brooks. Call me Dale if you like, Tom."

"Well, Dale, would ya like a little drink? A little shot, maybe, 'fore supper? Katie! Katie, bring me a drink a brandy. And one fer Dale."

"Good God, Tom, d'ya have ta drink when the minister's here?" Katie scolds. "Act sensible, will ya!"

"It's okay, Mrs. Moar, I'll have one, too. Just a small one."

Katie fills two tumblers, mixing the brandy with hot water and a dash of white sugar, and sits near the doorway with me, a basket of mending by her side. With his glass in hand and a new audience, Tom is set to talk all afternoon. He knows that Danny and I stopped listening to his old stories a long time ago.

"Well sir," he starts, "we went west on a boxcar once. Slept in barns and shimshacks along the way. Worked the harvest out there and came back in the big coach first class."

"Imagine . . ."

"But wait a minute, wait'll I tell ya 'bout the time me and Ben Jacobs was sleepin' in a barn over in Maine. Well, sir, we was on our way ta pick potatoes and we was sleepin' in a haymow. There was this big ol' rooster, roostin' up on a beam up high over Ben. Well, sir, I let out a whoop in the night an' that rooster shit — pardon me, he let 'er go — right down on Ben's face!"

"Now, Tom," Katie chides, "don't get into the storytellin'. The man'll think yer crazy."

"Don't worry, Mrs. Moar, I like a good story." Mr. Brooks says, and sips on his brandy. He pats an empty jacket pocket. "Would you have a cigarette, Tom?"

"How's that?"

"Cigarettes, do you smoke?"

"No, I don't touch 'em. I smoke a pipe. The boys might have some tobacco, I dunno."

"It's okay, never mind. But I like the railroad stories, and railroad songs. My father used to sing the Jim Rodgers songs. Ever heard of him?"

"Rodgers? Hell yes, killed 'imself singin' and yodelin'. His throat give out, I guess, and he had TB they say." Tom thinks for a moment, comes up with lines from a Jim Rodgers song, then goes straight into an old hobo poem:

> *"I bet my way from Mexico to the rockbound coast of Maine*
> *To Canada and wandered back again . . ."*

"Tom, don't ya get into the rhymin' now. The man don't wanna hear that ol' stuff."

> *"I met Tom Colfords and Tom Connors Bull*
> *I was tough as a cop could be*
> *And I been in every calaboose*
> *In this land of liberty . . ."*

"That's quite a poem, Tom. Who wrote that?"

"I dunno. Some hobo. Bring me in a drink, Stevie." I go to the kitchen and pour him a light drink while he searches his memory for more words.

> *"I've chopped the spruce and built the sluice*
> *And taken a turn at the plow*
> *And I searched for gold in rain and cold*
> *And fell in a river slow . . .*
> *Sleepin' in the daisies after hitchhikin' all day*
> *Some folks like a feathered bed*
> *But give me new mowed hay."*

Tom takes a drink of the watered brandy. He fills his pipe. Settling in to recite every line he ever heard and make up new ones when he runs out, I think, and I wonder what impression of our family this stranger must have now.

> *"As I was walkin' down the road to pass the time away*
> *A man stepped up and asked me to help him pitch some hay*
> *He said his land was rollin' and I said, 'If that is true*
> *Roll me to a shady spot and I'll see what I can do.'*

> *"Early in the mornin' when the dew is on the ground*
> *The bum raises from his nest and gazes all around*

> *From the boxcar to the haystack, he gazes everywhere*
> *He never gets back upon his tracks until he gets a spare . . ."*

He stops only long enough to cough, harshly, deep in his chest.

> *"One day I met John Palmer, he stopped me on my way*
> *He said he had some potatoes that he wanted dug today*
> *'I can't dig no potatoes because I'm gettin' fat —*
> *Get the man that planted them, for he knows where they're at!'* "

"You have a great memory, Tom," says Mr. Brooks.

"I could word that stuff off all day."

"I see what you mean."

Katie puts aside her handwork and moves behind Dale Brooks, dusting off the Bible and putting a hymn book on the organ in the corner. "Reverend," she says, "will ya stay fer a bite a supper?"

"Oh, I really shouldn't, Mrs. Moar."

"Pretty likely yer stayin'," Tom interrupts. "He's stayin', Katie."

"It's no bother, sir. We're eatin' anyway, shad an' potatoes," Katie says. "Hope ya don't mind shad."

"They're bony lads, but good tastin'," Tom says, and winks, "but we have no bones ta pick with them fellas."

Tom laughs at his own joke, and the minister chuckles politely. Katie pulls me into the dining room. "Run over ta Coopers' place and borrow me somethin' sweet fer supper, with Mr. Brooks here, Steve. I've got no bakin' at all."

When I return, balancing a chocolate cake and a few molasses cookies, the dining room table is set and Katie's grey hair curls forward over one eye like Danny's. She's pinning her brooch on her dress, the brass spider with blue eyes she's worn for dress-up as long as I can remember. Tom is still talking with our visitor in the front room, about everything but religion, almost as if Mr. Brooks was a friend of the family, I think, or a relative.

Katie calls the men to come eat, and sets a plate of fried shad on the table beside another of steaming potatoes.

"Would you like me to give thanks?" The minister asks.

"Oh, yes, sure thing," Tom says, realizing he should have asked.

"Where's Danny? I called him," says Katie. "Steve, go get him down here —" There's a clattering on the narrow stairs and Danny bursts in.

"There comes Adolph now," says Tom.

We bow our heads for the long blessing. All of our names are in the prayer: he has researched the family. Then Tom passes a plate to the minister, pitch still streaked on his hands. The stubble of his beard is white, and his cheeks look as if the outdoor colour was layered on over pale skin. It was a long day, I think suddenly, and hard work for an old man.

"Help yerself, Dale," Tom says, passing things around. "There's plenty."

Danny and I are hungry from fresh air and labour, and could eat more than we do. We use our best table manners for Mr. Brooks, sitting up straight with elbows in and hands never touching the food. Danny gobbles his first few mouthfuls, and I kick his ankle under the table to slow him down. He grins and kicks back. Funny kid, with the half-grown slanted teeth very white and his face dark with suntan and freckles.

Tom finishes his meal first, and lights his pipe. He slurps tea, leaning back in his chair and blowing smoke over the table, talking again with the minister who is still picking bones carefully from a piece of fish.

"Oh, we do the best we can, that's all the Lord can expect of us," Tom says. "We try ta be honest an' earn our keep by the sweat of our brows."

"Have you spent most of your life here on the farm, then, Tom? When you weren't travelling the trains, I mean?"

"Yessir, I was born here and so was my father. Right in this house. Well, there was the trips workin' away, like ya said, and I went overseas in '39. After the war I met Katie here. Me lucky day. Yessir, met 'er in Fredericton, married 'er, brought 'er home here with me." Tom reaches across and pinches the plump fold at Katie's elbow. "Hated 'er fer a while, didn't yer, Kate? Hated 'er till she got used ta it. By'n'by she got ta likin' it and then she didn't wanna leave. Now she loves it here, don't ya, Katie?" He pinches her again and smiles broadly.

"A person gets used ta anything after a while, I s'pose, if ya stay long enough," Katie says, and sips her tea very properly from a delicate china cup, playing the lady. Tom laughs, and she won't look at him. "When I was a girl growin' up in Fredericton, I took music lessons and I played the piano. I even played at the schools and churches and I went to all the recitals. I went to Normal School for a year but never used it. When I married Tom and came here, there was no piano, just an old pump organ that never played, mice ate off the levers inside. I never used my education either, the bit I had." Suddenly she looks like her comfortable self again, and pinches Tom back. "But I always encouraged my boys to get educated and get out of here. Tom doesn't agree."

"I wouldn't live anywhere else meself. And I didn't need the education ta do it. We all lived well enough. Worked hard and lived well, read the Bible on Sundays. I guess life is kinda like the lad that kissed the cow. He said it was everyone for his own fancy."

"Wild horses couldn't haul that man outta here," Katie tells the young minister. "He thinks city life an' books go hand in hand, they're not genuine."

"Well, my father sold our old farm to the corporation," Mr. Brooks says, "so I couldn't go back there if I wanted to, not to that place. But I do plan to go back to college someday, maybe in Halifax."

"Now why the hell would ya wanna go back ta school at yer age?" Tom asks. "Yer workin' ain't ya? Have a job, ya must be doin' alright, drivin' around in a big car all dressed up, big pay cheque comin' in every week."

"True enough, but I still want the degree — the Master's degree, the thesis. I'd like to write on Thomas Aquinas." Suddenly he turns to me. "What about you, Steve? Are you in school?"

I explain to him how I quit to help out Tom around the farm, but that I'm taking correspondence courses. I even tell him my own hope to go to college. "Maybe next year," I say.

"And a great help he is, too, betimes anyway," Tom puts in. "A good boy ta work. When he's not up readin' all night, eh, Steve?"

"Steve, sometimes things don't work out easily, and you have to fight for your dreams. Things have a way of getting postponed. My father didn't go to college until he was forty, after the corporation bought out the farm. But he got there." Mr. Brooks was looking at me very seriously, and I felt as if he was waiting for something from me.

"Well, I guess there's hope for me then," I say.

"Keep the flame burning," he tells me, sounding more like a preacher than he had since he'd come in. "The kind of thing you're doing is done with the best of intentions, and correspondence courses are okay, but you've got to get to university to get it all. A dream can fade after a while and get lost in the more immediate turmoil of life. Don't let that happen, Steve."

I nod my head.

After supper we all move back into the parlour and Mr. Brooks reads from the Bible, short passages, leafing the pages back and forth — John 3:16, Romans 12, and the 23rd Psalm. Tom sits for a while with his hand behind his ear, straining to hear the reading. Then he folds his arms and drifts off to sleep, his chin dropping onto his chest.

"Do you get out to church often, Mrs. Moar? The boys to Sunday School?"

"No, I'm afraid we don't much," Katie answers. "We listen to the preachers on the radio, but Tom is not a religious man. Oh, he reads his Bible now and then and does the best he can ta be a good neighbour. He's a good provider. You know how it is."

"Yes."

"We read the Bible," Tom says, waking suddenly and catching some of their words.

"And I hope you all get the Holy Spirit some day," Mr. Brooks says gently, getting up, then kneeling on the floor with his elbows on the chair. Katie follows, pulling a cushion down under her knees. Then Tom gets down, groaning as his joints creak. Danny snickers, and then it is silent. The prayer is for our household, for each of us by name, for our crops and our woods and for the river.

"Amen. Amen."

"Well done," Tom says, "that's lovely."

The minister gets to his feet and gives Katie his hand. "Well, come out to church when you can," he says, smiling.

Katie smiles back. "Oh yes, we will for sure. We'll be gettin' back ta church now that the weather's nice and the road's dried up. I'm ashamed we haven't been there for sa long."

Tom slips Mr. Brooks five dollars, "Here, fer the church . . ." and goes back to the summer kitchen and his couch.

Our visitor drives away, his car rumbling on the gravel road and curling a cloud of dust into the red sky. The dust boils into the woods, settling lightly in the bushes, the leaves of the alder, the needles of the spruce and the juniper. It sifts through the trees and clings to the damp grass on the flat, and it circles with fallen blossoms on the eddies of the river. And there is silence.

Then, as if silence on a weekday is a sin, work at the new house begins again. First one hammer thumps, then several together, faster, pausing, beginning again in slow staccato strokes. It sounds, I think, like someone trying to learn a strange new dance.

CHAPTER 10

At eight o'clock there are already a few cars at David Cain's new house, but the dance won't start until dusk. From out in the yard we hear the boys tuning up, the scrape of the fiddle, the hollow wooden tone of a guitar as it is bumped, the occasional burst of laughter. The house has been framed and boxed in with plywood, but there's no roof and the windows are still empty.

"She's a good size place," someone remarks. "Dave must be glad ta be back after sa long in the big city."

David was in St. Catharines for five years, worked at Kimberly-Clark's making toilet paper and Kleenex, made good money and hated it. Last summer, when he was home, he got the promise of a job selling furniture in town. And his father offered him the field between the railway and the river.

When he came back for good, early this spring, David tried to find a carpenter. They were all at the mill or in the woods, so he and his brother started the job, with old Henry, eighty-seven now, sitting by in a chair and telling them what to do.

"I'll have a dance in 'er, boys, soon as she's boarded in," Dave had promised. "Meet everyone and raise some money ta finish 'er with." He kept his word.

In the gold light of sunset dandelions and buttercups dominate the fields. The shrubs and blossoms on the riverbank are yellow. Everything is yellow except the river itself. The smells of lilac and cherry hang in the air, heavy with black flies and mosquitoes, and the neighbours gathering in David Cain's yard slap at their arms and trade news and watch cars pull off the road in rolls of dust. Three men in work clothes drive up in a pulp truck, its chains rattling and banging as they park off to the side. Strolling over to the group near the house, they push and wrestle good-naturedly with the men who are dressed for the dance.

"Yer dressed up sa good I hardly knew ya. I thought ya was a finance man. Or are ya a preacher?"

"Ha haar, I got the words fer it. I ken rattle 'em off!"

"Boys, we'll go way inside after we have a drink er two," says a man in a tight white shirt, his hair combed back and slick with tonic.

"I hope the Cole boys don't show up," says David Cain, looking down to the road. "They can start trouble and spoil a time."

The men in the yard stand in a circle, smoking. The strong smell of aftershave drifts with the cloud of smoke toward the river. Then they go to a car and pass the bottle, talk louder, jostle each other and laugh. Some dig their hands in their pockets, round-shouldered, their lighted cigarettes hanging carelessly on a lip. I've tried that, no hands and casual, but I can't talk and laugh around the smoke the way they do.

Nick and Cindy come up the hill from the river. Cindy is slim and brown in her white blouse and pleated skirt, with smooth tanned legs and her new sandals showing off pink toenails. She tosses her blonde hair away from her face and smiles at me on her way inside. But there's no sign of Howard. He told me that he'd be here and stay until dark, before his night-blindness comes on. Some more people come down the railway, their heads down, talking and kicking the loose gravel between the ties. I'll wait for Howard a while longer, I tell myself, but I'm suddenly excited. The night is full of possibilities and music and Cindy.

"Come way inside, boys, don't be shy," someone calls from the doorway. "Gimme a hand with all these women! Let's get 'er rollin'!"

The music starts, the fiddler sawing a jig, and I move to the doorway to watch. The guitar player in his western shirt taps a foot and puts some fancy runs into his chords, like he's heard Hank Snow do. They play "Under the Double Eagle," already starting to sweat. Old Henry Cain can't contain himself. He hobbles to the middle of the floor and tries a few steps, picking up one foot at a time with hands linked behind his knee. It's been a while since he had a dance. Out of breath, he kicks one foot in the air and gives a fragile old-man's whoop; everyone claps. Out here, in the dusk of the yard, someone whoops louder and someone else whistles. The dance is under way.

More cars drive onto the field. Horns honk and the beams of headlights probe the clouds of dust as they bob over the crossing. In the downriver sky, gold-fringed black clouds are covering the sunset.

Through the doorway, I can see someone swinging Cindy, her skirt fanned out and showing her legs. Men and women crowd the house as the fiddler plays the "St. Anne's Reel," "Ragtime Annie" and the "Taylor Mountain Hornpipe." They call for tunes to dance the Circle and the Lancer. As they swing each other, heavy work boots shake the floor. A few of the men push past me, going to cool off and pass the bottle.

"Here, young fella, have a swig a this. It'll put lead in yer pencil," a man calls from the shadows. The others laugh, and I turn back towards the dancers. The smell of whiskey and sweat is carried on a haze of cigarette smoke. Everyone is dancing and whooping like the two are meant to be done together, and the men call to each other.

"How's yer bird?"

"All feathers an' no tail t'night!"

They scuff around a little awkwardly, taking turns with the women, swinging until their shirts are wet with sweat. They stop only long enough for another drink or a cigarette. Sometimes they go outside in twos or threes, stay a while, and come in red-faced and laughing.

The musicians put their heads together, then the fiddler shouts, "Get yer sets fer a Lancer!" I'm waiting for a waltz so I can ask Cindy to dance; so I stay where I am, leaning in the doorway, until the fiddler stops, lights a smoke and is treated to a drink. Outside, someone calls my name.

"Steve!" I step outside. "Steve, c'm'ere!"

I follow the voice behind the house. Nick is slouched against the wall, his hand under his shirt.

"Have a little drink," he says.

"What is it?"

"Rum!"

"Where'd you get this?"

"Found it. Never mind. Look, it was never opened."

"You found it? Where?"

"There, under the step. I could see it from here. Have a good one, Steve."

"I don't think we should. Look, maybe you better put it back."

"No, Jesus, no. I'm not puttin' it back. C'mon, have a drink. What's the matter with ya? If ya don't help me, I'll drink 'er all meself."

I take the pint he holds out and swallow cautiously. The rum burns my throat and it's bitter, almost sickening. My stomach tingles as it hits.

"There, I've had a drink. Now put it back before someone misses it."

Nick tips the bottle and his jaws swell, and when he swallows he gives a "Ha whoo!" He staggers slightly, but braces his feet apart and holds the rum high, like a torch or a trophy. "Have another swig," he says, "just one more. C'mon, just a little one. What ails ya?"

"Now put it back, before someone comes."

We have another drink and put the empty bottle back under the step before we go inside. Finally, the fiddler is starting a waltz. Nick heads straight for an older woman from downriver, smiling broadly, and I make my way across to Cindy. I feel confident, the rum tingling. Cindy sees me coming and springs to her feet, both hands held out to me. We dance, moving carefully to get in rhythm with each other, keeping it smooth.

"Never sway yer arm up and down that way," Katie had told me when we danced in the kitchen. "Yer not pumpin' water."

The fiddle scrapes louder and slightly off key as it grinds out the tunes "Over the Waves," "Smile a While," and "My Wild Irish Rose." Cindy is snug in my arms, her head on my chest. I can feel her breathing, smell the perfume. I want to kiss her but she doesn't raise her head. Her smooth thigh moves against me like a signal.

Crack! The music stops. Heads turn towards the door.

"Now what the hell was that?" David Cain asks.

Someone has put his fist through the wall. It's one of the Cole boys — Ted. He staggers to the middle of the floor, eyes glassy and shirt undone. He's drunk, and angry, and waving an empty rum bottle. Against the far wall, Ted's sister Tina shrugs her shoulders: at least he's here alone. I look over at Nick, who has frozen with his arms still around the downriver woman.

"Who drunk me fuckin' bottle a rum, boys?" Ted roars. The whole house is silent, everyone staring at the clenched fists. "Now who da fuck was she, boys?"

Nobody speaks.

"Come outside! Come outside! Ya yella son-of-a-whore, whoever ya are," he shouts. "Come out an' fight like a fuckin' man!"

Silence. I feel the taste of warm rum rise in the back of my throat, like fear.

"I'll beat every thievin' son-of-a-whore in this house if I have to, ya yella-belly sons-a-whores."

"Mention some names!" a big man shouts.

"I'll not mention names! I'll beat the whole fuckin' bunch!"

Some of the men grab Ted and pull him outside. Everyone jams through the doorway after them, two and three at once like the house is on fire.

"Fight!"

"Hit the son-of-a-whore!" someone shouts.

"Don't break up the man's time. He's tryin' ta build a house here," someone else pleads.

Fight! The word is shouted. Is this what everyone's been waiting for?

Two men are clutching the shoulders of Ted's shirt. He twists and they jostle and tug but no one's throwing punches. Ted's shirt rips, and he reaches around the tangled men to pull off the shreds of cloth, throws them into the cellar pit and kicks sand in on top. His stomach and chest have scabs of pitch like he has spent the day in the woods. Reeling from one part of the yard to another, the wrestling men are just holding Ted back, now, and talking it out. Gradually Ted's fury fades and the bunched muscles relax. Then they're all sitting together on the grass, sharing a smoke and a drink as if nothing has happened.

"Boys, let's get the music goin'," someone shouts. "She's early, the night's young and yer sa beautiful. Start 'er up, boys!"

The music starts up again and we all go back in, ready to grab a partner and swing faster than ever before.

"Whoop an' drive 'er!" David shouts.

And someone shouts back, "Don't crowd the fiddler!"

Some men stand at one end of the house. They are passing their last bottle openly now; huddling, they light cigarettes from one match. Someone goes outside to vomit beside the step. There is a smell of beer and sweat and the smoke that settles waist-high in the room. In a while, they run out of rum, and there's talk of going to the bootleggers. Drinks of any kind at any price will keep the dance going, the dance that is going to peak with the next drink. They pool their change and someone leaves.

"Now, boys! We're gonna auction off these here little baskets," David Cain shouts from the fiddler's stand in the corner. "Tell the boys outside ta come in here."

Some of the women have brought small baskets of food. The highest bidder gets to lunch with whoever brought the basket, and Dave gets the money to help out with his house. He holds the first basket over his head.

"Now, boys, what am I offered?"

The men stand silent, hands in their pockets. Some are waiting eagerly for a certain basket to come up, or for someone else to make the first bid; others are bored with this ritual: feeling the drink, they want to dance. The women sit on the bench around the walls, watching, their legs folded beneath their pleated skirts, toes moving up and down in their open sandals.

"Do I have a bid? Does no one wanna eat with a beautiful lady?"

"One dollar!"

"One dollar. Do I hear more?"

"Two dollars!"

"Two twenty-five"

"Is there bright salmon in 'er, boys?" calls a man from near the back. "I'd give ten dollars for a good feed a bright salmon."

"No," David answers, "but this basket was brought here by that lovely lady, right over there, in the bare feet."

"Five dollars!"

"Goin' once, goin' twice, three times, five takes 'er, boys!"

Dave's reaching for another basket, and I'm looking around casually for Cindy's blonde hair in the crowd, when I see Nick slide out of the house arm-in-arm with his dancing partner. They stroll into the shadows beyond the yard.

Suddenly Jess Cole leaps into the centre of the floor. He is Ted Cole's big brother, and he has a thirty-thirty rifle in his hand.

"By the Lord God," he says, trembling, "I'll shoot the first son-of-a-whore that moves."

Nobody moves.

"Who stole me brother's fuckin' bottle a rum?" Jess is glassy-eyed, his hair greasy and falling over his eyes.

Tina, his sister, pushes through the crowd and runs to Jess, crying. She tugs at his sleeve. "Jess, put it down," she begs, "put Ralphie's gun away!"

"Fuck off, Tina!"

"But you, ya said! Ya did, y' said ya wouldn't drink again after ya took the pledge. Y' said ya wouldn't, so ya did!"

"Shut up, Tina!"

"No, you shut up! Stealin' Ralphie's fuckin' new gun. He'll get the blame fer this if the Mounties come. Ya know they blame everythin' on Ralphie, just cuz he's on suspension."

"They're not gonna blame this on Ralphie."

"Yes, he'll get it. The Mounties'll do it to 'im again, ya know they will."

I can't tell if her words are making any difference. But Tina's a big girl, and she takes Jess by surprise. She grabs the gun and levers the action: it is empty. Three men grab Jess and take him outside, shouting and crying and cursing everyone in the house. I follow, with some of the others.

"Boys, who in the name a God took the man's rum anyway?" David Cain appeals, irritated now.

"I did."

"Who said that?" Jess asks, swinging his head around.

"I did. I drank some of it," I say, stepping into the light. My knees are weak and my head is throbbing. A voice inside me has taken over and is saying things I can't stop. I look around for Nick, but he's nowhere at the dance, no help to me now.

"You? Steven?"

"Yes, it was me. I drank most of it."

"Yer lyin', ya wouldn't take a drink. The Moars don't drink."

"I drank it."

"Then step up an' fight like a man, ya skinny fuckin' book-readin' wimp."

"Hit 'im, Steve!" someone cheers.

"Hit 'im, Jess!" Tina shouts. "No one can stand the Jesus big-feelin' Moars anyway. Hit 'im!"

Jess takes a swing, slow and awkward, that brushes me on the shoulder at the same instant as he kicks me on the shin. Then he takes another telegraphed swing and the big work boot just misses my crotch. He seems drunk and fighting for his pride. Suddenly he turns and sits down on a pile of boards.

"That's enough a that foolishness," he says. "Let's have a drink."

Ted Cole comes across the yard with wheel wrench in his hand. When he sees us sitting together, he throws the wrench in the pit and sits beside us.

"Friends?" Jess offers me his hand.

"No hard feelin's?" Ted says.

"Friends," I say, shaking hands with them both. Everyone goes back inside, the fight over. The music starts, but the dance is almost done and people are starting to trail away. Cindy comes toward me with her hand out, and I walk with her down the path to the river. Neither of us mention the Cole brothers or the rum. In the distance we can hear the mellow strains of late waltzes, and the whooping of the men as they go to their cars.

"All feathers an' no tail t'night!"

"Yer mother was a bear."

I can feel the warmth of Cindy's body and her movements against me. The stolen rum and the relief flood happily through me, and the river is silent, with only the occasional toad singing. Across the bridge we follow the gravel road with its pockets of warm air left over from the hot day. The smell of blossoms is strong and touched with a taste of dust that settles in the ditches and powders the broken pop bottles and the empty potato chip bags.

"Steve, yer awful nice ta me," Cindy says, and I lean towards her cheek for a kiss as we walk. "Yer moochin' with me, Steven Moar."

"I enjoy your company. I really do."

"Steve, I love you."

"Really?"

"Yes, I do. I love you. Would I swim the river if I didn't?"

"I don't know."

"Must be love, when you think of someone all the time, ain't it?"

"I suppose it is."

"Then I love you, Steve."

"I think about you, too, Cindy." How carefully I choose words! I don't love her, she makes it too easy. But I'm attracted to her, a feeling that is exaggerated now by the drink.

When we reach the Longs' house, it's in darkness. Cindy says her parents are gone for the weekend, and she holds onto my arm and leads me inside to the sofa. Listening to Howard and the boys talking, I used to wonder if I'd know what to do. But this is how it goes — the dance, the rum, the girl, the empty house and the sweet breeze of summer through the screen door as we kiss with new passion.

Cindy pulls away and steps out of her new white skirt, folding it across the back of a chair. Then her smooth legs are against me like warm satin and I think — it's loneliness, she's lonely — before our lips devour all thought and that lesser force, conscience.

The night is cool when I start for home. As I walk, guilt and pride keep step with me. It wasn't quite like I imagined it would be, and I'm not sure now whether I'm disappointed or pleased. Still, I feel I've now had an experience many wish they'd had. Only my footsteps are audible as they keep time with the moving memories. The bridge looms high in the darkness, stretching across a pond that reflects of body of twinkling stars; a mirrored galaxy.

As I pass David Cain's house, I see the cars have gone, the empty house a cube open to the night. But the memories of the dance are strong, and the box is a black entanglement of feelings — spirits that whoop and dance — they mix their smells like animals, their hates and joys, they smoke the same tobacco, drink from the same urns, and share the same desires and torments. As they have for generations, they dance on in the darkness.

CHAPTER 11

Through the next days, everyone talks of the dance and how half the men there were fighting and wrangling all night. As the story spreads, it grows so that it's hardly recognizable to those of us who were there. They say that a crowd of men from downriver beat Ted Cole. They say that a man with a broken rum bottle attacked Tina. They say that Ralph Cole went to the dance with a gun, looking for revenge. He fired the gun, they say, and the community buzzes with alarmed gossip — Ralph is on a suspended sentence, everybody knows. Finally, someone calls the Mounties.

Two days later they come to our place. The black car, with buffalo-head crests on the doors and a whip aerial on the back fender, glistens under the elms beside our Chev. The Mounties have been to David Cain's and the Coles' and have talked to Ralphie. Brass buttons sparkle as the officers stride across the dooryard, their brown boots polished, their clipped necks sunburned below the tilted hats. The tallest one loses his hat when he walks under the clothesline, and Danny, watching from the window, snickers. They don't talk much and they never smile. Tom knows the older man, a Corporal Brown, and together they walk through the garden, looking at the vegetables. The Mounties stay only minutes, but it seems like hours to me. I expect to be questioned — yes sir, I confess, I drank the man's rum — but they talk only with Tom. Corporal Brown orders a hamper of cucumbers for the fall. When they're gone, Danny strides around the house, arms swinging. He says he wants to be a Mountie someday.

By now the grass has lengthened and the oats are thick and dark; the trees are weighted with new growth. Cranes stand one-footed on the gravel points of the summer-slow river, labouring away on huge wings when we come near the shore. Dead shad come adrift and circle in the eddies, catching in the scrub bushes to decay; their smell mixing oddly with that of the sweet shore roses.

And there are bright salmon in the river. They school past in widening Vs, the occasional one jumping, leaving a doughnut-like wake to widen and drift away. Sometimes they stop in the cold water at the mouth of the brook. Howard has a new fishing rod; on hot days, when he comes from the woods, he hurries straight to the river to flyfish and jig. It's his whole life.

One Indian Summer

I've been driving the new car for a couple of weeks — and lucky I wasn't out on the road when the Mounties came! Since then, Tom has taken me to town to take my driver's test with Corporal Brown, going around town and parking on the hill. I passed. But to get the license I had to lie about my age — the same way I lied when I was being sworn in for a guide's license, and the warden added "and are you positive yer eighteen?" to the end of the oath. When Corporal Brown asked my age, I told him I was eighteen and showed him my guide pin for proof.

Tom has never asked about it. I've never told him. I wonder if he even knows the legal age to get a driver's license; but sometimes he lets certain things pass, maybe thinking he's helping me get on with growing up. Whatever his reason, I'm grateful that he lets me use the car as though it's my own.

It is Saturday evening when Nick comes, dressed in jeans and T-shirt, wanting to go to the circus in town. He waits while I dress and borrow money from Tom.

"Now hang on ta yer money, lad," Tom says. "It's just a place ta lose money, a jeezless circus."

The heat of the day is withdrawing and the sun has dropped behind the trees on the top-hill when we drive away, leaving Danny and Tom hand-weeding the potatoes. They disappear in a cloud of dust in my rearview mirror.

Nick has hitchhiked to town twice since we went together on the train. He knows the hangouts. He has met town girls — even walked some home from the Delux Grill, though others refused him because he's from so far upriver. It's a reverse of when we came here together in the spring. This time, Nick's the one with confidence.

We get to town at dusk, circle the main streets, then go to the grill for cigarettes. The restaurant is warm but empty — everyone's at the circus. Nick leans against the jukebox and plays Hank Williams' "Lovesick Blues," and we have a smoke before we leave.

The midway is set in a ballfield back of town. One bingo tent is crowded around with booths and a dozen rides, including a merry-go-round and roller coaster. carnival music is everywhere, and children scream above the clatter of machines. Yellow lights stretch around trailers where tattooed men in black T-shirts serve soggy hot dogs and french fries, their stained aprons loose and faces glowing with grease. A sign in front of one tent advertises the freaks: a half-man half-woman and the World's Shortest Man. Another tent has the girlie show. The circus has plenty of ways to take the river's money.

"Now step right up folks. Three for a dime, nine for a quarter, step this way and win a prize," someone calls.

"Here's the game right here, friend."

"Ring the bell and win a cigar."

A crowd gathers at the girlie show, where three women dance on a platform in front of the tent. A man in a rhinestone-studded shirt urges the grinning men to come inside and see Tina the Terrible "shake it to the east, shake it to the west, shake it the way you like it best." The dancers wiggle their hips and breasts and pale skin peeps through their black dresses, inviting us in to see more.

"C'mon, let's go in," Nick says.

"No way."

"C'mon. Why not?"

"Someone might see us, Nick."

"So what? Whoever sees us will be just as guilty, right?"

"It's going in and coming out."

"We'll go out the back way," Nick says, dragging on my arm. "No one knows us anyway."

"Still . . ." I hesitate.

"Aw, c'mon."

We pay the man in the rhinestones and go in to see the strippers. Inside there's a small board stage and some benches, where a small crowd waits. Some are drinking, boisterous. Others seem as embarrassed as I feel. I'm looking around, relieved to see only strangers, when the music starts up and the women strut out onto the stage. Moving their hips to the heavy downbeat, they undo layers of skirts and let them drop to whoops and whistles. Bits of clothing drop until they wear only necklaces and G-strings; they tug at the straps, one side at a time, to give a peek to the row of mesmerized men up front. Tina the Terrible teases them with near touches.

"Holy Christ!" Nick says, "did ya see that? Shy thing, ain't she?"

Tina the Terrible calls out to a man standing alone at the back, "Come here, big fella, come closer an' smell the roses."

"I can smell ya from here," he answers. Everyone laughs.

"What a Jesus tramp, though," Nick says.

The show lasts only a few minutes, then we're back out on the grounds. I'm uncomfortable now and everyone is looking at us like they know we've been in the strippers' tent.

Two girls in particular are looking at us, strolling our way. One has long brown hair and a smile I remember: Amanda Reid. The midway crowds fade and I see only her. It seems a long time ago that Nick and I had lunch at her family's inn, but the same feeling overtakes me, her singing and the music of the piano playing again in my head. Amanda looks plain, though, beneath the yellow lights; almost unattractive, I think.

The other girl knows Nick and introduces herself as Anna. "And this is Amanda," she says.

"Hello, Nick and Steve. I remember you from somewhere," Amanda nods at us and smiles.

We fall in step behind the girls and they joke as we pass the strippers' tent, daring us to go in. At a booth I throw darts and win a stuffed rabbit for Amanda. "Oh, he's beautiful, Steve," she says. "I'll put him in my room, thank you."

When Amanda says my name, I'm full of myself. And when I stand beside her it's like I've known her for years. Her personality bubbles and overflows and she smiles to people passing, who smile back warmly. I hear them call her "Mandy." She is slim, and smaller than I had remembered, and I'm pleased with her. I gain confidence as we walk.

"C'mon, let's get on the roller coaster!" Nick says.

"Nick . . ." I don't want to lose this chance with Amanda. The circus rides can wait.

"Aw, c'mon," he says, "Let's all share one of the cars."

"Let's get on with them," Anna says to Amanda.

Anna and Amanda take the seats facing us, a motor blats, and the small train moves over the rails. Amanda fastens the web seatbelt as the cars begin to rock, gaining speed, licking around the tight turns of the steel frame hills. Her knees are almost touching mine, and her long hair catches the wind, whipping across her face as she laughs. A fast turn or sudden drop over an incline, and the girls scream. When the ride stops, I take Amanda's hand to help her down.

I'm dizzy and the grounds are hot with a rank smell of candy apples and popcorn. "Let's go on the Ferris wheel," Amanda says.

But something has changed. "No, we have to go," Anna says. "Remember, I'm expected home to babysit." She glances at Amanda. And I wonder if she is so suddenly ready to leave because of Nick. Maybe she's one of the girls that refused to go with Nick because he's from upriver; is she that kind? I can't tell. "Remember, Mandy?" she says again.

"Oh, yes, I remember now."

Anna lives near the fair grounds, a block from Amanda's. We offer to walk them home, and they exchange glances. But they neither accept nor refuse, so we follow the sidewalk with them. And shortly Anna and Nick break away. I'm walking alone with Amanda.

"Do you go to school, Amanda?" It's all I can think of to say.

"Call me Mandy, everyone calls me Mandy. Actually, I just finished, graduated this year. What about you, Steve? Are you in school still?"

I hear myself talking, spilling out words so she'll know I'm different, I won't always be an awkward guy from the farm: "Me? No, not really, but I'm going back next year. To university. At least I want to. If I can raise the money. I've had to take a year off, to help my father at home. His health . . . but I'm taking a correspondence course: English literature. And I'm reading."

"Where will you go then, when you go?"

"Fredericton, probably. I have some relatives there, my mother's sister, she'll put me up. But I might go to Halifax — King's."

And suddenly there's the rock wall by the inn, and there's her front door. I'm out of time. I take her hand, warm and sort of tingling, and she leans against the door, looking at me with brown eyes. Hugging the stuffed rabbit, she says, "Thank you for this, Steve."

"Thank you, Mandy. Look, maybe we could do something sometime, go out to something maybe."

"Maybe," she says, "sometime."

"I'll call you," I say, touching her on the arm.

"Okay. Thanks again, Steve."

I want to kiss her, but the way things are going there isn't time. She backs through the door into the house. The door closes. I walk back to my parked car, acceptance of my disappointment mixed with a gentle yearning. Whenever I see Amanda, I love her, I think, and slightly more each time. I get into the car and light up a cigarette, waiting for Nick, leaning back through the open window to look up at the stars. The music of the circus carousel drifts towards me, with screams of laughter from the roller coaster.

Nick comes strutting, bubbling with confidence that he has made progress with Anna. "I kissed 'er good night," he grins. "She let me kiss her."

"Good for you."

"You?"

"No."

"Let's get some beer," Nick says. "A nice cool Moosehead."

"The liquor store would be closed by now."

"We'll go to the bootleggers. I know a lad who'll sell us."

I drive to the waterfront and park behind a taxi stand. Nick runs inside and comes out with two green quart bottles of Moosehead. Then I drive out of town, find a woods road, and shut off the car. We listen to the radio as we drink. The ale is bitter and cold and froth streams down the bottles. We peel off the wrinkled labels, curl them into little balls and toss them out the window. The bottles are damp between our legs and we keep the windows up because of the flies, though there's a little night breeze in the poplars.

"That Anna's a bit stand-offish," Nick says, "but I think she likes me. She let me kiss her after a while."

"I got to know Mandy a bit. Her friends call her Mandy."

"But that Tina was a terrible sassy thing, though."

The radio is playing WWVA out of Wheeling, West Virginia. Fiddling and guitar picking. Doc Williams sings "My Old Brown Coat and Me," all twelve verses.

Then a car drives up behind us, so close its lights shine under our bumper. Nothing happens for a long time. We are uneasy with the empty bottles on the seat between us.

"Throw the bottles out. Quick! Out your side!" Nick cranks down the window and drops the empty bottles into the breaks.

"Get out, please. Walk back to the patrol car!" An RCMP officer is picking up the bottles on Nick's side of the car; I think it's Corporal Brown. His partner comes to my window, taps, and asks me to step out. He turns his flashlight to search the car.

"Who owns the beer?" the younger Mountie asks.

One Indian Summer

"What beer is that now?"

"The Moosehead, the bottles you threw out."

"I don't know. They must belong to Nick," I say.

"You don't know?"

"My friend Nick, here, it's his." Nick will have to claim the beer. I'm driving.

"Where did you get it?"

I mutter that I don't know for sure, he got it someplace, at the liquor store, I guessed.

"Was it a bootlegger?"

"I don't think so."

"Was it the taxi stand?"

"I don't know," I say again, very respectfully. "Look, we have to be going. They're expecting us home."

"Where's home?"

"Up river."

We go back and get into the police car, where Nick is being questioned by Corporal Brown.

"Well, this man purchased the liquor," Corporal Brown nods at Nick.

"That's right, she's mine," Nick says nervously. "I'll claim 'er."

"But he won't say where he got it. Now, the liquor is opened, which is a criminal offence. I could book you both on three or four charges." Corporal Brown frowns, writing in a black notebook. "The fine for illegal possession is fifteen dollars. Now you can pay me here or appear in court."

Court!

How could we explain something like that to Tom? Our whole evening would come out — the girlie show, our dates, the bootleggers. Our names would be in the newspapers.

"If I pay ya now, would that be the end of it?" Nick pleads, digging into his wallet.

"Yes, you can pay me. I'll give you a receipt."

We both sigh. I have only a bit of change left.

"I'll pay you half when my wood sells," I tell Nick. His hand is trembling as he pockets the receipt and opens the car door to get out.

"Just a minute! I'm not through with you fellas yet. Now, I'll be keeping an eye on you both for the rest of the summer. Don't let me catch you boys in trouble here in town. I'm giving you fair warning. Now go straight home and don't be on the highway at this time of night, and don't be drinking on the highway. If I catch you again I'll lock you up."

"Yessir."

"Are you the driver?" Corporal Brown turns to me.

"Yes, sir," I say.

"Let me see the ownership and your driver's license."

I pass him Tom's car registration and the paper he had signed for me after my test just days ago.

"Remember me?" I smile.

"I remember. Drive carefully, Steven Moar."

CHAPTER 12

To think of someone isn't love. It's the intensity, the turbulence that determines true love. When I think of Amanda, everything turns over inside me. The pleasure I find is a joy ride that overshadows anything that may dampen my spirits through days of bad weather, back-breaking labour, or the rejection of a story. The feelings prevail. And as this new spirit intensifies, I know it has to be love and that it's real and growing.

We've had three days of east wind and rain, and it is cold and damp in the main house. In the mornings, we huddle by the range in the summer kitchen. We lift the stove covers and make toast over the flame. When the fire dies, we run to the shed for more sticks to keep it going. On the back of the stove, the tea pot simmers, its gooseneck spout clogged with tea leaves. It is warm and cosy and the darkness behind the stove makes the cot there inviting. I lie and think of Amanda and listen to the snap of the fire and the rain on the roof.

Katie has made bread in the morning, as she often does before the day gets hot, and has taken the loaves to the dining room, turned them upside down and buttered their crusts with a piece of waxed paper. Then she starts the molasses cookies. She cuts them out with a drinking glass and places them carefully on the pan, leaving room for them to rise and spread. Then she puts the pan in the oven and puts just the right size stick on the fire to cook them. When they start to rise, she tests them by puncturing their surface with a straw from the broom, and when they are done she carries them in from the summer kitchen and sits them by the bread, under a dish towel.

On one such trip to the dining room, Katie drops the towel.

"Oh, good Lord, a stranger'll come to the door."

She goes back outside, sits at the table, and eats one of the warm cookies, buttering it and breaking it in two pieces, dipping it in her cup of raw tea. Finished, she turns the cup and studies the pattern of tea leaves.

"Oh my goodness," she says to herself, "a death in the settlement." And she goes back about her work, humming now, "Bless'd be the ties that bind."

Through the wet spell, the summer kitchen remains warm; the fragrance of the baking blends with the fire and together they smell like home. Outside, the wind wails at the eaves, lashing the drops of rain into blotted patterns on the screen door. Smoke swirls over the dooryard, the stovepipe moaning like someone blowing across the top of an empty bottle.

The hay is nearly full grown and the fields have clumps of daisies and buttercups. Furry-stemmed devil's paintbrush, orange and black, nod in the rain, and there are patches of caraway waist-high behind the woodshed. In the run-out field above the barn, wild strawberries look like tiny red beads scattered in the open hay. The tiny brook, now hidden in the grass, divides the field between the fine-top and the timothy, lodged now by the rain and wind. The swamp grass awaits the scythe.

Danny brings in the mail, and there is an envelope from the *Star Weekly*. I tear it open, anxious to learn that my story has been accepted for publication. But no, the manuscript has been returned intact, with a typed letter that reads:

> *Dear Mr. Moar,*
> *At present we are unable to use your submission as it is not quite suited to our present needs. We seldom use western stories. Perhaps you should consider a more regional publication . . .*

I carry the letter and my story up to my room. I'd set out to revise the manuscript, but I know that I'll get into trouble with Tom if I write in the daytime, so I lay it away and go to help him.

Tom works in the barn, cleaning out the mows and preparing the scaffold for haying. He puts a new rung in the hayrack, whittles a new tooth for the rake, and oils the wood pulleys and trip lever on the pitching machine fork. He'll work in here for as long as it rains. The doors are propped open but still the thrashing floor is dark, save where a reflection of light extends from the feeding hole into the empty mow. In spite of the overcast day, there is light between the horizontal boards in the gable that resembles a near-closed venetian blind. Swallows squeak in mud nests along the eaves and sparrows flit near the roof, painting the hand-hewn beams with splatters of white. The cattle are across the road in the swamp pasture, crowded against the gate, bawling to be put in out of the rain.

"Lad, run to the house an' fetch me the spikes like a good boy," Tom says. "They're there by the wash stand in the cookhouse."

I put a jacket over my head and run to the outside kitchen. The long grass in the dooryard is beaded with raindrops and the clothes on the line droop to the ground. My pant legs are wet as I search for the brown paper bag containing the spikes.

A knock comes on the kitchen door. Katie, wiping her hands on her apron, goes to answer it. It's George Cooper.

"Well, good God, look who's here. Come in, George," she says, "you're quite a stranger."

"I have bad news, Kate, bad news," he says, coming through the door, taking off his hat. "Poor ol' Henry, Henry Cain passed away last night. Where's Tom?"

"Now hold yer tongue, surely he didn't!" Katie says. "Tom's at the barn."

"Yessir, he had a big feed a corn beef fer supper, like any of us would, took gas, had a drink a soda, went ta bed and died, he did. Just slept away!"

"Well, God, poor Henry's dead. It's hard ta believe it," Katie says. "Poor dear Martha must be in an awful way, surely ta the Lord."

"Poor ol' thing's near crazy."

"Well, well, a person never knows what they're gonna hear when ya get up in the mornin', do ya?"

"No sir, we don't know the day, none of us."

"I saw Henry jest the other day, alive and well as any of us. How old was he?" Katie asks, even though she knows.

"Eighty-eight, come fall."

"Yes, I thought he would be. No spring chicken. I knew he was older than Martha. He'll be laid out there at the house, I 'spect. A small place, too."

"Yes, the wake's t'night, tomarra night, and Sa'rday. The funeral's Sunday afternoon," George says.

There seems to be no end to the comfortable platitudes George and Katie exchange. It's a ritual, I think, without which no neighbour on the river can be allowed to pass on.

"The man's time jest come I s'pose."

"Yes, surely. It says in the Bible, like a thief in the night."

Katie walks to the window and looks out at the barn. "I jest knew something bad was gonna happen." She is wringing her hands, twisting them in her apron. "I had such awful dreams. And Tom said something knocked off his hat in the barn — a forerunner. I could feel it in my bones, something bad was gonna happen."

"Don't fret now," George says awkwardly. "It coulda been worse."

"I worry about Tom," Katie says. "He coughs sa bad and he smokes an' coughs, wouldn't go to a doctor if he was dyin'."

"Tom's healthier than any of us, Kate. The man's strong as a horse."

"Oh, it's no use in talkin', surely ta the Lord," she says briskly, turning back to the room, "and Martha, the poor dear ol' soul, sa frail herself. I'll send down some bakin'. George, now you tell Martha, if she needs a hand, Tom an' the boys can come, dig the grave an' the like. But we don't wanna butt in, ya understand what I'm sayin'."

"I'll tell 'er."

George is gone by the time Tom comes in from the barn, looking for me and the spikes. He takes the news as if it was of no more importance than if the milk had gone sour or the cookies had burned. It's no secret that the two men weren't close, having had a falling out some years ago over a horse Tom bought from

Henry. Tom shakes his raincoat and hat and hangs them on a nail behind the door.

"Boys, she's rainin' pitchforks out there, pitchforks and dung forks," he says, pulling off his rubbers.

"So Henry's dead, eh? Good fer him. He's been dead fer years, he jest wouldn't lay down."

"Good God, Tom, be serious will ya. It's a wonder the Lord don't strike ya down," Katie scolds.

"Well, 'is time jest come, I s'pose. The poor ol' son-of-a-whore, he never was a well man. As long as I knew 'im he had something the matter with 'im, an' lazy, oh, oh, oh!"

"Tom, don't talk about the dead that way!"

"I told 'im that to 'is face," Tom protests. "But I always liked Martha. How's she taken it?"

"Oh, she'll miss 'im. They were always together, ya know."

"What killed 'im, I wonder? He didn't kill 'imself workin', that's fer sure. Eatin' maybe, but not workin'. It wouldn't be his heart — I never knew the man ta have a heart." Tom wanders around the kitchen in his wool socks, gesturing with the stem of his pipe as he talks. "A sad place down there t'night. Where'd ya s'pose they'll find pallbearers?"

"He had friends, now, Tom. Everyone has friends an' relatives."

"Well, they may have ta hire someone ta cry. Oh, I s'pose the poor ol' bastard was all right in his own way. A good 'nuff fella, hurt nobody or helped nobody. Stole a bit. An' drank a bit. An' cheated whoever he could. An' ya can't fault a man fer bein' lazy."

We eat dinner with the spectre of Henry Cain beside the table, and I think that the old man's death is like a warning to us all. We are humbled. All except Tom, who makes cracks about Henry, dead though the man is, all the old bad feelings coming to the surface. Still, I haven't heard Tom swear, not using the Lord's name, since he got the news. Young or old, we all take a look at ourselves today.

"With a corpse right here in the community," Tom grumbles, "I s'pose we'll have ta send flowers."

By late afternoon, the rain has stopped and the clearing light wind has left only a few small clouds that drift and make moving shadows across the oat field on the flat. In the lee of the breeze, the sun is hot and the air is steamy. As evening approaches a mist lifts from the rain-soaked fields.

We are all inside getting dressed for the wake. Katie has put on her wine-coloured dress but she doesn't wear the brooch. She fixes her hair in a wave over the left eye and puts on a hair net.

"Poor, dear Martha, she'll need our prayers tonight," Katie says. "When ya say yer prayers, say one fer Martha."

She wraps two loaves of bread and a dozen molasses cookies to take with us.

"I hate like hell ta go down and inta that wake house t'night," Tom says, tightening his necktie at the kitchen mirror. "I never know what ta say and I might get ta coughin' in the crowd."

"Martha would 'spect ya ta be there. They're sa handy home."

"It's fer her sake I'm goin'. She had no picnic livin' with that lazy son-of-a-whore, I can tell ya. She told me once she could count her good times on the fingers of one hand."

"Still an' all, she'll miss him."

"Poor ol' Martha don't know the difference between a good time an' a bad, she's been sheltered with him sa long. But she'll be a full house, I s'pose, nothin' else goin' on."

Katie goes behind Tom and fixes his white shirt collar, brushes lint and dust from his suit. The grey suit is snug, bulging at the buttons, but Tom looks distinguished with his grey hair and dark tie. He walks through the house stiff and uncomfortable, yet enjoying the dress clothes.

I bring the car around to the front door and Danny and Tom get in the front seat beside me, Katie in the back alone. We drive slowly down the road to the wake house. Tom sits with his arm out the window and as a car passes us, we are blown with pebbles. I park at the highway and we walk in the lane to the Cain house. Tom steps along like a neighbouring squire, his iron-grey hair contrasted with his wind-blown complexion. As we near the house, we stop talking, and as we single out to go through the gate, a kind of spirit overtakes us.

Henry's farmhouse is quaint and white and the neat sheds around it are stained black from the rain. The dooryard is hand-mown and tidy, the only machinery out of doors is Henry's grindstone in the tall grass near the henhouse.

Some of the men gather around the grindstone, putting their fine shoes on its bench and giving the crank a turn. This is almost like shaking hands with Henry; it has more to do with him than the corpse laid out in the parlour of the house. They mumble and whisper together. The setting sun creates an unbalanced sky, red like stained glass.

Among the men are Charlie, and Howard, who has on a new western shirt but the same pitchy overalls and workboots. His hair is wet and combed into a wave. He comes to meet us, as Tom and Danny and I go to stand by the grindstone.

"Steve, ya goin' in? Ya goin' way in ta see ol' Henry?" he asks.

"Yes, I think we're all going in. Coming in with us, Howard?"

"Oh, no, Jesus, no, not me. I don't wanna see 'im. I couldn't look at a dead man that way."

"Sure you could. Come in with me."

"Oh, no, Jesus, no. It'd keep me up all night. I couldn't sleep. Besides, it's a lot cooler out here."

"I'm stayin' out here with you, Howard," Danny says. "We'll be right here at the grindstone."

"Poor ol' Henry's grindstone," says Charlie, "right where 'e's left 'er. Boys, if she could talk, she'd tell a sad tale."

"A lotta miles on that wheel," George Cooper puts in. "Henry could sharpen an axe."

We walk toward the house, slowly, exchanging greetings with other neighbours.

"Evenin' Tom, Katie, boys."

"Daresay the rain's 'bout over, d'ya think?"

"Soon be hayin', eh Tom?"

"Poor ol' Henry went outta her fast."

"Sad thing."

The veranda is full of people, older people in chairs and children along the railing, half-hidden by the smothering wild pumpkin vines. There is a plastic wreath on the front door, and the parlour curtains are closed.

"Go right in, go right in, Martha's there," someone says.

"Sudden, eh?" Tom says, nodding.

"Yah, slept away."

Inside, the kitchen is sitting full and folks are standing in the hall and perched on the stairs. The parlour is crowded. Martha and her grown children, Marie and David, sit beside a grey coffin. Flowers are everywhere. A round basin lamp shines pink against the ceiling and the wallpaper is purple, and there are pictures on the wall behind the massed flowers. That's all I see, besides Henry.

The dead man lies in the satin nest, hands folded, skin the colour of clay. With the dark suit and neat tie, he looks more like a rich relative than Henry Cain. His lips are pink beneath the tea-stained moustache. I've never seen Henry dressed up before, or without his glasses.

Following Katie, Tom and I shake hands with the family.

"Sorry fer yer troubles."

"Thank you."

"Sorry fer yer troubles."

"Thank you."

Katie and Martha hug each other and cry just a little.

"Katie, I haven't been up ta see ya in a spell" Martha says, forcing a smile. "Such a cold backward spring. Henry and . . ." She catches herself. "Oh, my God, poor Henry, it's hard ta believe." She cries.

"Marie, you've grown like a bean," Katie says, to break the tension. "I hardly knew ya, yer sa good-lookin'."

There's silence, and the smell of flowers, perfume, and death.

"If there's anything, Martha . . ." Katie offers. "We have a car now, ya know."

"He doesn't look a day over seventy" Tom puts in. "Do ya have someone ta set up with the remains? Steve here could stay, eh Steve?"

"I . . ."

"George is stayin', thanks jest the same. I'll be alright."

More people are pressing through the front door, among them the minister and a group of church women. Someone carries a portable organ. As I slip out through the crowd, into the yard, I hear the Bible reading and praying begin. Through the open door comes the singing, the organ wheezing, "Bless'd be the ties that bind." I move further from the house.

Howard comes up behind me, so close I can smell the tobacco on his breath.

"How'd ya make out, Steve?" he whispers. "With the big Reid one? Nick said ya walked 'er home from the circus. Bad rig, too, ain't she? Jesus, ya musta wanted ta get yer hands on that, though, didn't ya?"

"Yes, she's very beautiful."

"Jesus, but what a man would do with it, though."

As dusk comes down, Howard leaves. I sit on the fender of our car, waiting for Tom and Katie, half-watching Danny, who's chasing a bad-tempered tabby around the sheds. People drift out of the house, and the dooryard fills with people. Among them is Cindy; she sees me and smiles, moves purposefully towards me.

"So when are ya takin' me ta town in yer new car here?"

"Oh, one of these evenings."

"I wanna go ta the drive-in with ya."

"We'll do it some night."

"Nick said ya went home with, what's 'er name, Angela."

"Amanda Reid."

"Yeh, that's it."

"Yes, we walked to her house from the circus. Just a step really. From here to the river."

"I know about the Mounties, too."

"What do you know about the Mounties?"

"They caught you and Nick with beer opened," Cindy grinned.

"Where'd you hear that?"

"Nick told us. Dad made him explain where he spent all 'is money."

"I'm paying half."

"Now that ya got yer license and a nice car ta drive, I s'pose ya'll be goin' to town to see the Reid one."

"Maybe I will. I don't know." I'm feeling pretty uncomfortable now, and catch myself edging slowly towards the house, looking over the crowd for Tom and Katie.

"I'd like ta go in the new car with ya," Cindy says, "Everyone says the Reid girl's a town snob. Do ya like my hair this way?"

"Yes, your hair looks good tonight," I say, not sure how it's different from usual. "But Amanda seemed nice to me."

"You'll find 'er out."

"We'll go for a spin, you and I."

"Promise?"

"I promise."

Danny comes running then, Katie and Tom walking behind him, looking tired. I open the car door for them, wave to Cindy, and turn the car onto the road. There are pockets of fog now, and some late owls fly over the fields towards the barns.

"Henry was a good 'nuff lad in a lot of ways, I guess," Tom says. "He's more popular now that he's dead — I never knew he was such a great man."

"A handsome corpse," Katie says.

It has been an upsetting day. But Henry Cain is already gone from my mind, his wake half-forgotten. Howard and Cindy have turned my mind to town, to Amanda. And Amanda is firmly in my mind. She wears the white pants, the soft denim shirt; she smiles at me as she did on the roller coaster, and in the darkness of the car I smile back at the memory. I hardly hear Tom and Katie in the background.

"But where'll they bury 'im, I wonder? I never knew the man ta darken a church door."

"St. Peter's. Martha used ta go. Hope ya didn't count the cars t'night, Tom. It's bad luck."

CHAPTER 13

It is hot and the sun shines through the window of the summer kitchen, throwing a beam onto the board floor. Katie sweeps and a million particles of dust hang in the sunbeam. As she passes the window the light catches the grey hair beneath her hair net and it glistens like steel wool. She uses a newspaper for a dust pan and lifts the stove cover, throws paper and all into the flame. The stove rumbles for a minute and is quiet again. Kneeling on an old coat of Tom's, Katie scours the floor with the scrub brush. She scrapes away gum and patches of grime, using a case knife to dig into the cracks, scouring until the floor is bleached to the colour of honey.

Tom hand-mows the dooryard, cutting the white clover in half-circle swaths. He bears down on the scythe, leaving only the transparent stubble. I carry forksfull to the pigpen and watch the pig smack it up. When the yard is mowed, Tom puts another edge on the scythe and mows the front garden, taking care not to run the blade on the white rocks Katie has piled around the beds of dahlia. Finished, he sits on a bench in the shade of the barn and lights his pipe, blowing out the match with an exhalation of smoke. He coughs, mops his face with his handkerchief, and coughs again. I bring him a dipper of cold water from the house.

"God bless ya, Stevie," he says. "Boys, that's lovely, lovely altogether. Yer a great lad ta work."

He has taken his shirt off and his flannel undershirt is soaked with sweat. I notice that he trembles a little as he drinks, and water runs down his chin. Then he smokes with more ease, taking a drink once in a while and waving his handkerchief at the flies.

"A great man in 'is day, that ol' Henry. The preacher said so," he mutters. "Good God, doesn't the man know anything? Henry Cain weren't worth his feed."

Throughout the day, I try to reach Amanda, telephoning the inn a dozen times only to get a busy signal. By afternoon, I'm calling at twenty minute intervals or when someone isn't talking on our own party line.

"Now stay in or out," Katie warns. "Make up yer mind. You're trackin' me floors and lettin' in the flies."

Finally I get through and my heart pounds as the phone at the other end rings. I'm ready to hang up when someone answers.

"Hello — Elm Inn!"

"Yes, hello, is Amanda in?"

"This is she."

"Mandy, this is Steven Moar." I try to sound calm. "Remember me? From the circus?"

"Oh, yes, of course. I remember you. How are you doing?"

"Fine, thanks. I just thought I'd give you a call." Does she sound glad to hear from me? I can't tell. There's a long pause. But my urge to see her again carries me into the silence.

"I called really to ask you out." I say all the words in a rush. "Would you like to come out with me? I have a car and there's a good movie at the drive-in."

"Movie? Oh, you mean a show. What's it called?"

"*Maccumba*."

"Oh, yes, with Grace Kelly."

"And Clark Gable."

"If I come out with you, it's as a friend."

"Okay, as a friend. If that's what you want."

"As a friend, yes, I'll come."

"What time can I pick you up? Seven, seven-thirty?"

"No, you better make it eight or eight-thirty. I may have to help out here at dinner."

When I hang up the receiver, it is like a new day. Suddenly everything is right, everyone is happy. Working with Tom is good, sharing the labour and the reasons for doing it, accepting the responsibility — two men together — of getting the work done.

We're taking the haying machinery out of the shed when Howard comes looking for someone to go blueberry picking with him. He has pitch on his face, must have just come from the woods, working in the same shirt he wore to the wake.

"Way in callin' 'er up, were ya?" he says.

"Who's that now?" I ask.

"Oh, Tom said. He said ya were on a callin' spree. That ya was, oh, a callin' 'er all day like that, that's all. Was it the big Reid one, down in town, yer callin'?"

"Maybe."

"Nice ta see a lad in love. Ya in love wit' 'er?"

"C'mon boys," Tom calls, "gimme a lift here. Don't stand around with yer hands in yer pockets. Christ, yer both lazier 'n Henry Cain,"

We put planks on the ground and lift the pole, backing the clinking mowing machine out the shed door. The spiked wheels make staggered notches on the plank. Then we wrap the raker's axles with bran sacks and carry it, Tom on one end and Howard and I on the other. We move it on short nudges, half lifting, half dragging it to the door as Tom gasps "Heave!" each time. The raker's teeth scrape the sand floor.

"Now heave," puffs Tom. "Christ, heave! Steve can't lift worth a damn. He's got a girlfriend, ya know, Howard. His back is bad."

I can feel the tips of my ears turning red, and say nothing.

"Oh, yah, Jesus, yah," Howard says. "He's in love with a big one in town. Ya should see 'er, Tom."

"You see 'er, Howard? Is she one of the nice ones?" Tom asks.

"No, but I heard tell a her."

"Steve, explain yerself," says Tom, pleased now that he's getting some help and has an ally in Howard. "Was it love at first sight? How did it happen?"

"No, I don't think so. Nothing much happened anyway," I answer.

"What's 'er name, boys?"

"Amanda Reid," says Howard. "Big Amanda."

"She's not big."

"What religion is she, boys?"

"I don't know."

"But did he get inta her pants," Howard says. "That's what I wanna know."

"You'll never know."

"Reid's a Catholic name," says Tom. "Don't waste yer time goin' with a Catholic. They won't turn."

"I'm not marrying the girl."

We roll out the iron raker's wheels and Tom greases the hubs before we fit them on the axles and put the pins through. Then he bolts the shafts to the frame.

"Thank ya, boys," he says. "Next time I see ya I'll thank ya some more."

By early evening the smell from the pigyard is strong and it mixes with the scent of the cut grass so that the dooryard smells like the inside of a barn. Already the short stubbled yard is starting to bake in the calm heat. Howard and Danny wander off to the railway for blueberries and I oil the raker's trip levers and the blade levers on the mower. Tom has taken the mower blade to the woodshed and is resting it across the wheelbarrow staves, filing the sections until the slanted edges gleam silver. When it's completed, he takes his crooked knife and whittles a hardwood tooth for the spare hand rake.

"Tomarra, if it's fine, we'll mow that ol' run-out field above the barn, knock down those bull's eyes," Tom tells me. "The hay's sa poor up there now, ya have ta drive stakes ta see where the mower goes."

While he works in the shed, I carry buckets of water from the kitchen and wash the car.

"Now, when yer in town, pick me up a scythe stone, coarse grain, and a straw hat, size seven. Would ya have time?"

"Yes, I will. If the stores are open."

Tom goes into the house, sits in the leather rocking chair in the parlour, and goes to sleep. He's still there when I leave for town.

A little salty breeze drifts in from the river, rattling the leaves on the California maple and the elm, filling the streets with the smell of mill sulphur as I wait in the car for Amanda. I've arrived early but it is nine o'clock before she comes out. As she walks across the lawn to the car, she tosses her hair away from her face and smiles. She gets in beside me.

"You should have come to the door," she says. "I was held up at dinner but you could have waited inside. I didn't know you were here."

"Yes, I should have gone in. I'm sorry. I did honk."

We drive across the bridge and down the shore road, past the golf club to the drive-in theatre. Amanda rides facing me, her back against the door. She has spent the day in the sun and is tanned, almost matching her eyes. She wears only a touch of makeup, white knee-length shorts and a red blouse. She slips off her sandals, stretching her legs across the seat, and her bare feet touch my thigh. I notice that her legs are smooth and well-proportioned, the toenails a delicate pink. I try to shield my feelings, which are now overpowering me. I let myself love her, and secretly believe that she loves me. She is electrifying, and her spirit moves me; I want her more as I know her better. I have to fight to make sensible conversation, and fight against my feelings, presenting an image which I know is false.

"So, do you have a steady boyfriend, Mandy?" I ask as if it doesn't really matter.

"Well, sort of. We're not exactly steady except when he's home. He's in the Navy and not home that much."

I swallow the disappointment, act the happy-go-lucky person I wish I were, but the effect of those words stays just below the surface like a strange illness that comes on you in the night and disturbs your rest.

"So what's his name?"

"Gordon Collins."

"From here?"

"Yes, town here. Tardy Avenue."

"I guess you've known him for a long time then."

"Yes, we grew up together. He's a real nice guy. Quite a clown, fun to be with. He's never serious about anything. You'd really like him, Steve."

"Does he have a car, too?"

"A white convertible. He lets me drive it. But I haven't seen him now since the prom."

"Did Gordon . . ." the name sticks in my throat, but she doesn't seem to notice, "Did Gordon go with you to the prom?"

"Yes. We were out all night. We went to a beach party down at Oak Point."

"Sounds like quite a time, this prom."

"Yes. And I went to his last year. It was fun, too, but there was an accident on the Boulevard and one of Gordon's classmates was killed."

"I'm sorry. I remember reading about it."

"Did you go to a prom this year?"

"No, I've had to drop out of school for a while."

"Oh, yes, I remember, you told me. Your father's illness."

"But I'm taking a correspondence course at home — English — and next year I'm going to university," I say, turning into the short dirt road to the drive-in gate.

"But what if your father's no better?"

"My brother, Danny, is helping him next year."

After stopping at the shack to get a speaker, we follow the lane to a mounded field and park. I hang the speaker on the edge of the car window and plug it into the post beside the car. It echoes and blats a soft static, while advertisements cross the huge screen before the preview of next week's feature, *Rebel Without a Cause*, starring James Dean, Sal Minio, and Natalie Wood.

Mandy is intent on the screen now, but her slim hand with pink fingernails is on the seat beside her. I reach out and squeeze it gently. She responds with a firm touch that has my heart beating like a drum. I kiss her cheek. She makes no attempt to move away so I kiss her again, moving down her cheek toward her mouth. She closes her eyes and turns toward my lips, and my arms come around her. The grey lights from the screen play against her face. We kiss again.

"So, what does this Gordon fellow look like?"

"Oh, let me see now. He's tall, blond, the athletic type. He played football for the school team. He's a lot of fun to be with. You'd like him."

"Yes, you said that."

"He's getting his degree in the Navy."

"Sounds like quite a guy."

"Yes, he is, quite a guy indeed."

I kiss her again, touching her face, moving my fingertips over the long eyelashes, the hair that falls over her shoulders.

"So when's he coming home again, this sailor with the white convertible?"

"Tomorrow. I expected him today, actually. That's why I wasn't sure if I could come out tonight."

"Home on leave? How long?"

"He has two weeks."

"I guess you're not really looking forward to it, then," I say, thinking that I must not call her until Gordon is gone again.

"Oh, yes, I'm looking forward to seeing him," she corrects me.

"Do you love him, Mandy?"

"Steve, I don't think you're supposed to ask questions like that. Well, we're close, but I don't know if it's love or not."

"You're right, I'm sorry. It's none of my business. I just wondered how close you were, that's all." And I wondered why she was kissing me back, with this Gordon fellow having a claim on her feelings. Almost experimentally, I kiss her lips again, trying to measure the response. Is it a little less? A little cooler? Something less than whole, as though she were preoccupied now with Gordon. Maybe this is why she said she'd only come out with me as friends.

"You're a good kisser," she says suddenly, smiling.

"Good enough for a friend, anyway."

"But you're a good friend, Steve. Everyone needs good friends."

"But is a friend's kiss worth that much?"

"Sure it is."

"How much?"

"What do you mean?"

"Equal to, say, Gordon's"

"Steve! Don't ask me that. I can't compare you. You're you and Gordon's Gordon. Two different people."

"Different people, different feelings." I can hear the roughness of growing pain at the edge of my voice.

"That's right. I've known Gordon for years. We went to the same school, the same band, the same sports; I was a cheerleader at the football games. I hardly know you, Steve."

"I'm sorry."

"But you do seem very nice."

"Thank you. You're very nice too." I can't talk about this any longer. "Look, Mandy, do you feel like something to eat? I could go to the canteen for a hot dog or fries."

"No, thanks. Well . . . maybe just a Coke."

When I come back to the car, the show is mostly over; only the romantic ending remains. We watch the screen and sip our Cokes. Grace Kelly is leaving the jungle on a riverboat. Clark Gable stands on the shore, shouts to the boat's crew to take good care of her. She jumps overboard and swims back to him; she can't bear to leave. They embrace in a jungle sunset. A happy ending.

On our way back into town, Amanda finds a favourite station on the radio and turns it way up, singing along with the music. She moves closer, her hand resting on my leg. "You're awfully quiet," she says.

"Just thinking."

"A penny for your thoughts."

"You."

"Just me?"

"Could I see you again sometime?"

"I don't know. I enjoyed tonight. But Gordon will be here for some time. Look, Steve, thanks for asking me out. I've had a nice time. Really."

"I'd like to see you again. Maybe after Gordon goes? Could I call you then?"

"Well, I suppose we could do something together. Call me then. If I can make it," I'll go out.

As I walk her across the wide yard to her house, I have a sudden impulse to confess. To tell her I love her, as hopeless as it all seems. I fight back the urge, kiss her once more, and leave.

CHAPTER 14

"Oh, Steve, I love you. I love you so much it hurts." Amanda snuggles against me and I caress her bare back to the soft curve of her buttocks.

"I love you, too, Mandy. I always will."

We are like one. I can taste her lips, smell her hair, but as our passion peaks she is gone. My arms are empty. And I'm running after her through hayfields to the river. She's on a riverboat, just like Grace Kelly, and waves to me from the deck. I shout to the crew, "Take good care of her," and she's in the water, swimming toward me with long overhead strokes, splashing. I run to the water and put out my hand for hers. But it's Cindy who comes out of the river, and the disappointment stings. I set out after the riverboat, paddling Tom's canoe, but it escapes me, disappearing around a bend in the river. I can smell the popple smoke from its stack and I keep paddling, paddling frantically against the emptiness growing inside me from losing her.

"Steve, Steve! Get up!" Katie is shaking me. "Get outta bed now. Tom'll need a hand with the hayin', and Danny's up and gone long ago."

She hurries about the room, gathering bits of clothing for the wash. Then she raises my window, propping it open with a flower pot. A light morning breeze makes a belly in the curtain and the room fills with the scents of popple smoke from the kitchen pipe and of freshly cut hay. I lie in bed and try to put my dream back together, group it into a package that I can hold on to. I search for those wonderful moments, but already it has started to fade like pieces of old film. Reality is too strong. I can hear a rooster's muffled crowing from inside the henhouse and the clinking of the mowing machine as it turns at the corner of the field. Tom shouts at the horses, "Ho ho hooo, ya sons-a-whores! Hooo now!"

I get up and look out the window at the soft summer morning. The season has advanced almost overnight. The oatfield on the flat is a dark green, its petals starting to break open. Below the house, the purple-top timothy and wild flowers nod ripe with seed and the Queen's Choice crabs outside the window are the size of marbles. In the old field above the barn, the fine-top has been raked and bunched. The stunted blueberry bushes along the railroad carry dusty black and purple berries. I've been so preoccupied with Mandy, I have to stop and grasp the passing season. Haying time. The hottest part of the summer.

I watch Tom going past on the mower, still working the long day, chasing the seasons.

"Once the hay's cut, the summer's over," he always says. "When yer feet get wet from the dew in the aftergrass, she's all over, all over but the whoopin'."

Dressing, I think of Amanda, her soft cheek next to mine, the smooth bare back; I want to hold her. I can see her deep brown eyes, the curved smile, hear the lyrics in her voice. My heart aches. She is like a sickness to me, I think, one that grows more intense each day. On our next date, I will tell her I love her. And I can only hope that doing so will give me some comfort.

In the kitchen, Katie has her hands in the wash. The wringer-washer hums and splashes, surrounded by piles of dirty clothes. More are soaking in a boiler that sits on two chairs, and pots of water are heating on the stove. I take off a stove cover to make toast.

"Tom said a cow freshened in the swamp," Katie says. "She brought it to the bars this morning, a nice Jersey heifer. We'll need the milk 'fore long."

"When was it born?"

"A few days ago."

"I wonder what Tom wants me to do this morning?"

"Do some ho-daggin', he said, an' shakin' away from the mower down by the brook in the heavy clover."

"I have an assignment for my course I should be working on."

"I know, but Stevie, dear, the hayin' has ta come first. While the weather's fine. Tom'll have a fit if yer not out there soon."

"He's the only man I know who enjoys himself haying."

"Well, he knows it has to be done anyway, so he may as well like it. He does enjoy farmin', I do know that. And he won't let anything go undone about the place, or farm any less than he ever did."

"He'd chase a sprig of hay into a cedar swamp."

"Steve, now I know how ya hate the hayin' with yer allergies an' all. But Danny'll be more able ta help next year — if Tom's still able ta do it, that is."

"He'll be doing it as long as he's able to work."

"It's all the man knows, I guess. You have to understand that. He had no learnin' and couldn't do much else."

"He's happy as long as he's sitting behind an old horse."

Katie pours herself a cup of tea and settles down across the table from me.

"Stevie, ya seem a bit down in the mouth lately. Is anything wrong?"

"Oh, no, everything's fine. Things are fine."

"Yer mind seems ta be somewhere else."

"Don't mind me."

"Tom said ya have a girlfriend. Is that so?" I shrug and give a kind of sideways nod: maybe. "Well, try not ta get serious about 'er. You always said yer goin' ta college as soon as ya could. Does she go ta school?"

"Just graduated from high school. She's going to university in the fall."

"What's her name?"

"Amanda Reid."

"That's a Catholic name. Is she Catholic? Not that it matters ta me, ya understand me now. I never cared about religion myself, ya know that, Steve."

"I know."

"There's worse things 'n marryin' someone the wrong religion."

"Yes, like marrying the wrong person."

"I just want ya ta be happy, Steve. C'mon now, get a wiggle on and finish yer toast. Tom'll be wonderin' what's keepin' ya."

"We'll be out there until dark, no doubt."

"If it doesn't rain. I heard a blue jay this morning. Sign a rain."

"What would a bird know about the weather."

"Everyone knows a blue jay's the sign a rain. D'ya have ta question everything?"

I finish breakfast and go out to the barnyard. It is early, but already hot with a grey haze above the river. The spruce on the top-hill are blue and the air full of the warm hay smell. It is that season when we tell the time of day not by watches but by the sun.

I see that Tom's propped the barn doors open, and the breeze blows through sweeping the thrashing floor clean of chaff. The truck wagon has been pushed out into the yard, its rung hayrack facing the sky like an open basket. Nearby is the rib-toothed raker, with its ribs of teeth, hunch-backed against the sky like a peacock bustle, its shafts pointing into the ground. I get the pitchfork and scythe and start for the flat.

Of the standing hay in the field, only an island remains at the centre. Grasshoppers fly before me as I approach the mower, the long swaths of fallen hay catching around my feet. The horses haul at a steady gait and Tom sits straight, the seat's supporting bar bouncing him where the ground is uneven. The worm-like blossoms of timothy reach the horses' sides, and old Prince stretches for them as they fall and are tossed aside by the mould board, leaving the wheel-spiked grooves.

Danny comes across the field. I notice that the galvanized bucket he is carrying has beads of sweat running down the outside: water. Tom stops the horses and scoops a drink with the tin dipper. He slurps and gulps, his throat moving up and down as water drops from his stubbled chin.

"Boys, that's lovely altogether," he says. "Yer a great boy, Danny, a great boy fer work," and slops what's left of the water on the horses' rumps, making the great leg muscles twitch. He checks the harness, walking around the animals, checking under the collars for sores. Then he knots the traces on one side and hooks the end links to the harness.

"There now," he says to the younger horse, "that'll keep ya in yer place."

He pats the old horse on the neck and fixes the lock of hair twisted under the bridle straps, between the pointed ears.

"Steve, you can do some ho-daggin' along there by the fence," he says, "but don't run the scythe on the wire — and be careful for piss-mire knolls." He gets back on the mower and, wiping his face with his handkerchief, clucks his tongue to start the horses. They follow the wheel tracks, around clumps of swamp, dipping into small gulleys, keeping the gait even.

"Steve, get that corner the mower missed over by the plum bushes," Tom shouts to me as he goes past. "Now get a wiggle on. No, no, over by the plum bushes. That's the stuff."

I mow the breaks and fine-top hay at the field's edge and the scythe slips through it, cutting the breaks and leaving the hay. Near the plum trees, I stop and taste the red cherries. Nearby there are half-red plums in the shade of the leaves and half-orange choke cherries ripening on lower bushes.

"Good God, look at 'im, would ya," says Tom, getting off the mower again. He takes a scythe stone from the mowing machine box, comes to me in three long strides, and lifts the scythe from my hand. Standing the tool on its handle end, he sights along the blade. Then he runs the stone along it in long slapping motions, making the metal ring.

"There!" He runs his thumb along the edge and swings the scythe. "Now, listen! Bear down, hold against yer handle and give 'er a pull t'ward ya this way." He makes a clean swath. tripping the smaller bush and the breaks and the fine-top. "How in Christ are ya ever gonna learn, if ya don't listen?" He gets back on the mower and cuts the last strip of hay at the centre of the field before taking the horses to the barn.

For dinner we have corned beef and potatoes and a wedge of blueberry pie. Then we go out on the back step and sit in the breeze that always seems to blow in the alley between the outside kitchen and the woodshed. Tom whittles a flute from a swamp reed, carving holes a finger's width apart. He tries to play "Danny Boy," then whittles some more until his instrument is accurate to scale, and plays "Nellie Grey." He passes the flute to Danny and lights his pipe.

"Boys, she's swung around from the sou'west," Tom says, testing the wind with a wet finger. "She'll blow up rain 'fore long, sure as hell. Let's get that ol' hay above the barn in. We don't wanna shake 'er out agin."

We hurry, all three of us, putting the horses on the wagon, hooking the neck yoke and fastening the traces. Tom climbs onto the wagon, braces his feet and leans back on the reins. Danny and I sit on the rack's floor, our feet hanging through the rungs. The horses trot with their sense of storm-fear, and the iron-soled wheels bump over rocks and tip the rack as they dip into dead furrows. We circle and stop in the bunched hay.

I throw the dry fine-top onto the rack and Tom pushes it about, tramping and building the load. Danny clears behind the wagon with the wooden hand rake.

"Good beddin' is all she is, eh, Prince?" Tom says to the older horse, "but it looks bad ta leave 'er out in the rain." He tweaks the rein with a prong of his fork.

*"Some folks like a feathered bed
But give me the new mown hay . . ."*

Tom throws out pertinent bits of old poems as the horses move methodically from bunch to bunch. I pitch the hay on until the rack is full and the strands droop over the spoked wheels.

*"Cherries are ripe and so today
We'll gather them while you make the hay . . ."*

There is a rumble downriver that makes the horses' ears twitch and Tom points to a black cloud, silver-lined, like a mountain range on the horizon.

"Let's get what we can on 'fore she rains. There's gonna be an old dandy by the looks of 'er."

George Cooper comes quickly across the field with a pitchfork in his hand, and falls into place on the opposite side of the wagon, helping to load.

"Build 'er wider, Tom," George says. "Push 'er out over the rack or ya won't get 'er all on."

"Christ, she's wider now 'n Nellie's arse. But roll 'er to a shady spot an' I'll see what I can do."

"That Steve hasn't set himself yet," George says. "You can pitch faster 'n that, can't you, Steve?"

"I don't know."

"The girls keepin' 'im up all night," snorts Tom. "He's draggin' 'is arse."

We work on in silence, keeping a watchful eye on the darkening sky. When the load is so high that I can't reach Tom with the forkloads, he calls a halt.

"That's good 'nuff, boys. Ta hell with what's left there."

"Another bunch or two," George urges. "It's a shame ta leave it out."

"Nah, ta hell with it," says Tom; I feel the blister at the base of my thumb and echo his words.

"Yes, to hell with it."

Tom shouts to the horses and cracks the reins across their rumps. I wonder if he's trying to impress George Cooper with his horsemanship. As the sky lowers, the sultry air gathers into a freshening breeze. Chain lightning flashes over the river, and a rumble sets the horses whinnying and tossing their heads. As the wagon comes near the barn, Tom clambers down and leads the horses by their bridles, up the pole ramp to the barn doors. Hoofs drive hard against the planking, the sound like far-off thunder or potatoes bouncing down a chute. And the rain starts.

"She's too wide fer the doors. She's not gonna go!" George says. "They can't haul 'er, Tom."

The horses stop, puffing. The rain drives down, running off the roof onto the wagonload of hay. Another flash of lightning, a cannon-like crack, and the young horse snorts, the traces rattle.

"Easy, now, easy," Tom says, holding the bridles down nearer the bits.

"Let's pitch some of it off," I suggest. "The top hay is wet now anyway."

"She'll go, I think. Once they've winded," Tom says, "they'll bring 'er in."

"Christ, yes, it's only a bit of fine-top," George agrees.

The team appears very nervous, I think, but Tom lets go of their bridles and goes behind the horses. He takes up the reins and twists them into a whip, and brings it down with a snap across the broad rumps. The horses lunge forward, straining their weight against the whiffle tree and clawing splinters from the floor. The traces stretch bow-tight. *Crack*! The whiffle tree snaps at the centre bolt. The horses fall forward, stumble down onto their knees, up again; getting their footing again, they bolt through the barn, out the opposite doors. Reins dragging, they gallop through the downpour towards the upper field.

The wagon rolls backward down the ramp and comes to a stop on the flat. Danny stands behind me, holding his breath. The rain makes a wall of spilling water, running off the eaves. We watch it fall, and wait silently for the storm to stop.

Tom strokes his stubble of beard and scoops up oats in a half-bushel tin to go after the horses. "Whatta ya s'pose gets inta a man that way?" he asks.

CHAPTER 15

We are in the last days of haying and George Cooper, Charlie, and some others have come to help Tom hand-mow the swamps. The mows have been filled with the good hay, and this other will have to be stacked outside. It's a mixture of cattails, weeds and rushes the mowing machine couldn't reach, and Tom mows it only to keep the bushes back. The men pace themselves, moving in short strides one slightly behind the other, and drag their feet to make runner-like tracks through the fallen hay which is raked into near windrows by the action of the scythes. They take turns passing their scythes to Tom who "puts a bit of an edge" on them, the scythe stone clanging at intervals throughout the morning. Once in a while, someone stops and rolls a cigarette, leans on the scythe and smokes, sending tiny puffs drifting across the field. Sometimes the field rings with hearty laughter as a joke is passed around.

Already, the stubbled fields have clumps of aftergrass. The choke cherries have turned soft and black, and Katie warns we'll get appendicitis if we eat too many. Behind the woodshed, current bushes have clusters of the sweet transparent beads, their seeds visible inside. Knuckled cucumbers hide beneath a network of vines in the garden and the pumpkins at the edge are rank bulbs. It is humid. The cattle stand beneath the trees, switching at flies and bawling. By now the river is so low it's clogged with algae and the dry gravel bars hold small stagnant pools with sandpipers running among the rocks.

I have rewritten my short story, seeing some of the clichés and cutting them, tightening it all. I've sent it to the *Family Herald*; maybe they'll publish it. I'm sitting at the dining room table, working on an essay and dreaming of college when I hear Cindy's voice in the summer kitchen. She talks with Katie for a while — I hear the rise and fall of their conversation, but not the words — then she comes in to me.

"I have a pack of tailor-mades," she whispers.

"Okay, let's go and have a smoke."

We walk over the hill together and along the edge of the oatfield toward the millshed, keeping out of sight of the mowing men. Cindy is pensive. I'm certain she has more on her mind than sharing a cigarette. It's like she has stayed away and has starved her feelings, and has come now to let them surface or release them. She wears a boy's T-shirt, and I can't help noticing she's without a bra beneath it. She's wearing a lot of lipstick, and her jeans are tight. I think of last spring, when we were last in the shed together; and of the night of the dance, when we made love. My expectations now have me breathing a little fast.

Beside us, the ripening oatfield is grey and whispering in the sun; inside, the shed cool with the same musty cat-urine smell.

We sit again on the old car seat, and light two of her cigarettes.

"How ya been makin' out, anyways?"

"Lovely. Nice morning, isn't it?"

"Yah, ya wanna go in swimmin'?"

"No, the water's bad. You could catch polio from that water. Besides, I'm tired."

"Up late readin'?"

"Yes, and writing."

"Whatta ya readin' all night?"

"Last night, Kipling."

"Sounds like some kinda fish," she giggles.

The cigarette relieves some of the tension and I hurry it, making its coal long and the paper warm and damp, getting a little dizzy.

"You look lovely today," I tell Cindy. "If you want to go swimming, I'll go down and watch and wait for you."

"No, it's not important. I'm afraid of catchin' somethin' too."

We're sitting closer now, and I move even closer. Something pulls me to her, and I kiss her, my hand moving beneath her shirt.

"You're moochin' with me, Steven Moar."

I move my lips to her small ear, to the softness of her neck, her shoulder.

"Oh, Steve, don't do that."

"Why not?"

"Not unless you mean it."

"I always mean what I'm doing."

"That's not what I meant."

"What did you mean?"

"When you make love, you're supposed to really love. Mean it. So do ya really love me. I have ta know that first."

"Of course," I say soothingly, gathering her close again. But she pulls back and looks at me closely, a little frown between her brows.

"No, ya don't. You only pretend till ya get yer way."

"Well, you could say that I love you in a kind of way."

"What kind of way? Tell me that!"

"Well, it's like . . ." but my inspiration fails.

"Steve!" Cindy sits up and straightens her T-shirt, and tosses her hair away from her face. "We have ta talk." Then she lights another cigarette.

"We can always talk. That's all we ever do."

"No, I'm serious. I have ta talk now, right now, about something important."

"What's so important?" I ask.

"Us. You and me, and how we feel about each other."

I stroke her arm encouragingly and wait for her to continue. She has to say whatever it is she came to say. I might as well have another cigarette.

"Steve, now, ya must know how it is between us. Remember? Don't ya remember how I said I loved ya an' everything. Well, I really do. My heart aches, Steve. I can't sleep some nights, and sometimes I can't eat."

"I didn't know you meant it like that, that seriously. Cindy, I just don't love you in that sense. I like you a lot, but I don't really love you, not to that degree."

"But you said you did. On the night of the dance, before we did it."

"I said that?"

"Yes, that night. On the way home."

"I must have been drinking! Cindy, I was drinking — Nick treated me, remember?"

"But we did it that night. Now, Steve, you remember that. And you said you loved me and then we did it and you said how good it felt when we did it."

I begin to wonder where this is headed. I nod, yes, I remember making love, rum or no rum, I couldn't forget that. But . . .

"You said ya loved me. Enough to marry me?"

"No. You have to love someone an awful lot to marry them. I mean really love them."

"What if I was . . . you know . . ."

"No, Cindy. I wouldn't."

Suddenly her voice is low and furious, with a desperate edge that strikes me cold. "You just love someone enough ta get them in trouble!"

The silence stretches tense between us. Trouble.

"What the hell do you mean, in trouble?" I demand, each word coming out clipped and distinct. But I know. Those words only have one meaning in this kind of conversation.

"Steve, I'm expectin' a baby. Is that in trouble or not? And it's your baby too! Yours an' mine." She stands to face me. I want to run. The words fall over me and my face burns, and I can feel my forehead tighten: a throbbing headache begins. The sky has come down on me, and pushed me into a shell of guilt — a shell smaller than my true self. I want to run, to get free, to stop the words. But I have to ask.

"How do you know?"

"I'm way overdue. Six weeks. I'm expectin', alright. It's that simple."

"God." I can't take this in. "But how do you know it belongs to me?"

"You were the only one, Steve. There was nobody else but you."

"Now look, Cindy, look at me," I say, facing her, gripping her shoulders. "Does anyone else know this?"

"Not yet. But I can't hide it very long. Not from Mum."

"But maybe it will start, your period. Look! Why don't you go to the doctor? He would start it."

"No Jesus way! I can't do that, go ta see a doctor an' me expectin' this way and not married. I'd be ashamed ta death." She raises her voice. "I'd just be shamed ta go in."

"So what can you do, for fuck's sake? What can we do?"

"Oh, Stevie, I don't know what ta do! It's the disgrace, Stevie, for our families an' all. Unless we get married. You an' me. We could, ya know, we could get married. That would make it all legal and proper. I love you anyway and you said that you . . ."

"No! I don't love you, Cindy. Let's get that straight right now. I never did. I was drinking that night, that's all."

"But ya did do it!" She is crying now. "You did do this to me."

"I know, I know. Let me think. Let me think about it and I'll figure something out."

We leave the shed and pace along the edge of the oatfield, Cindy with her head down and arms folded. The edges of her eyes are red, and she dabs at them with a Kleenex.

"Keep this a secret," I tell her. "Don't tell. Promise you won't tell this to anyone until we can work something out."

"OK," she sniffs, "I promise." And I give her a hug, because she needs one.

When Cindy is gone, I want to turn to someone for help. But I know I have to keep the secret. I will have to marry Cindy. Give the baby a father. And that means that Amanda is lost to me; I will have to live with only the few memories of her I carry now. I try to visualize myself married to Cindy. I see myself overpowered, swamped by her needs, and I think of divorce. I will marry her, give the baby my name, make it all nice and legal and proper, and then get a divorce. I'll do it. I'll marry her. Tomorrow I'll go over and tell her so, tell her parents.

Some of the guilt starts to lift. I know I can't leave Cindy alone to raise this child. My own flesh and blood. It would not be a good marriage, and I will be unhappy, I know that; but at least it won't be guilt; at least I will be honourable.

I spend the rest of the day making plans. Try to get a job at the mill, I think, maybe even go to work for Tom, cutting pulp. I can get some property from Tom, build a house and be Tom and Katie's next-door neighbour. Try to be a good husband. Try to be a good father.

Cindy's more in my class anyway, I tell myself when my thoughts slide back to Amanda. Things are meant to be this way. Planned. My fate is to marry a good country girl. I try to see happiness with Cindy, but the good spirit just won't come. I don't love her. I get a trapped feeling and my head aches and my dreams of Amanda slip further and further out of grasp.

In the evening, Cindy's parents come to visit with Tom and Katie. I greet them in the dooryard, but they walk past me without speaking. The thought comes to me, frightening, that maybe this is not a social call. They are sober, like people going into a wake house. I watch from outside as they talk briefly with my parents in the outside kitchen and then go into the dining room and close the door. I stay around the yard, waiting to be called inside. But they don't call. After what seems like endless time, the Longs leave. Again they walk past me; again they don't speak.

"Steve! Steve!" Katie's voice is pitched much higher than usual. "Stevie, would you come in here a minute?"

The words fall onto me like a death sentence.

"Yes, get ta hell in here, God damnit," Tom shouts.

I walk into the dining room, trying to keep my face smooth, unworried, innocent. Katie closes the door firmly.

"What's going on?" I ask.

"You don't know?"

"Know what?"

"Now listen to 'im would ya, fer Jesus sake, listen to 'im," Tom says. "He don't know what's goin' on, I s'pose."

"Well, what is going on?"

"She's in trouble. The Long girl." Tom strikes the table with a fist. "And good God, she's blamin' it on you, of all the goddamn nerve."

"In trouble?"

"Well, yes, she's that way, you know," Katie puts in. "She's expectin' a child and the poor thing has ta blame it on someone, I s'pose. But we know it wouldn't be yours, Steve, and we told the Longs so. You've never slept with 'er, we know that. Well did ya?"

I take a deep breath. Their faith in me hurts.

"Yes. I did. It's mine."

"What's that?" Tom asks, his voice almost kind, pleading, hoping he heard me wrong.

"It's my baby. I'll marry her."

"Yers? Well, Christ only knows. I never knew ya was hangin' around over on that side of the river."

"I took her home on the night of David Cain's dance. We . . ."

"Say na more. Good God, say na more," Katie says. "Oh, God, God, the shame. The shame of it all, ta this family, and after all we done fer you. Ta disgrace yer own family this way."

"Christ! Ya musta went over in a fog an' back 'fore mornin'. that's all I can say. It didn't take ya long," Tom says.

"That's about how it happened, alright."

"Well, glory be ta God. Ya got the girl in trouble. Ya'll have ta marry 'er," says Katie, "that's all. And the sooner the better."

"Yessir, lad. Ya got ta pay fer yer fun. But how in damnation ta hell did ya get mixed up with that, oh, oh, oh . . ."

"I'll marry her. Don't worry. I told you I would."

"Pay is right. Christ, she could put ya behind bars. I believe the girl's underage at that. Is she fourteen or fifteen?"

"She's eighteen," I say impatiently. "She finished school last spring. I'll marry her. I know she's poor, but there's no disgrace in being poor."

"No," Tom answers, "yer right. There's no disgrace in bein' poor, but disgrace in bein' a whore."

"She's no whore. I know that much."

"Well, well, well. It's too damn bad altogether. Gettin' mixed up with that Long girl, a jeezless tramp. Oh, oh, oh, that oh, that dyin' tramp. All I can say is yer walkin' inta a ready-made family and how d'ya know if it's yers?"

"She told me. I believe her."

"Was she a virgin, boy? Or would ya know if ya had one?"

I shrug, I wouldn't know, not for sure. But there's no point in questioning all that now. I've been trapped, caught, landed like a salmon. Katie opens the dining room door. The ordeal is over, for now.

"I knew you'd face the music, Steve," she says, as much to Tom as to me. "Stevie has always been honourable with us."

Everyone moves about the house, Katie and Tom grim and silent, Danny restless but afraid to ask what has happened. We bump into each other nervously: the house seems too small. There are little flare-ups throughout the long evening.

"But where'll ya live?"

"I'll build down in the corner of the field, next spring."

"And where'll ya get work?"

"I'll try to get on at the mill. Or work with you in the woods. We always have the woods."

"What about the college learnin' ya thought ya needed?"

"I have to forget about that now, I guess."

Tom doesn't answer.

"We'll go ta see the minister tomorrow," Katie says a little later. "But I'd be ashamed ta go inta church once this gets around."

"Find out who all slept with 'er," says Tom.

"I'm the only one, according to her."

"She's lying. They all lie when they're in a scrap."

"I believe her."

"And her knocked up, imagine!"

"Tom!" Katie puts in sharply, "that's enough of that kind of talk. Accidents happen."

At bedtime, I go to my room and hide under the covers, or try to hide. But my thoughts, even on the edge of sleep, are lifelike and cruel, and much more clear than my magic dreams of Amanda. I try to cry, but the tears won't come. And then I think of Cindy, that she had to face this alone, and suddenly I want to marry her, save her, give her baby a name. Maybe I could love her after all?

But then I remember. We had agreed to keep our secret, promised each other to keep it private; and she went right home and told her folks. I'm disappointed in her. I know I can't ever truly love her, or trust her. And my night is filled with confusion, suspicion, guilt, and the crushing weight of my new responsibilities.

Waking often through the night, I can hear Tom and Katie's talk across the hall. Katie's voice is loud, so Tom can hear, but I can't quite catch the words through our closed doors. Then there is the rough hacking of his cough, and swearing.

Sometime after midnight, Danny wakes too. He tiptoes into my room in his striped pyjamas, looking like a old man with his hair tousled. He has been listening, and now he knows the secret too. He sits on the side of the bed, watching me in the pale light of the moon beyond my window.

"But how did ya come ta do what ya did?"

"I don't know, Danny."

"But what about university? You'll have ta go. What about that, Stevie?"

"That's off, too, I guess."

"Sure, and I was goin' ta stay home from school next year ta help Tom, just so you could go. I s'pose that's off, too, now."

"I suppose it is."

And in the morning, when I come down to the kitchen, Katie is sipping tea, hands cupping the mug beneath her chin, elbows on the table. She greets me from somewhere far away in her thoughts — "Oh, good morning, Stevie dear" — and goes to the stove to prepare my breakfast.

"Where's everyone this morning?"

"Tom and Danny went down ta rake off the marsh."

"I'd better hurry down there."

"Steven, yer father works hard and all he wants is the best for you. He don't want ta see ya gettin' in a rut and not gettin' out. You're so young ta get tied down. Try ta understand yer father: he means well. He's good in a lot of ways."

"I know. I feel I've let you all down. Ruined the respect of us all."

"We'll manage. We'll pull together."

"She's really a good kid, you know," I say.

Katie sets down across the table and pours herself some more tea. "Would Cindy move in here with us, stay fer the winter, say, till after the baby comes and yer own place is ready?"

"I don't think that would work out."

"Sure it would. Tom said in the night it would be alright with him. We have the spare room. Come spring, he'll help ya build a place in the lower field. He'll take the lumber he's been keepin' ta build a garage with."

"I have to get a steady job now, first."

"Tom's gonna speak to the man down at the mill, next time he's in town, and see if he'll give ya a job. He owes Tom a favour or two."

"I suppose I could fix up our old millshed and live in that."

Katie forces a smile but erases it quickly. "This is no time ta be funny," she says, almost to herself. "Somethin' like this needs plannin'."

"I won't live on the other side of the river, I know that much."

"You've hardly touched yer breakfast."

"Where did you say Tom is?"

"Down rakin' off the marsh."

"I'd better get down there, give him a hand."

As I swing open the screen door, Katie pulls at my sleeve and says, "Stevie, now don't ya worry about the other business any more. She's a nice little thing. I always liked her; her folks are decent people; it could be worse. We all have our health and if we trust in the Lord, things will work out. I can just feel it in my bones."

I know, now, that Katie and Tom wanted more for me than this. I walk down to the swamp meadow through a beautiful morning, seeing only my own guilt, and the silent support for my dreams that I never saw before. I've let them down. I had wanted so much out of life. Now I would be a burden on my family, as well as a shame.

Tom is lifting the forkfuls of half-dried swamp hay into the field and scattering it on the stubble to dry. Danny comes behind him with the long-handled wooden rake.

"Here comes a lad lookin' fer a job," Tom says, without looking up. "I hear he's gettin' married and needs work."

"Yes, a married man needs a job," nods Danny, grinning. "Here, take the rake and finish this."

"Boys, she's not worth haulin' ta the barn," Tom grumbles, whacking a clump of hay. "She's all sticks an' weeds. Next year we'll leave 'er."

Tom does not mention Cindy, but he's kind today and I wonder if he's sorry for how he spoke about her. All day, working together in pensive quiet, talking little, I can feel the kindness and sympathy pouring from Tom. We're trying to adjust to the sudden twist in my life. It isn't until evening that we talk. Tom comes up to my bedroom and sits for a minute before he goes to his own room to bed.

"Ya best get over an' talk to 'er, lad, an' the sooner the better," he tells me, and I nod agreement. "An' talk to old Will 'imself. Now he's a strange old coot, but he may take a likin' to ya."

I come down from my room the next morning to find Cindy sitting in the parlour, swinging around on the swivel organ stool, her hands under her. Her blonde hair is almost white in the curtain-darkened room. I open my mouth to tell her of my decision to marry her, but she speaks first.

"Steve? Could we talk?"

"Just about everything's been said around here by now."

"No, it hasn't. I couldn't sleep, Steve, I felt so guilty. That was an awful thing I did to ya."

"You mean telling your folks?"

"Yes, that. But there's more. I lied to ya, Steve."

Still standing in the doorway, frozen in place, I stare at her.

"And I feel awful," she goes on. "It's true I'm expectin' a baby, but . . . but it's not yer baby, Steve."

"Not mine?" Her words sink in slowly, her tone soft and soothing and terribly kind.

"No, you're not the one," she says. "It was Dale Canter from town. I was expectin' when ya took me home from the dance. But I love ya, Steve," and her words come out in a rush now, "I love ya, so I wanted to marry you, not Dale. But I just couldn't lie to ya any more. I wish the baby was yours, but it's not. I love you, Steve. I'm sorry."

Tears run down her pale cheeks, shining in the dim light, and I go to her to take her in my arms and wipe them away. When I try to release her, she clings to me like a frightened child.

"Oh, Stevie, I love you," she whispers tearfully. "Please marry me. I could make you happy, I know I could. Please gimme a chance. I'll do whatever you want, always I would. I'd look after ya, worship ya. no one would ever know the baby isn't yours. It would have your name. Oh, Steve, please! Please!"

"But it wouldn't be any good, can't you see? Even without the baby, it wouldn't be any good. It wouldn't be fair to you, either."

"And why not?"

"You don't have to be anyone's slave. You're a beautiful person. Someday you'll find someone who really loves you. Can't you see, I'd only be pretending?"

"But you could learn to love me, if you let yourself." She looks up at me from behind the curtain of blonde hair. "I'd always be yer girl, for ever and ever and ever. I'd never let you down, I promise."

"Cindy, oh, Cindy, please try to understand."

"Oh, you're right. I know it. Damnit, yer always right!" She pushes me away and gets to her feet, turning to the wall. She wipes her eyes and nose, sniffing just a little.

"Cindy," I say, suddenly realizing what all this means, "you have to tell your folks. Tell my folks."

"I did tell my folks, already. They sent me over to beg forgiveness. Will you forgive me, Steve? Oh, please forgive me fer lyin' to ya. It's only because I love ya so much and I wanted . . . Will ya forgive me fer lovin' ya this much, Steve?'

"Yes. Okay. I forgive you. I honestly forgive you. But go now, please, and tell Katie."

Cindy walks slowly to the outside kitchen, red-eyed and ashamed, frightened, to talk with Katie. And I sink slowly into a chair, staring at the door. A weight is lifting from me, and the morning brightens with hope for the future I thought I'd lost. I hear the voices coming and going beyond me, and still I sit there in the parlour, feeling the joy and relief spread through the house. A new kind of spirit is growing among us, like people waking at last from the same paralysing nightmare.

CHAPTER 16

Since haying time, the stubble fields have turned from grey-green to a patchwork of red clovers and dandelion, fertilized by the mouldering hay remnants left by the rake. The potato stocks are yellowing and along the line fences the withering choke cherries droop in clusters above the small pairs of hazelnuts smothered by the bush. In the dooryard, the crab apples at the top of the tree are orange and the rhubarb patch has seeded sentinels that tower a jungle of elephant's ears.

We have spent a full day in the woods, and after we have finished supper and Tom has done the milking and separated the cream, Danny and I take turns pushing the churn dasher up and down until the first glimpse of butter appears around it. Katie then scoops the floating chunks from the buttermilk and kneads it with the ladle until it's free of water. Then she packs it into the small wooden boxes to harden, I carry water from the kitchen to wash the car, and as I work, Amanda's spirit overtakes me and carries me, so the work goes unnoticed. The feeling grows out of those dreams, more than from actual life, so I'm half lost in fantasy. When Tom comes out with the pail of buttermilk, I don't even see him.

"Mix that with hog grower and give it ta the pig, would ya like a good lad? Oh, never mind," he huffs, seeing I'm miles away in my mind, "Christ, I'll do it myself!"

As the night comes on, I feel my need to be with Amanda grow. I'm edgy, tense, restless. I want to be with Amanda. But what if I do something wrong, or say something to turn her away? The feeling's too strong. I borrow money from Katie and go.

I drive the gravel highway to town as the August evening fades to brown with thin layers of fog settling into the hollows. I push sideways the two small levers that turn on the car's heater and the warm air carries the strange sweetness of radiator rust to mix with the scents of my shaving lotion and Brylcream. I light a cigarette and switch on the radio. The rear speakers are thin against the rumble of the car, as Hank Williams sings "Why don't you love me like you used to do." I try to relax, dragging on the cigarette and taking glances at myself in the rearview mirror. I turn my shirt collar up to hide the peeling sunburn. I need a haircut.

In town, I turn onto the main street and drive around the business district. There are other teenagers on the sidewalks and a line-up in front of the uptown movie house. The name of the show, I notice, is *High Noon*, starring Gary Cooper and Grace Kelly. Another group stands in front of the Delux Grill. Neon signs blink and the windows are lit, people shopping in the stores. I drive to the Elm Inn. Amanda's expecting me.

I pull into the driveway and honk, but it's a long half hour before the yellow porch light comes on, and by then there are several cigarette butts on the ground beside the car. Amanda almost runs across the lawn, smiling brilliantly, her hair blowing behind her. Getting into the car, she sits close, and I can smell her perfume.

"Why didn't you come inside and wait? I was tied up with dinner again."

She talks on, but I don't listen, and I fight myself to be casual, driving in no apparent direction. Her sideways glances are flattering; I want desperately to stop the car right here and pull her into my arms. We pass the Delux Grill.

"Oh, let's go in," she says, "I'm thirsty. And my friends are in there." I park and we go in.

The old grill has dark sideboards and fans revolve overhead; under the dim lights, in the haze of tobacco smoke, it's warm and intimate and soft with the smell of burnt onions. I find a nickel for the jukebox and Amanda leafs through the songs, selecting Buddy Holly, "That'll Be The Day."

The Grill's owner is an older woman whose name is Georgina: George, they call her. She drags one foot when she walks, and the smell of boiled cabbage comes from her clothing. It's clear that she loves young people, joking with the crowd, calling Amanda by name, asking who I might be.

"So, who's this fine looker ya found, Mandy?"

"Oh, George, I thought you'd met. This is Steve, Steve Moar."

"Hi, George," I say, meeting her smile.

"From these parts, are ya?"

"Yes, upriver a few miles."

"In a village or the country?"

"A farm, actually."

"Oh, fer goodness sake. On a farm! What d'ya do there?"

"Not much."

"He's taken a year off from school to help his father," Mandy says. "He's going to university next year."

"Do ya have pigs an' cows an' chickens an' horses out there?"

"Yes, I guess we do."

"She's very nosy," Amanda whispers, laughing a little, when Georgina moves on to fuss over another table.

We sip our drinks and I smoke a cigarette. The guys in the next booth shout bold remarks to Georgina, and joke tentatively with Amanda. It's clear they know her, but they're being polite in my presence. I'm set apart. I admire their openness and their self-confidence. I want to join in the conversation, but I don't know what to say, what we'd have in common. Pigs and cows and chickens and horses? Hardly! Town guys aren't loners, they all have each other, like a family. And they're so sharp: hair uncombed and uncreamed, fresh slacks and suede shoes. I'm dressed all wrong, I think. Plaid shirt, jeans and Wellington boots. I have to stop wearing the hair cream. I turn my collar down and wonder why Amanda is with me at all. I wonder if these town guys have dated her. It would all be so easy for them. I wish I were from town.

I reach across the table and squeeze Amanda's hand. I love her so much I have to watch how I talk and act around other people: I look into her eyes and I want to go parking.

"Are you guys coming to the corn boil?" someone in the next booth asks. It's the leader, the popular one, looking like Sal Minio in his black leather jacket.

"Where is it, Smitty?" Amanda asks him.

"Oak Point. Why don't you come down?"

"Would you like to go, Steve?"

"I don't really care."

"They have plenty of corn. But you're driving, it's up to you."

"If you'd like to go, we'll go. Personally, I'd be just as happy to stay around here."

"I'd kind of like to go."

"Okay, if you like."

We drive down the river road, past the golf course and the drive-in theatre, and out a long lane to the river. There are four other cars here, one a '53 Chev like ours except that it's brown with a white convertible top. There's a motorcycle — Smitty's, I guess correctly — the model with the big Indian chief's head stencilled on the gas tank.

On the shore they stand around a driftwood fire, blasting music from the radio of a Buick parked nearby. Two girls, one looking like Natalie Wood, dance between the fire and the water, beer bottles in their hands. All the rest are guys, and everyone has beer. As we step down the bank and approach the group, Smitty turns and holds out his arms.

"Oh, great, Mandy's here," he says, and they all turn to greet her, two fellows swinging her around and chasing her around the fire and down the beach. One of the others hands me a beer. Someone turns up the radio: Jim Lowe is singing on the hit parade, "Green door, what's that secret you're keeping . . ."

Smitty calls to Amanda. "C'mon, Mandy, let's dance!" He pulls her into his arms and they waltz out of the circle of firelight, pressing close. I am jealous. I watch the dancing shadows from the corner of my eye, and smile, and listen to the other guys talk. They talk about the local football team that two of them play for, and they talk about the movies they've seen at the uptown theatre. They joke with each other about girls they all know and most have dated.

Amanda comes back to stand beside me, but she's only there for a minute; someone asks her to dance and she's gone again. When she comes back to me the next time, I'm quick to ask her myself. But someone calls that the corn is done, and we go back to the fire, where the hot cobs are dripping with butter and the car's fender makes a table.

Smitty goes to the parking area and starts up his motorcycle. It makes a roar and backfires as he drives it up to the fire.

"C'mon, Mandy, jump on and come for a ride," Smitty says.

"I'd like to go for a ride with Smitty," she says to me, smiling.

"Sure. Go ahead. Be careful."

"We'll just go for a short ride."

Amanda gets on the wide leather seat behind Smitty and puts her arms around his waist. The big bike idles away, out the lane, and heads up the highway toward town, its motor blatting.

I stand by the fire with the group and drink another beer. It seems like hours before I hear the bike return. She shouldn't have left me there for so long. I'm a bit embarrassed, and again I feel jealousy churning inside. But Amanda comes to me laughing, her hand out for a beer, and she stands beside me until the fire burns low and it's time to leave.

We drive back to town and there is a din of passing vehicles and the lights make halos in the night like projector lamps reflecting in a mirror. We cruise around town and find a dark lane running up the hill toward the railway yard. I park behind some freight sheds and spin the dial of the radio to find music.

When I put my arms around Amanda, she turns to me, inviting me to kiss her. We close our eyes and I hold my lips to hers in a long breathless embrace. I can feel the fullness of her lips and for a long time we are as close as one. I become warm inside now, and proud of myself for getting this far with her.

She turns and lies across my legs, linking her arms around my shoulders. Her full breasts rise as she holds me. I hold her tightly and wonder when the time will be right to tell her how I feel. I kiss her forehead, her nose, her chin, and finally her mouth. I move my hand down the front of her blouse and touch the softness of her breasts above the limiting bra. She pulls my hand away and holds it tight. "Now you're being naughty," she says.

I relax and light a cigarette, gathering my courage, smoothing the back of her small hand. When I turn to look into her eyes, there is a special chemistry in what I'm feeling.

"Mandy, I love you," I say, squeezing her hand as the words spill out. "I can't help it, I just love you."

"You're kidding!" She's surprised by my outburst. "You actually love me? I mean, you're in love with me?" But her voice isn't right. It is as if I haven't said anything serious. I say the words again to make the point more strongly this time.

"Oh, yes. I love you," I tell her, "I really do." Amanda is silent. I feel cheap, overly sensitive, easily moved. And I wish I hadn't said the words that can't be retracted now. I hold her, saying nothing more, wondering if my timing was bad. It was like some power overtook me and said the words I couldn't stop from coming out.

Amanda sits quietly in the circle of my arms, just hugging me a little, still saying nothing. I feel drained and disappointed. She has not returned the compliment. I've been blinded by my love for her, I think; I can't see reality.

"Well, Mandy," I say, trying to make my voice light, "do you love me? Just a little?"

"Oh, Steve, don't mind me. I'm not sure how I feel sometimes. Actually, most of the time. Sometimes I wonder what the word 'love' means."

"But you must love someone, sometimes. Have you never been in love?"

"No, I don't believe so. I've never really been lovesick for anyone, if that's what you mean."

"Not even with Gordon?" I ask, remembering the absent boyfriend.

"No! Look, Gordon's a good friend and I like him a lot, but I'm not madly in love with him. We've been friends for years. It's not love, for cripes sake. At least, I never thought if it as love." She turns a serious face to me in the grey darkness of the car. "How does someone know when it's really love anyway?"

"When it happens, you know."

I try to turn the conversation around, lead it in a new direction. We leave the word love somewhat disputed. Amanda knows how I feel about her. And, while she didn't say that she loved me, she did say that she wasn't in love with Gordon.

"Steve, look, you're very nice," she says suddenly. "Oh, don't mind me. I just need some time that's all. Time to think. Okay?"

I kiss her again, trying now to control my feelings. Maybe I'm overly hungry for a lover, I think. We lie on the seat, looking through the windshield at the late summer sky. The stars are tiny pebbles of gold scattered in the darkness. There will be a chance of frost before morning.

"Steve, it's awfully late. I should be going in."

"It seems we just got here."

"Father will worry. It really is quite late."

I hug her again and start the car, and we listen to the radio as I drive through town with my arm around Amanda. Already I'm wondering when I can see her again.

The Elm Inn is in darkness when we arrive, but the yellow porch light is on. We stand against the door, my arms around her tightly.

"Would you like to come in for a coffee before you drive all that way upriver?"

"No, I don't think so. We might wake your father."

"So?"
"I don't think he would like me."
"Nonsense. Why do you say that, Steve?"
"It's just a feeling I have."
"He doesn't even know you."
"We've talked on the phone once or twice, when I've called for you."
"I have to go in, really I do. Thank you for taking me out."
"Thank you for coming out. Will you again?"
"I suppose."
"Next Saturday night?"
"Maybe. But call first. I may have to work."

I kiss her and her lips are firm and kissable; I have to force myself to release her. She pushes herself away from me and disappears inside in a series of gently closing doors. The car is parked on the street, the motor still running, and as I walk towards it clouds of vapour drift across the lawn.

Amanda's spirit is still in the car as I drive. I search the evening's experiences for something that might reveal her feelings. Her eyes seemed to show a kind of want, I think: yes, there was a definite chemistry when our eyes met. I try to keep the image of her as close as the smell of her perfume lingering on my shirt. I will relive these memories through the week ahead, and cling to it, and count the days until I'm with her and everything is bright again.

CHAPTER 17

Danny has received a notice from the Customs office saying there is a parcel to be picked up. It is obviously the Union Cavalry saddle ordered in the early summer. While he's been waiting for our trip to town, he's been cutting poles in the swamp and dragging them to the barnyard to build a corral. This will be like the horse corral in the Red Ryder comic strips in the *Family Herald*. It will extend from the cow stable to the highway and back to the barn. According to Tom, this is quite an undertaking for a lad Danny's age and one that shows great promise.

It is late morning when Tom, Howard and I leave home in Charlie's half-ton truck to go downriver to pick up a cow. We will stop in town and go to the Customs office and then to the hardware store to get spikes for Danny. As we drive, the day is crisp and breezy with scattered fluffy clouds. Sometimes a few drops sprinkle the windshield and the wipers are turned on. Then the sun shines and the windshield dries so the build-up of dead flies and dust along with the faulty wiper blades makes it almost impossible to see. Howard has a strong urine smell on his clothing, and he smokes, squinting through the smoke and the windshield. His nicotine-stained fingers clutch the wheel, making the veins in his arms bulge. Pitch speckles his hands and wrists. I sit in the middle, trying to get something on the radio. Tom wears his big straw hat, flannel shirt and braces. He fusses with his pipe, coughs and spits out the window. It is that kind of day when it is too warm with the window up and too cool with it down. So he leaves it down and his arm lies out the window and the dust boils into a cloud behind the truck, and the breeze — which according to Tom is coming from the north-northeast — carries dust across the fields. Tom keeps up a commentary on the scenery as we go.

"Boys, looka ol' Jack Haines, still hayin'. He'll be at it till Christmas. His boys were a worthless bunch, ya know." And further on, "Boys, that's the old Smith place, fallin' down — third generation."

Tom has purchased a cow over the phone after reading an ad in the *North Shore Leader*. He has agreed to pay fifty dollars, sight unseen, and the owner is throwing in an almost-new churn. We have given Howard five dollars for gas and the sideboards from our old truck. He is just happy to be asked, and proud of his new sideboards. Charlie's truck is a '50 GMC which Howard has decorated with coloured cab lights, stringing them along each bumper and into the shape of a tree in the grill. Because he is night-blind, we want to get back before dark.

"Boys, I shot a deer in that field once, right there by the apple tree."

"So why'd ya buy a cow that way, Tom?" Howard pries.

"It's a good deal at the price."

"But what ya s'pose ya bought?"

"A cow, I hope."

"But what ya s'pose she'll look like?"

"Like a cow. Boys, look fer a field a oats."

"But how'd ya know she's good fer milkin' without tryin' 'er?"

"I can tell when I see 'er if she's a milker."

"But how could ya tell?"

"By the size of 'er bag, pretty Jesus likely." Tom is losing his patience, and I hide a smile.

"But a cow could be forty an' gone dry, an' still have a big bag," Howard persists. "How would a lad know?"

"I can tell when I see 'er, I tell ya."

"But how could a lad tell?"

"Ya can tell a cow's age by counting the wrinkles on 'er horns."

"But what if she don't have no horns?"

"Did ya ever see a cow with no horns? I never did."

"They could be knocked off, that's all."

"Then it's the grey hair on 'er nose, I guess."

"If'n she's not a grey cow ta start with."

"Go ta hell, Howard."

Near town, the static disappears from the radio and we listen to *Hayshakers' Hoe-Down* with host Art Matchett. There is singing by Hank Snow and old-time fiddling by Ward Allen. Tom drums his fingers on the dashboard, keeping time. With Howard and Tom both smoking, there is a haze in the cab even with the windows down. I'm craving a cigarette and can't smoke in front of Tom, so I take Howard's makings from his shirt pocket, roll a smoke, and light it with a deep drag before passing it to Howard. He throws his butt out the window and takes the fresh one.

Downtown, Howard pulls over and goes into the liquor store to get a little jug. I haven't shaved in three days and my overalls are pitchy, with holes in the knees, so I stay in the truck where I won't be seen. Tom goes to the Customs office and picks up Danny's saddle, which is a basic seat without straps or stirrups. He tosses it in the back of the truck. As we leave town, heading downriver, Howard opens the top of his brown bag and has "a little toddy fer the body" as he drives. Then he passes the bag past me to Tom, who takes a swig, coughs, and spits again out the window.

"Boys, that's lovely," he says. "Lovely stuff, sa strong she'll stand alone."

"Christ, take a good one, Tom. Ta do this job a man's gotta be half-drunk."

We drive downriver past the golf course and the lane to Oak Point, and at a small farm with falling-down buildings we pull in for Tom to ask directions.

"It's in here, boys," Tom says, recognizing the place from the description he got on the phone.

An old man on the veranda stands, stretches, and comes to meet us unshaven and dirty, smelling of wine. "Yer here fer ol' Sadie, are ya?" he asks. We follow him around the house to where the cow is tethered on a pole and chain. His old suit coat and baggy pants are too short and they reveal his heavy wool socks jammed into plaid bedroom slippers. "Here fer ol' Sadie," he murmurs, "I hate ta part with 'er."

Sadie is thin with exaggerated hip bones, and her chain is caught around her horns so that the pole tether extends from her head to the ground.

"Ya got 'er propped up have ya?" Tom walks around the cow. "Will she stand up without the brace?"

Howard laughs loudly, appreciatively. "That's tellin' 'im," he grins.

"How old did ya say she is?"

"Six."

"Six, by Jesus!"

"No more 'n eight," the old man shrugs.

"Look!" says Tom, "ya'll soon have ta tie sticks on 'er horns fer the wrinkles ta climb!"

"Ha haa, Jesus, that's tellin' 'im."

"Shut up, Howard. You're drunk."

Tom agrees on a price of forty dollars, if the old man throws in the tether as well as the churn, and reluctantly hands over two crumpled twenties. "Let's get 'er loaded an' get ta Jesus outta here," he tells us.

Howard goes behind the truck and has another drink. Then he backs the truck across the road, dropping its rear wheels into the ditch. Tom leads the cow up the tailgate ramp but she braces herself when her front feet reach the box.

"Take a kink on 'er tail!"

Howard twists the cow's tail and she lunges forward, into the truck. Tom throws the churn and tether in behind her, and we drive back toward town. Howard finishes the rum and throws the bottle out. Near town he turns a switch and the many lights come on, making the front of the truck look like a Christmas tree. He's singing as he pulls up in front of the liquor store to get more rum.

"Horny in the mornin', horny in the evenin', horny at suppertime . . ."

Tom leaves his hat on the seat beside me and goes into the hardware store, to buy a new sink with the money he's saved from the cow deal. I smoke from Howard's tobacco and watch the crowd gathered at the Delux Grill. The cow jostles and twists her head under the sideboards, lifting the stakes and rocking the truck. Then she bawls and splatters the box; I sink low in the seat.

One Indian Summer

A group of girls walk past to join some guys in front of the Grill. I watch them push and tease and chase a girl with long hair that looks like Amanda's, and I pull Tom's hat down over my face, watching through a hole in the brim. It *is* Amanda, bold and loud. My heart thumps. My face burns. I wish I were somewhere else, but I can't take my eyes off Mandy, and I want to be a part of her group. I've never seen this side of her, so bold, even tomboyish.

One of the boys with her is Smitty, from the cornboil. Amanda pushes her hands through his hair, so he takes a comb from his back pocket and puts it in place, looking at his reflection in the window of the Grill. Then another helps Smitty hold Amanda while he unties her ponytail; she chases them into the Grill, and the door drifts shut behind them, sending the smell of burnt onions into the warm street.

I am burning with jealousy; I curse myself for being here and tilt the hat completely over my face. Waiting for Tom and Howard, I try to make myself invisible. People pass on the sidewalk.

"Phew! Smell the cow shit!" someone says.

"Lookit the antique cow," says another. "I bet she's going to get it."

"Must be from upriver. Lookit all the stupid lights."

"Would ya come for a ride in me truck?" comes another voice, jeering, a town boy's imitation of someone who'd own this ridiculous cow-laden rig. The cow bawls again, long and loud, then arches her back, curls her tail, and urinates into the box. I sit very still, face hidden, and hear laughter.

"Shh. Someone's in the truck. Look."

The voices fade off down the sidewalk, and I pull the brim of the hat up to wipe my forehead. Tom and another man are coming out with a large sink, humping it against their hips to swing it up behind the cow.

"Thank ya ever sa much," Tom says to the clerk. "The next time I see ya I'll thank ya some more."

Howard opens the driver's door and hands me his brown-bagged bottle while he hits the ignition. Nothing happens. No life is left in the battery. So Tom and I push the truck out into traffic and down the street. Some strangers come over from the sidewalk to help, chuckling. The truck jerks, and we run behind it. Howard feeds it gas, and the lights brighten again across the front end, and black smoke pours from the exhaust; we run and jump in. I have a headache now. Howard's into the rum again.

"But Tom bought 'imself an antique cow fer forty dollars, ha haa!"

"Go ta hell, Howard, yer drunk."

"Steve, Steve, Stevie, take me to a whorehouse!" Howard hollers, turning around in his seat to breathe rum at me and wink, "Ya must know one, yer always down here."

"I don't know of any," I say. But Howard isn't listening. He pulls the truck suddenly off the road and reels into the woods, unbuttoning his fly as he goes. When he returns, I get out and push him into the middle, and take over the wheel. Howard is content: he sings and rambles and laughs for a while, then slumps against me, asleep. Tom sips from the bottle, fusses with his pipe. He cranks down the window to spit and the cold air blows through the cab, making Howard mumble and laugh to himself in his sleep.

"Did ya see that field?" Tom asks, pointing to a flat field with a rock pile and raspberry bushes in the centre. "That's the old Cain property. Ol' Henry's folks, I s'pose, I don't know what relation they be, let me think . . ."

"It doesn't matter," I tell him.

"Well, sir, they had a nice house in there and a big barn over there by the rock pile. They sold cream an' raised horses. Belgiums."

"What happened to their place?"

"Well, when me and Katie first got married, I bought a mare from him. Prettiest thing ya ever saw ta look at, round as a barrel."

"Ride 'er home?"

"No, me an' George Cooper come down an' got 'er with his ol' three-ton. She went on the truck hard, too, like the cow did today. Hated ta leave home I s'pose. Well, she balked goin' onto the truck an' it took four of us ta push 'er on."

"What would you pay for a horse like that, then?"

"Eighty dollars. But eighty dollars then was a lot of money."

"Still is," I remind him.

"Well, sir, we took 'er up home there an' stood 'er in the stable an' everyone came in and sized 'er up, just like they did this summer with the new car, an' they all thought she was a great buy."

"Did she become Prince's mother?" I ask, thinking of the solid old horse with the fine-boned head.

"No, Christ, no wait 'til I tell ya."

"But a good haulin' horse?"

"No. Son-of-a-whore wasn't worth 'er feed."

"Why's that?"

"Well, sir, the next day I hooked 'er up to the express wagon an' me an' Katie got on ta go pickin' berries, an' she couldn't haul us."

"Couldn't haul the express wagon?"

"Couldn't haul a sick whore off a piss-pot." Tom takes another swallow of Howard's rum, and screws the top on the bottle. "Strong stuff, stand alone," he says, and puts the bag back on Howard's lap.

"What did you do with the horse?" I ask.

"We got Jack the vet ta come look at 'er. He said 'er back was broke."

"Holy shit!"

"So next day we took 'er back an' me an' George, we unloaded 'er right where we put 'er on, an' was she ever glad ta get home. But the ol' man was away that day, or hidin' someplace."

"Did he give you back the money?"

"Well, sir, it took me a long time, but I got it. I had ta chase 'im fer weeks, till he sold the ol' mare ta some other poor bastard, I s'pose. I never trusted 'im after that, but we never held a grudge."

"What became of his farm?" I am interested now.

"Wait'll I tell ya now. Bad luck seemed ta follow the man in some way. Maybe it was just 'is way of thinkin', or bad management that made bad luck follow 'im."

"So what happened?"

"Wait now, yer gettin' ahead a me. Well, sir, a few years after the horse deal, his wife lost 'er mind an' killed 'erself. Went crazy from puttin' up with 'im, I s'pose. They say she drank stove pipe polish."

"And him?"

"That ol' man was more deep rooted than any of us. Ya'd see 'im out pickin' wildflowers there in the back field on Sundays. But he just couldn't be stayin' there alone on the farm, day in and day out. An' his mind went. So he took ta the bottle an' stayed drunk day an' night."

"Did he make his own brew?"

"No, Christ, no. He drunk nothing but the best Haig scotch. Expensive as anything. He sold 'is animals off one at a time an' drunk the money an' then he sold the machinery an' then the lumber off the place, and drunk that. An' one night when he was three sheets ta the wind, he knocked over a lamp an' set fire ta the place. house an' barn burnt down, and he burnt in 'er."

"Holy shit!" I shake my head.

"Yessir, boys, he came ta sad end. A sad tale. But life can be that way if ya stop ta look at 'er. An' all it takes is one little flaw in a man ta start the ball rollin' downhill. That ol' lad we got the cow from is likely in the same boat."

As we drive into our dooryard, Howard snoring happily between us, Danny comes running out of the house, looking for his new saddle. Katie comes behind him, smiling, to see the bawling cow standing now with her back feet in the dung-splattered new sink.

CHAPTER 18

The nights are cold now and the dew is heavy in the aftergrass, with frost lingering in the shade of buildings until mid-morning. The sun fights the breeze and by mid-day it is hot. But it is a different kind of heat from the long days of high summer, and we savour it, blocking out thoughts of approaching autumn. But the dooryard is burnt brown and in the air we can taste the ripe weeds and the pig manure and the decaying raspberries that cling to purple stems behind the outhouse.

We watch the oatfield as the last shades of green fade, and the blackbirds, spooked by the slam of a screen door, come and go in wavering flocks between the swamp alders and the field. The oats whisper in the breeze and their kernels rattle like the feet of a million mice scampering through the grain.

As the day declines, the old millshed hunches low and black against the sunset as though it were smothered and crowded into the field's corner by the thriving oatfield. After supper the sky becomes forlorn and rigid, and a charcoal creeps in like an invisible smoke so the trees on the horizon are a sawblade, supporting the superlative moon. The little night breeze follows, rattling the apple tree and dropping the first red crab to the ground, and with this comes the hollow feeling that we have let the best days of another summer slip by us and we are uneasy and restless, like the one who is always going to leave for some far-off paradise, but never really goes, or the one whose heart aches for some love they never really find.

We've moved from the summer kitchen back to the main house. Our lights go on at suppertime now. The kitchen is bright and warm, with comforts to rediscover. In the slanting rectangle of light outside its window, we stand and talk and dodge the bats that dive across the dooryard after flies.

And I have a hunger for new books, something deeper and more mystical than any I've read, and I go to the dining room, close the door, and fill out the application form for another correspondence course. I start to write the short story that I hope will be made into a radio show by the CBC, to be aired on Sunday nights replacing *Jake and the Kid*. I mail it to the *Atlantic Advocate* and the Fredericton *Gleaner*'s weekend magazine, and then I am all hollow inside from writing for too long. I have to fight myself to keep from going across the river to see Cindy. At least I know Cindy, know where I am with her. The trip downriver with Tom and Howard has shaken my confidence. Do I know the real Amanda? That bold laughing girl with the boys at the Delux Grill was a stranger; and neither does she know the real me. If she did, if she knew me, would she still come out with me? I can't help feeling a surge of love when I think of her, but now I wonder if I see only what I want to see in her. Certainly, my love for her has grown in spite of everything, but when I think of it, I see only what I want to see in her. If only she loved me enough to do the same. But the declining summer is now haunting, with its melancholy touch of blues and I know that now, even more than before, I want to strengthen our relationship. So far, all I have is a few precious memories and the hope I keep hidden.

Tom is not the kind of person who can talk about a thing like love. He is silent so much of the time, his mind is a mystery to me. Sometimes he works all day alone in the field or the woods and just thinks. Maybe he has no dream now and just looks back. When I stop to think of it, I have not often heard him laugh, and his face lights up only when we speak of the old days. But I have heard him say a hundred times, "A man can be happy anywhere if he has the right woman, content in a swamp in a tar paper shack."

Katie's belief is different. "Trade up," She says. "Up, or don't trade at all. Someone to grow up to."

I go to bed and wonder if the mind that wouldn't grow could love the mind that does, and maybe bind into a sensible chemistry. Would the two let it happen? Could they ever be close?

"Do you want me now, this way?" she asks, coming out of the shadows in my dream. "Do you want all of me?"

"Yes," I whisper, "I want you both."

"But I'm only me. Did you think there was someone else?"

In the dim dream light, I strain to see the pale shape which is her face, strain to discern her features. This is the woman. Who is she? Who is she?

"I thought you were someone else. I thought there were two of you."

"Who else would it be? Who do you want?"

"I just want you."

"You mean like this?"

"This way is fine. As long as you're here, is what's important."

"Are you glad I came across tonight?"

"Yes, I'm glad — across or up or however you came."

"Kiss me. Everyone starts with a kiss."

She is neither Amanda nor Cindy, but both. Her skin is soft and tender and she bends over and kisses me with her wet mouth and I can feel her smooth legs against my sides and I rub her back up to the shoulders and around to the front.

When I awake, I'm holding my pillow and the house is cool in the dull light of morning.

"Now, where's that Danny got to this time," Tom grumbles as he walks the kitchen floor. "He's been hard ta find lately."

"He's gone hunting. I saw him gathering rocks."

Danny is uptight about having to go back to school soon, because he is repeating Grade Four and will have new classmates. He counts his free days and fills every hour. Sometimes he's up and gone just after daybreak. I've written another order to New York for him, this one for the Manly Art of Self-defence home course, advertised on the back cover of a *Ringo Kid* comic book. While he waits, he's collecting money from Howard, Nick, and some of the others, and has ordered a set of ten-ounce boxing gloves from Eaton's. He wants to take down the pitching machine rope to build a ring in the dooryard, but Tom won't let him. Already the Eaton's Fall and Winter catalogue has arrived, and Danny wants the Red Ryder Daisy air rifle featured in it.

Danny comes from the swamp carrying a spruce partridge he has killed with his slingshot. He takes the bird into the house and gives it to Katie, and then comes to help us as the Deering binder is taken out of the shed to set on its trucks in the dooryard. Tom wants to get the oats cut and hauled in as quickly as possible. He fears the blackbirds will take them all or a wind or rain will lodge them so they can't be picked up by the binder. We crank down the driving wheel and take off the trucks. Then I use the same crank to turn the gears as he oils the square-linked chain that rolls the table's canvas and the fingers that tie the sheaves. He uses a gooseneck can to oil the unreachable areas, belching its bottom with his thumb until the yard is thick with the smell of oil. We put a new ball of binder twine in its container and thread the twine into the fingers and crank the sheave-throwing levers by hand until they work smoothly.

"A work of genius, the binder," says Tom.

When we have the horses hooked up, Tom gets up on the seat and I pass the reins to him through the iron ring on the front. The team pulls the out-of-gear rattling binder with ease, rattling as it goes to the flat. Its driving wheel cuts slashes in the sod. At the edge of the oats, he kicks the machine into gear and the binder eats into the standing oats as the big grey wheel tilts the standing grain against the cutting blades. The side levers kick, throwing out the sheaves, and Danny and I walk behind to pick them up by the twine and stook them in wigwams. Blue jays flit among the stubble, and Danny gathers rocks for his slingshot to hunt them. He wants the feathers to make flyhooks.

The first load of oats hauled in and tiered on a temporary scaffold above the barn floor, we go back to the flat. I stick the pitchfork into the butt end of the sheaves and toss them high in the hayrack, where Tom pushes them around, ends out, to make a nice square load. He grumbles about the blackbirds stealing part of our crop.

A white station wagon drives up to the edge of the field — it has pink license plates — and its driver gets out and walks toward us cautiously over the stubble. He's grey-haired, dressed in khaki, with a huge belly pushing out over his belt.

"Now, who in hell is that comin'," Tom says, "the High Sheriff?"

"Is this the Moar farm?"

"Yes, sir," Tom answers, eyes never leaving his work.

"Would you be Mr. Moar?"

"Yes, sir."

"My name is Sam Eagles. I'm from Connecticut. Someone said you folks might have a place to fish."

"Yes, sir."

Eagles is around fifty years of age and he puffs on a big cigar. I smile to myself because he seems intimidated by Tom.

"How's the fishing out front here?"

"The very best! But it depends what yer lookin' for. Chubs? Eels?"

"Salmon?"

"Yessir."

"You mean there's salmon out front here?"

"Sure. We have fishin', an' good fishin'. They'd be salmon at the rock today, don't ya think, boys?"

"I saw one jump this mornin'," Danny says.

"Would you mind, Mr. Moar, if I took a cast or two?"

"No, no, go ahead. but ya'll need a guide." Tom moves the sheaves about without looking now. "Danny, you go with 'im an' show 'im where ta fish."

"Beautiful, beautiful," the American says. "Come along, Danny."

He drives over near the millshed and Danny helps him assemble his equipment. He puts together a long split-bamboo fishing rod and pulls on long wading boots. Then he takes a landing net from the car and hands it to Danny. He also sets a tackle box on the ground, and with a small hand pump begins to inflate a rubber raft.

"He's got enough riggin' ta go after a whale," Tom says. "He must have money. But we'll have ta see if he's a tipper."

When the oats are in, Tom feeds each horse a sheaf and I go to the river to watch the American fish. Danny has anchored the raft near the opposite shore and Mr. Eagles is casting into the eddy. Danny has anchored him in the wrong place on purpose, and when he sees me on the shore he gestures that he has seen fish at the rock behind the raft. I watch for a while and when the salmon breaks water I go to the house to look for my fishing rod.

My rod has not been used since Danny fished with it in the spring, and I find it now standing among the raspberry bushes behind the outhouse. The reel contains very little line and the rod's tip has been broken and repaired with electrical tape. I thread the line through the guides and pull down on its tip; it seems to bow evenly but the rusted reel squeaks of grit and sand as I crank it and make casts in the yard. I go to Danny's room and find one of his blue jay flies. Knowing there is a salmon at the rock I feel the pull of the river as strongly as I have ever done.

Beneath the overhanging grass, Tom's boat is moored on the rocks with its paddle and pole afloat inside. I bail, and set the rock we use for an anchor on the bow, chain coiled nearby. Adrift, I pole toward centre stream. I brace myself in the stern, manoeuvring the old boat among the rocks. Half-way, the water is swift, frothing over boulders and the shallows of the gravel bar. I push the anchor overboard and its chain rattles over the gunwales like a machine gun. The boat sways, tugs, holds fast. I hunch on my knees to keep the balance.

I cast the feathered flyhook to where the water boils up behind the salmon rock and it is followed by something deep that makes a swell as the line tightens.

"Fish on!"

"Ha whoo, hu hu! Hold his head up!" Danny shouts.

The fish goes to the bottom and there is a screech from the reel as the old rod bends double. The fish lies still for a few seconds, then swims downstream, making the reel hammer in its frame. Then it leaps above the water and shakes its head.

"Look! Look! Your brother's got one on! He's got a big fish on!" Mr. Eagles points and shouts. "Let's help him land it!"

I push to shore, paddling at intervals, keeping the line tight and the fish away from the boat. At one point I hold the rod cork in my teeth and paddle. When the boat reaches shore, I scramble through the tall grass to regain some of the line, but can do little better than hold my own in the rough-going until the fish swims into an eddy. Danny and Mr. Eagles follow.

The salmon rises to the surface, and we can see its back. An old hookbill, the biggest I've ever seen. A kind of panic comes over me.

The fish leaps clear, showing its deep silver sides. "How about that!" Mr. Eagles says, "Look at the size of that fish!"

I sway the rod back and forth, trying to move the fish close. Danny has the scoop net, and paces beside me downstream.

"But did you boys actually see the size of that fish?"

"He's going upstream," Danny shouts. "Let's run up the shore and get in some line."

"It's okay," I answer, feeling the fish move my line, "he's swung with the current." The salmon comes back into deep water, and we watch the slant of the yellow casting line as it disappears into the depths.

And then the rod begins to buckle. Where it was repaired, the tape is giving way. As the fish moves deep and shakes its head, the outer half of my rod collapses and falls into the water, following the line toward my salmon.

"The rod's breaking," Eagles cries. "Oh, hell, your rod's gone into the water!"

I'm losing my salmon, the biggest salmon ever! I have only the rod's butt end and reel, and as I crank I find I have no control. I try to grab up the slack as the fish swims toward us. It comes so close that Danny is reaching to scoop it, has the net beneath its belly, when it turns quickly and swims into the deep water with the rod's end trailing from its jaw.

"This should be his last run."

"Danny, get ready with the scoop net!" Mr. Eagles shouts. He has a camera on a string around his neck, and he takes pictures of Danny and me.

The fish comes into the shallows and this time Danny scoops. We all help carry the thrashing salmon to shore. Danny hits it with a rock and it convulses on the ground, then lies barely quivering, blood and shoregrass clinging to its sides.

"That's remarkable," Mr. Eagles says, his booming voice quietened with awe. "It must be twenty pounds."

We take pictures of each other holding up the salmon.

"You boys need a decent fishing rod."

There is dew now, making our tracks visible as we cross the field to the house. I have my hand in the salmon's gills and its tail drags. For the first time this year, the evening brings the sour damp smell of autumn. We lay the fish on the floor of the outside kitchen and go in for Tom.

"Well, well, well," Tom says when he sees it. "Ya got one after all. Didn't think there was a fish in the river."

Mr. Eagles gives Danny ten dollars for guiding and he leaves us a new fishing rod and reel of his. Then he draws Tom aside.

"Consider it, Mr. Moar," he says. "I'll give you more than it's worth."

"Oh, I don't think I'd ever sell me shore."

"I'll buy it and the family can still use it like it was your own."

"Oh hell, I don't care about sellin' 'er. You can always fish 'er, any time ya like, I don't care a damn, ya know."

"But you could probably use the money. And you never use the shore yourself, anyway."

"Oh, I don't think we'd ever sell 'er."

"Think it over. It would still be yours when I'm not here. Hell, I'm in New Haven most of the time." He moves slowly across the dooryard, staring through the twilight to the shore. "I'd build a cabin, right out there where that old shed is. There would be a job for you and the boys, helping to build it, and then afterwards I'd need a caretaker.

"We'll think 'er over," Tom says finally, "and let ya know."

"I'll buy the whole farm, Tom. Do you mind if I call you Tom?"

"Hell, I don't care what ya call me."

"Just call me Sam. You boys, too, call me Sam. Okay? Tom, I'll buy the farm and you can live here just like you are and use the farm and house. You can probably use the money. We all need a bit of security at our age, eh?" He passes Tom a white business card. "Call me collect, anytime."

"No, now, I won't sell ya me farm. But now, if ya wanna come ta fish, yer more'n welcome. Welcome as th' flowers in May. An' there's plenty a fish fer us all. I don't bother with 'em myself, till October, when I take a drift an' get a few ta salt."

"That Steve is quite a fisherman, a great boy," Sam Eagles says, slapping Tom on the back.

"Good 'nuff, Sam," Tom answers. "We'll think about what ya said about th' shore."

They walk to the flat, to the white station wagon, mumbling together like old friends, and Danny and I trail behind. Sam reaches into his car and brings out a handful of feathered pattern flies for us. He gives Tom a can of pipe tobacco, a good sweater and a landing net. Then he shakes hands all round and calls each of us by name.

The American honks as he turns onto the highway, and waves an arm, and we wave until he's out of sight.

"Wow! What a guy!" Danny exclaims. "Look at all the stuff he gave us!"

Tom smiles at him, ruffles his hair. "Nice likeable lad, though, wasn't he, boys?"

CHAPTER 19

We've brought the cattle from the swamp and turned them on the aftergrass for the fall, fencing the potato field and garden by running page wire from the barnyard to the binder shed and along the hill to the lower swamp, with a set of bars at the road to the river. By now, the heavy frost has deadened the corn stalks, and the vines in the pumpkin patch have shrunk to a net of black twine, their loaf pumpkins exposed to ripen in the sun.

And by now school has opened, so Danny leaves reluctantly at eight-thirty: his new canvas bookbag, a picture of Joe Palooka on the flap, hangs on his shoulder. As he walks, he fires his slingshot at hydro insulators, at a squirrel and sparrows in the swamp. His new class has only two boys and two girls, and he hates the idea of not getting a new reader. But his boxing lessons have arrived and Katie has sewn the National Sports Council crest on the bookbag beside Palooka. The money Danny got from Sam Eagles has paid for the boxing gloves, and he's made a punching bag by tramping hay into Tom's old army duffle. For the time being, the empty woodshed is his gymnasium. After school, and on weekends, Howard and Nick come to box.

We have lengthened out the truck wagon, adjusting the stretcher to its longest possible wheel base, and Tom and I are hauling firewood from the ridge and piling it in the dooryard. This maple and birch, cut last winter, is dry now and free of sap, so we put stakes on the wagon's benches and throw the long pieces over until the load is rounded. Sometimes we throw on a pine stub or sleeper chips, then we put on the corner bind chains and tighten them to the rockers. Tom climbs on and sits on a sack of hay to drive. I walk behind.

We leave our last load of the afternoon on the wagon and Tom puts the horses in the barn for a feed of oats. Danny is in the woodshed, doing high push-ups with his feet up on a chair. He finishes in time to come inside with us to where Katie prepares supper. Tom turns up the radio as Ned Landry comes over the air, playing "The Fishers Hornpipe," and swings Katie through the kitchen and into the hall. Then he sits down on the rocking chair, and pulls her onto his knee, rubbing his stubbled chin across her cheek. I turn away, a little embarrassed.

"How's me beautiful Katie?" Tom says, and tickles her.

"Goodness sakes, Tom, don't be silly. Act yer age," she blushes. "The boys are watchin'." She slips off his knee and straightens her apron, and Tom jumps up to grab my elbows. He pushes me down on the cot and cuffs me with one of Danny's boxing gloves.

"He's down, start the count! It's another win for Marciano!"

Danny tackles him and there is pushing and shoving and we pile onto the kitchen floor, puffing and throwing punches. Katie kicks Tom in the seat of the pants, and doubles over with laughter.

In the height of the moment and quite on impulse, I go to the phone and call Amanda. She has to work and can't come out, but invites me to spend the evening at her house, so I'm going. I have gained some confidence because of my being accepted into the Reid's house. In fact, Amanda sounded like she really wanted to see me. Maybe she loves me after all, I think; at least she likes me enough to invite me in.

Floyd Patterson is fighting later tonight, and Tom gets me to find the New York radio station for him before I go. The signal is buried in static, fades in and out. As I shave at the kitchen sink, I can hear bits of a Hank Williams love song. The station gets stronger as fight time approaches.

Tom pours white liniment into a saucer and heats it on the stove while he makes himself a drink of hot peppermint, rubs his chest and throat. He was coughing a lot while we loaded firewood, I remember. He lies down on the cot behind the kitchen stove, staring at the ceiling and smoking. He has his hands behind his head and his boots are off, and he crosses his legs, rubbing his wool socks together.

Howard comes in, to listen to the fight. He leaves his unlit lantern by the door and finds a seat by the radio.

"Where's Tom?"

"I'm over here on the lounge, Howard."

"Do ya wanna go downriver fer another cow?"

"Not with a drunken bastard like you."

"Hello fer a spree, though, eh?" Howard laughs, and he snags my sleeve as I slip past. "Hey, Steve, did ya hear the latest? They say the one across the river is knocked up."

"Oh?"

"Oh, yeah, I guess she's up the stump."

"Really?"

"Yes, Jesus, she's up higher'n a kite. But who d'ya s'pose got into 'er pants?"

"I think she has a boyfriend in town," I say, edging away towards the door.

"Lucky son-of-a-whore, too, ain't he?"

Tom has heard us, and props himself up on his elbows.

"Do ya have a girlfriend yerself, then, Howard?"

"Nah, it's no use, Tom."

"What about the girl across the river, what's 'er name? She's a nice lookin' filly, though, boys. She's no slouch."

"She's got someone else by the looks a her, Tom. I used ta go with 'er a bit meself," Howard says.

"Ya might a went with 'er, but I bet she didn't know anything about it!"

"Ha, Jesus," Howard laughs, "he wouldn't tell a lad off, would he." He pushes the red hunting cap back on his forehead and shows all his large brown teeth in a grin as he rolls himself a cigarette. He licks the cigarette paper, twists the ends and torches it with his heavy lighter. "Nah, she's no use, boys. Everything on that side a th' river is knocked up."

"Speakin' a the fair sex," Tom says, "Steve's got a date t'night with the little one in town, what's 'er name?"

"Amanda. Big Amanda. Have ya though, Steve?"

"Yes, she's invited me to her place, the Elm Inn, to spend the evening with her." My own voice sounds strange to me, like someone on the radio.

"Christ, yer movin' up in the world, too, ain't ya?"

I borrow two dollars from Tom, and as I leave Howard and Danny sitting by the radio looking through one of Danny's books, *The Saga of Boxing*. On its cover there is a photograph of Jess Willards and Jack Dempsey in their Fourth of July, 1919 heavyweight title fight.

Amanda's father meets me at the door of the Elm Inn. He is dressed in a dark grey suit, white shirt and bow tie and he has a stern intolerant look about him.

"Yes?" He looks down over his glasses.

"Is Amanda in?"

"Oh, yes, it's Steve, is it? The boy from upriver. Mandy is inside. Take a seat; she'll be out in a moment."

I follow the sound of piano music to the big parlour, where a half-dozen elderly people are listening to Amanda play. When she sees me, she smiles, blushing and furrowing her forehead, but her hands move across the keys without error until the piece finishes in a cascade of quick high notes. I remember seeing her here in the spring, when I came with Nick. She's just as lovely tonight, I think, her hair fixed up some way short so her face is rounder, the dimples more exaggerated. She comes to me smiling, pretty in a red blouse and jeans, both hands outstretched. I kiss her cheek, and she leads me to the empty dining room.

"So, how have you been, Steve?" she asks, passing a cup of coffee.

"Oh, busy. Helping my father still. We've been into the harvest and getting up the firewood."

"That sounds like hard work. I thought you might be getting away to university this fall."

"Wish I were. But I can't, this year." I tell her about my new correspondence course, how hard it is to study at home, my frustration. It is easy to talk to her about these things, and the words come out with more intensity than I expect.

"Next year. I'm going next year. Danny — my brother — he'll be old enough to take a year off and help around home."

"It's a shame," she says softly, touching my hand.

"Well, I don't think Tom's all that well. Coughs all the time, but he says he's okay. Won't go to a doctor." I shrug, putting the small nagging worries to the back of my mind. "How about yourself? Have you decided what to major in?"

"Music. Well, I'm studying music for this year anyway."

"When do you go to college?"

"In about a week, Thursday."

"I won't be seeing much of you, then, will I?"

Amanda stands suddenly, gathering up the coffee cups. She turns back in the door of the kitchen. "We'll have to talk about that later."

"Okay," I say, uneasy. "Later."

For a while we play music on the living room grafanola — Perry Como, Frank Sinatra, Jimmy Dorsey — love songs, slow and sentimental; then Mr. Reid puts his head around the door.

"Mandy, your mother and I will be out for a time. Keep an eye on things, will you, dear? Steve, goodnight." He comes forward to shake my hand, briefly and formally, and I notice how white his shirt cuff is against the dark wool of his suit. Someday, I know, I'll have cufflinks like his.

"Good night, sir."

When the front door closes behind the Reids, I put on a Bing Crosby record and we waltz, and her small waist is snug and firm against me and she has a firm hold around my neck. Then we forget the music, our own electricity overpowering us, and we embrace, moving to the sofa where we rub each other's backs and kiss.

"Oh, Amanda, I love you, I do. I just can't help it."

She pushes me away, gets up and walks across the room. "Steve, you are much too serious. Why do you always have to be so serious?"

"I don't know. I can't seem to stop it."

"Love is a serious word. Do you know that?"

"I know, I know it is. I guess I can't stop loving you. I'm serious, but that's how I feel."

"That's what I wanted to talk to you about."

"Okay. We can always talk about it, but I don't think it will help."

"Oh, Steve, I don't know quite how to say this. I don't want to hurt your feelings."

"Just say what you have to say and see what happens."

"But you'll probably take it the wrong way. It's not really your fault and I know you'll be upset."

"Well, try me," I say, trying to relax. "Try me and see, that's all you can do."

"Oh, Steve, please understand. It's not you, it's just the way things are. Don't take it personal, but I just can't get serious with anyone right now. I won't be able to see you anymore. At least not this often."

"Oh, why is that now? What did I do? What brought all this on now?" I feel hollow and empty.

"You've done nothing. It's not you. I just can't go steady right now. Maybe we could go out once in awhile. You know how it is, you could drop by, like Gordon or Smitty does."

"How often?"

"Not regularly."

"Why is that now?"

"Oh, Steve, don't be mad. You're a beautiful guy and one of my best friends. You're the nicest guy I know, but I don't love you."

""Mr. Nice Guy, that's me."

"I'm sorry you fell in love with me."

"So am I."

"But I don't want to fall in love right now. Not with you or anyone else. It's nothing personal. I just have my education to think of right now."

"But I would never interfere with your education. I believe in that, too, remember?"

"I know, I don't know what I'm saying any more. The thing is, Steve, my folks don't want me seeing you either."

"So that's it."

"You know what old people are like. They want me to marry someone rich I suppose, like a doctor or lawyer or someone."

"Well, I'm certainly not rich, that's for sure."

"Steve, I'm sorry," she says, and her soft voice goes on and on, apologizing, trying to make something right that will never be right again. "I never meant to hurt you. I never wanted to hurt you. I didn't mean to lead you on."

Everything is happening so fast. I try to stop it, but as she talks it comes to me that this is real, that this is no bad dream. I'm not going to wake up and know she's my girl. It hurts, it hurts; and the worst of it is that I was led on by nothing more than my own wishful thinking.

"It's not your fault, Mandy," I tell her gently, trying to keep the bitterness from my voice. "You're beautiful and talented, and I did this to myself. I'm the blind one." I take a deep breath to steady myself and hide the pain that's crashing inside me. Keep it light. "Well, honey, we do have a time of it, don't we? I guess this is it. If I can't see you, I'll just have to get used to it, that's all."

"Oh, you can still come and see me sometimes," she says. "Once in awhile, maybe we can go out."

"I don't know about this once in awhile business."

"I'll be away at school now, anyway. You should get out with other girls. There are other fish in the sea."

"Well, if that's how it is, that's how it is. I know I do get serious, too damn serious. But I can't help it, I wish I could."

"Steve, don't be hard on yourself because of this. You're a real nice guy. There's nothing wrong with you, it was just bad timing."

"Yes, the story of my life."

"I'm actually flattered you've fallen in love with me. It's a compliment."

"Sure."

"You'll get over this. There'll be others. You'll find someone you'll probably love more than you do me. Someday you'll thank me for this."

It isn't late, but I know I have to leave right now. Amanda invited me here for a reason and I must make it easier on us both by leaving without further argument. She had been fair with me and I must put my feelings aside and be fair with her. At the risk of hurting her feelings by leaving too soon, I get up to go.

"Well, kid, you could at least walk me to the door or better still, walk me to the car."

"Sure, wait, I'll get my sweater. But must you leave so soon?"

"Oh, yes. I must be heading home. There's a fight on the radio later tonight. Some of us are staying up for it." I feel now that I belong at home with Howard, listening to the fight.

On our way to the car, I hide my feelings and try to be as charming as possible. "Well, could I give you one last hug?"

"Of course you can, silly." She hugs me.

"One last kiss, maybe?"

As we kiss, I hold her tighter than ever before. As I press my lips to hers, I realize it is my last, and I try to make it last, one last kiss from the only girl I will ever love. I release her.

"Mandy, I can't help it. I will always love you."

"Oh, Steve!"

"But that will always be our little secret, just yours and mine."

"Steve."

"Look, if you ever change your mind?"

"Oh, Steve, please don't say that. I feel so bad." She stands under the light and she looks pale and haggard and she cries, wiping the tears on the sleeve of her blouse. It makes me feel better to see her cry.

I force myself to start the car, every single movement an effort. I'm hoping she will run after me, say it's all a bad joke. But she stands firm, the prettiest girl in the world, crying. As I drive away, she waves, then turns to go inside.

As I drive, I try to cry. It will make me feel better, I think. But the tears won't come and the agony grows as the reality of the evening settles in. I must be strong about this. I must keep this hidden inside — a double fight, losing Amanda and keeping the feelings inside.

I would never love again. I would shield myself from letting it happen again. The risk in trusting someone is too great, the hurt too much. And love can't be bargained for. But at least I have the memories of sharing some precious moments with her and I moved her enough to make her cry. So she at least tried to love me. But nothing could justify this hurt.

Tom has gone to bed by the time I get home, and Howard and Danny are sitting by the radio, the fight well under way.

"Ya made 'er back, did ya?"

"Uh huh."

"We thought ya'd be way inta th' night gettin' back."

"How's the fight going?"

"Patterson's ahead on points."

The radio comes in clear, advertising Gillette razor blades between rounds. Then there's the clang of the bell and another round starts. We can hear the roar of the crowd, the sound of the punches as Don Dunphy calls the blow-by-blow in his fast, high-pitched voice.

"Well, good night, boys. I'm going to bed."

"What? Not stayin' up ta see how she ends?"

"No. I'm tired. Danny, turn off the radio when you come up."

"Not stayin' fer the big fight?" Howard raises his eyebrows, and winks at Danny. "Stevie must be in love. Are ya? The Reid one's got ya."

"I guess she did."

"One time he'd a set up all night ta listen to a fight," Howard mumbles to Danny as I go up the stairs.

My bedroom is an old friend, warm and inviting. My old comic books remain stacked on the bureau: *Kid Colt*, *Ringo Kid*, and *Matt Dillon*. The brown-flowered wallpaper tries to give me its old-time comfort, as does the church calendar with the photo of smiling Eskimo faces. Katie's houseplants sit on the windowsill, kindred and warm, and I try to find my real self, but there is no returning to it. I wonder what kind of fool I am and how Amanda will remember me. The house is quiet now, except for Tom's muffled coughing across the hall. I can smell his white liniment and Vicks. And my room tries to pull me to itself, comfort me as a mother takes a lonely child into her arms. But it doesn't work. I drop my shield now and the tears come at last, in a darkness deeper than the shadows of the bedroom.

CHAPTER 20

*"Along the line of smoky hills
the crimson forest stands..."*

It is morning, and Danny walks the floor with his reader, trying to remember the words of "Indian Summer." He peeks at the poem and puts the book behind his back.

*"And all the day the blue jay calls
throughout the autumn land"*

While he does his homework, I sit at the kitchen table ordering him a taxidermy course from the Northwestern School of Taxidermy in Omaha. Already he's lost interest in his boxing lessons; now he wants to be a full-time taxidermist, and he's been working in the swamp after school and on Saturdays to pay for the course. As I endorse the envelope, Tom carries in an armful of split wood and clatters it into the woodbox. Then he brushes off his sweater and goes out, slamming the door so the glass rattles in its putty.

"Now by the brook the maple leans..."

"Now by the brook the maple leans..."

Danny opens the brown-paper covered reader quickly, then closes his eyes and paces in a circle, thinking.

"With all his glory spread"

He's stuck again, and I try to help by supplying the next few lines.

*"And all the sumachs on the hill
have turned their green to red"*

"How come you know that ol' poem? Can you remember Grade Four stuff?"
"I've always liked it."
"But it's so long since ya took it."
"Eight years. But if you like a thing, it'll stay with you."
"It won't stay with me 'til I get ta school."
"You have to memorize it, use the rhythm as it was intended. Give it a little thought. Put your soul into it."
"Nah, I don't like it anyway. Ya have to like somethin' to put yer soul into it."
"You would like it if you let yourself."
"I'll learn enough ta keep outta trouble with the teacher. I hope she don't ask me the last part."

Tom kicks the door open and brings in another armload of wood. It spills from the woodbox, so he pushes the loose sticks into the stove, breathing heavily between his teeth. As he slams the door going out, the dishes rattle in the cupboard and the calendar drops from the wall.

"I've always liked Wilfred Campbell," I tell Danny.
"How d'ya know him?"
"Oh, just through his works. He's been dead for years, but I feel like I know him by his writing."
"How could ya know a man that way?"
"You learn his philosophy from the poems, and if you can you should learn as much as possible about the poet's life, his way of looking at things. It helps you to understand the poetry."
"If I could learn to word this off, I'd be happy."
"Still, you could find out something about the man. You'd get a better mark. Campbell was influenced by Byron and Tennyson. But you learn all that kind of thing in the higher grades."
"I'm not worryin' about the higher grades none."
"Mention them anyway."
"I'll write their names on my scribbler. But if I say it, the rest will think I'm weird an' laugh at me."
"Don't worry about the rest of the class."
"I'm quittin' anyway, when I get my course."
"What?"
"I'm quittin' school. I'm not the type. 'Sides, I'm gonna be a taxidermist."
"Everyone's the type to get educated, Danny."
"Not me. I'm a workin' man. My mind's made up, Steve, so save yer breath."
"Who do you know that's doing so great without an education?"
"Howard."
"Howard? Howard across the river?"

"That's right. He's doing good, workin' every day in the woods with his father. Since he quit school, he's enjoyin' life. He told me."

"And what happens to him when his father isn't around any more?"

"Work alone."

"And if they stop buying pulpwood?"

"Ya cross that bridge when ya come to it. Lookit Charlie an' George an' the Cains. They're all makin' 'er alright. None of them got education. They enjoy life, too."

"Danny," I say, concerned now. This isn't a kid's talk; he's serious. "Danny, those are not good role models. When you leave here, you'll see."

"Who says I'm leavin' here? Lookit Dave Cain. He had a good job in Ontario an' he quit an' come home to be with his own. The big city an' the big money wasn't fer him. Now he's got a new house an' he owns that front field, an' he's got a good job in the mill. Happy as a pig in shit."

"He didn't like the city because he couldn't adapt to it. He couldn't adjust. Maybe he was afraid: ignorance breeds fear." How can I get through to Danny? My little brother, he could put that imaginative mind to anything he chose. He sees the frustration tightening my face and challenges me, planting his feet wide, the reader forgotten in his hand.

"Well, I'm not afraid a nobody. I can look after meself anywhere — that's why I got the gloves."

"You don't need boxing gloves to get through life."

"I'm going to be a taxidermist, I said!"

"Okay, I guess you have it all figured out. You have all the answers."

"No, just know what I wanna do. 'Sides, Steve, what else is there? Some ol' teacher or salesman or maybe a tax man who chases after people fer their place? Who wants to be that, dressed up like an undertaker!"

"There's other things to be."

"Yah, always tryin' ta be proper like a gentleman. Turn yer back on a lad like that an' he'd steal ya blind. Stick a knife in, too, if he could."

"Well, poor and ignorant and honest don't always go together. You'll find that out."

"I just wanna be a real man, that's all, like Tom, like Rocky Marciano, or even Howard — that's why I got the gloves."

"You don't have to be a fighter to be a real man. In fact, it works the opposite."

"Well, not for this lad she don't."

"You'll find out someday, when it's too late, after you've gone to work in the woods or at the mill."

"So I s'pose ya know it all now, do ya? Ya read books, ya know 'er all?"

"I never said that. But maybe I do."

"Why don't ya shut up then?"

"You shut up."

"You shut up."

"Stop or I'll slap you, Danny Moar."

"Steve! Danny! Get ta Christ out here," Tom yells, swinging the kitchen door wide. "The men are here. And good God, yer settin' up readin' poetry. I'll have ta get yer lads a bonnet."

"It's for a test. Danny has a test today."

"Well, it kinda made me wonder. C'mon. It's gettin' on inta the mornin' and I need ya both at the barn."

"I'll be right there."

"You, too, Danny. I'll need ya ta stow away straw."

"Oh, great! Wow! I'm stayin' home from school!"

"But he has a test today," I protest.

"That's too damn bad."

"He's even got his homework done."

"Katie," called Tom, "write this lad an excuse. He can be sick fer a day. One day ain't gonna matter none. We have a teacher here in the house, by the look of 'er, boys."

I try once more: "We can thrash without him."

"I said we need him. He's stayin' home ta work. It ain't like he was stayin' home ta fish or hunt birds. It ain't hurtin' him, one day."

"It won't help him any, either."

"Good God, now listen to 'im. He's tellin' us all what ta do. Ya'll have the young lad wantin' ta do nothin' but set up an' read. There's a real world out there, boy, an' there's work ta be done."

"I hate poetry," Danny says. "And there's work to be done."

"C'mon, Danny," says Tom. "If yer a good boy ta work, I'll buy ya a new fiddle fer Christmas."

Katie puts her hand on my shoulder as the door closes behind them. "It's no use," she says, "you can't talk to that man. Scholarship is the last thing on his mind."

"It grieves me to discuss it with him," I say.

"Stevie, dear, now you work outside. You know how your allergies bother you when you go in with the dust and the chaff."

"I'll tend the engine."

The men shout to each other above the rumble of the separator as Tom cuts the twine and feeds the broken sheaves seed-end into the revolving drum. He waves the oats back and forth across the shiny steel table and the teeth eat into the kernels, slowing only when straw plugs the drum and makes the engine labour, the web-belt slipping on the pulleys.

"Yer belt's slipping, Tom!" George Cooper shouts. "She's pluggin' up!"

Tom turns from the table and waits until the drum gathers speed, and I pour molasses on the belt, making it slap as it sticks to the pulleys and drives the drum to new speeds. When Tom waves the grain into the drum again, the separator's side levers and the shakers hurry as if to make up for lost time. Tom always brags that his old Moody thrashing machine is 'clean' and does a better job than George's small undershot model, the Thomas Hall. But he slows the pace to one the machine can keep with and as he feeds the drum he coughs and spits on the barn floor, then takes his handkerchief and ties it around his face, covering his nose and mouth like a bandit. The thrasher spins, the chaff drifts through the open doors and catches in the breeze, and I pour gasoline into the engine's carburetor to keep it going like a pile-driver echoing between the pigpen and the binder shed.

George tends bushel, smoothing off the cool half-bushel tins as they fill beneath the shaking spouts and pouring them into sacks propped against the cow stable side of the thrashing floor. To keep tally, he marks crows feet on the shingled wall beside the tracks of other thrashing days: 50 bushel 1948; 65 bushel 1952; 80 bushel 1953, thrashed September 18th.

Charlie stows away at the tail end, falling behind at times and pitching in all directions until the floor is cleared. He hates this job, but he owes Tom a turn so he's here. Beneath the rumble of the machine, he curses the small barn, the aging separator, the engine, and he curses Danny who takes away the mow. He fights the machine like it was spoiling yet another small part of the day by keeping him buried in straw, and as he curses, Danny drops the huge forkfuls back down from the mow to slow him up and make him swear more.

"Lord liftin' Jesus, that boy's hazardous. He's dead from the arse up, 'pon-me-soul ta God."

Danny chokes in the dusty mow, where the only breeze filters through the cracks and knot holes in the gable end. To get fresh air he puts his face against the wall and breathes through a knot hole, and when he sees Tom using his handkerchief to breath through, he ties his own over his face.

Howard is sitting on the temporary scaffold above the thrashing floor, passing the sheaves down to Tom. With his sandy hair and faded tan, he's almost unnoticed in the straw. but he's enjoying the company of the thrashing crew, and he whoops and laughs through the long day.

At noon, Tom gives me the signal to cut off the engine's gas, and when the machinery stops everyone comes out into the barnyard to cool off and talk and have a smoke.

"Boys, them's tight quarters up there in the feedin' hole," Howard complains, rolling a cigarette with one hand. "Tight as a hen's arse."

"Yer black as the inside of a cow," George says, dropping down to the grass and tilting his felt hat over one eye.

"What time should we finish 'er up?" Howard asks. "Would it be around suppertime?"

"Finish? We just got started. Why?"

"There's a dance in town. I might run down."

We all know that Howard isn't going to the dance, but we play along with it.

"Dance?" George whoops, "Hell, I'd thrash that bit a oats an' walk ta Fredericton to a dance."

"That's tellin' 'im!"

"Don't ya worry none, young fella, we'll finish in plenty a time fer the dance."

Katie comes to the back door and waves a dish towel. Dinner is ready. There's a washtub of lukewarm water sitting on two chairs in the outside kitchen, and a new bar of Sunlight soap. Chaff floats on the water as we gather around to wash and share a towel. Then we file into the dining room, Tom and George hanging their hats in the porch and smoothing their damp white hair.

These are different men, in Katie's domain: polite and mannerly, gentlemen in the skins of rough workers. The table, extended to its full length, is completely covered with dishes of pickles and preserves, a potato scallop with ham, homemade rolls, sweet butter. Katie brings a pie from the pantry, then leaves us to eat. Awkward with Katie in the room, the men become themselves again and reach long arms for the salt and pepper.

"Dig in, young fella," George tells Howard, passing him the scallop. "You'll need all yer strength fer that dance t'night."

"I'm not going to the dance."

"How ya makin' 'er with the Reid girl? Ya readin' these nights, Steve?" The men roar with laughter.

"We're doing alright," I say, stretching my mouth in a smile. I have not told anyone about Amanda and me, about our splitting up. It would just give them fuel for tormenting me, I think. My heart aches now for what I've lost.

"Yessir, save yer energy," George says, and then he leans forward to whisper loudly, "ya may have ta do some comin' ashore." He winks. "But yer kinda gettin' inta high society there, ain't ya?"

"How's that?"

"Well, ain't she kinda a high-toned thing? A silver spoon thing?"

"I heard tell of 'er," Howard puts in. "She's a lot better lookin' than the Reids round here, the swamp Reids."

"Well, sir, them Reids always seemed ta have money an' a nice big place in town. If ya hang around 'er, ya won't know us a'tall pretty soon."

"I doubt that."

"Oh, yah, he'll be gettin' up in th' world."

"They say Ol' Man Reid got his start bootleggin'," Charlie says. "Now, that was years ago. Someone said he sold moonshine an' kept women there, too. At his ol' hotel, fer the men comin' outta the woods an' off the drives. Train stopped along there too."

"I've found Mr. Reid to be a scholar," I say stiffly, "and a fine gentleman."

"Oh yeah, I know. I know what yer sayin'. I'm just tellin' ya what I heard, that's all. An' they said he run a whorehouse."

"Well sir, I knew Reids upriver," Tom says. "Worked in the woods with 'em, all hard-workin' honest people."

"Sure, there's good Reids, too."

"Well, say what ya like, I found the Reids ta be a high-toned bunch," sniffs Charlie. "Big feelin' and overbearin'."

"I don't think yer goin' wit 'er anyway," George says. "She's just stringin' ya 'long."

"Maybe so."

"But ya know, boys, I always liked ol' Herb. Now I know he's a big-feelin' son-of-a-whore, but good-hearted. I stayed at his hotel one time years ago on me way home from the woods an' he wouldn't take a cent."

"What religion did ya say they are?"

"I don't know."

"Well, boys, I like ta see a man go ta church. Don't care what church he goes ta 'long as he goes."

"That's right, George," says Charlie. "A man tryin' ta live in this country without religion is like a man tryin' ta thrash without an engine."

"That's a good one, Charlie. Ya shoulda been a preacher."

When they finish eating, they light their pipes and tip back the wooden chairs. Conversation turns to calves, and then to pigs, and to horses. Katie walks around the table with a china tea pot, filling the delicate cups. Then she brings in a treat of hot stewed currants. I stare at the picture of the young Queen Elizabeth II hanging by the cupboard. We can hear the radio playing in the kitchen. Eddy Arnold is singing "I'm sending you a big bouquet of roses" as we go back out to work.

By mid-afternoon, the thrashing crew have gone. Tom works around the barn, putting things in, covering the engine and closing up doors. And I go to my bedroom to write a letter. The western short story I wrote in the early summer has been returned once again, with a note saying, "Try a local market." So I'm sending it to the *North Shore Leader*. I endorse the manuscript envelope and put it on my bureau to be mailed later. Then I go down to the parlour and lie on the folding bed. Exhausted, I drift off into a troubled dream.

The dining room at the Elm Inn. It's crowded and quietly humming with the murmur of well-bred conversation. There are silver spoons everywhere.

"Bring us a cuppa tea, would ya, an' make it snappy," Charlie shouts.

The whole thrashing crew sits around me at the big centre table, talking loudly and laughing and thumping their fists to make plates jump on the white linen tablecloth. The smell of our stale sweat blends with that of the dust and chaff crusting our workclothes, and Amanda doesn't seem to see me as she writes down our orders. Maybe this isn't part of our "once in a while" relationship, but I try to call her name. No sound comes out.

"An' bring me a glass a yer bootleg," Charlie howls.

"Who's that ol' undertaker over there?" asks Danny, pointing. "What's he readin' at this time of day?"

"It's Mr. Reid," I say, urgently trying to quiet the men. "He's reading poetry. By Wilfred Campbell." Howard snickers into his dirty handkerchief.

"I s'pose ol' Herb Reid wouldn't 'member me," says George, twisting around in his chair.

"Hardly. That's years ago you stayed here."

"There's one a his whores! Hey!"

"No! No, that's Amanda. That's his daughter. My girl. She's a fine lady, and she's going to study music. She's a scholar."

"I believe they're Anglican."

"I don't know."

"Or Catholic."

"I don't know."

"She smells like a peach orchard."

"I love her."

"Girlie, girl, c'mon over here."

Amanda moves slowly toward our table, graceful, her face pale and expressionless above the red blouse. "Yes?" she answers Charlie.

"Do ya know this lad here?"

"Do ya know him?" the others echo. "Do ya know this lad?"

"Do you know me, Amanda?" I ask her softly, trying to read her eyes and pleading with mine. White linen and silver spoons, the room spins around me for the long moment that she studies my face. I reach out to her, smiling. "Do you know me?"

"Not really," she says, and turns away.

CHAPTER 21

"Back up now, back up." Tom jerks on the reins, guiding Prince to the engine in front of the barn doors, an oat sack drooped over its carburetor. The old horse almost sits on his haunches, and his ears are upright and twitching, hearing the unaccustomed savagery in the old man's broken voice. "Back now, back," Tom insists, putting all of his weight against the bit, yanking the horse's frothing mouth sideways.

Tom hooks the chain into the ring on the engine's runners and slaps the reins across the horse's rump. Prince flattens into pulling stance and nudges the thousand-pound engine slowly forward. The runners cut shallow grooves across the dooryard to the woodpile. When the engine is in place, there's another trip to the shed for the table saw. I carry over the woodcutter belt, the car battery, the coil, and a tin of gasoline.

After he puts Prince in the barn, Tom sets up the woodcutter in the dooryard. In his ragged grey sweater and felt hat, he's almost invisible in the shadows of twilight.

Down the valley, the evening express clatters on, dropping the mail at whistle stops and tying the river communities together. Its whistle sounds in the distance, and Danny comes from the post office, grinning. He brings me another rejection, this time the return of the short story I sent to the local newspaper: "We don't use fiction." I slip into the dining room to have a closer look at the story; I haven't read it for some time. Now I can see that it's choppy with sentence fragments, so I sit down to rewrite it, tightening it and moving around entire sentences, sometimes reading aloud to see how it flows. I'm in the second paragraph when Tom opens the kitchen door and shouts.

"Gimme a lift out here, lad!"

I waste no time putting on my windbreaker and getting out to the yard. We carry a huge log across to the saw table, for a prop to keep it steady. Then Tom picks up the hammer to drive a spike into the end brace where a chain holds the table from tilting. Hurrying, he brings the hammer down on his thumb.

"Damnation ta hell!" he lashes out, flinging the hammer away. "The devil's here t'night." His last word is swallowed in a cough that bends him double. He spits, then mops his face with his handkerchief. As he straightens slowly, I see his hand trembling.

"Call it a day," I suggest. "It's too dark to do any more tonight."

"Yah, I guess yer right." Tom leads the way back to the house. A large moon rises above the tree-fringed horizon, glittering on the saw table and the steel roof of the barn. "Now be up early," Tom says. "Be up and around when the men get here. Don't be sleepin' all day."

Katie and Danny are in the dining room, going over Danny's lessons, so I take my story to the kitchen table to work on it. Tom goes to the cupboard and finds his full flask of brandy, in behind a box of oatmeal. He drinks on his feet, legs braced wide, his head tipped back for the liquor to slide down his throat. Recapping the flask and putting it away, he settles into the rocking chair with his pipe and hums quietly to himself. Bits and pieces of old Jim Rodgers songs, "My Rough and Rowdy Ways," and "He's in the Jail-house Now." Then he attempts the Wilf Carter song, "Swiss Moonlight Lullaby."

"Yer into the brandy?" Katie says on her way through the room.

"Come 'ere an' see me."

"Yer drinkin'."

"Just a taste."

"Why don't ya move inside and sing. The boys are tryin' ta study."

"Ya don't like my singin'."

"Not 'specially."

"My voice is a gift."

"Then you oughta give it back."

Tom grumbles, but he pulls himself up and goes off to bed. We can hear him in his room, coughing and singing and mumbling to himself, the smell of Sloan's Liniment filtering down the stairs.

I turn my attention back to my writing, but a sudden thought intrudes. Tom wants to show the men that he has raised a good worker. Tomorrow will be my test.

As dawn penetrates my bedroom, the window becomes a grey rectangle against a wall of black. I turn, half-conscious, pulling the heavy patch quilt over my shoulders, the room cold in the dull light. Downstairs, the furnacette and the kitchen range snap and crack contentedly and a soft warmth filters through the house, making the grey September fields of frost withdraw into themselves.

Muffled voices from the dooryard below penetrate the silence. George Cooper's laugh brings me fully awake. and I remember Tom's warning of the night before: "Be up early. Be around when the men get here." As I struggle into my clothing, I hear the hollow church bell sound of the saw's balance wheel as the table is moved into place. When I was Danny's age I looked forward to this day, when I would stay home from school to tend the engine. But today, I know, will be a day of the hardest labour on the farm. Still, I gulp my breakfast with rising excitement, anxious to join the men in the yard.

"Now be careful ya don't get hurt around that woodcutter," Katie warns, "an' keep an eye on Danny around that ol' engine. The boy should be in school."

"That's a lost argument. Tomorrow Tom wants him to stay home to pick the crabapples."

We exchange a silent look, then Katie smiles and takes my empty plate.

Danny has already eaten and is out in the yard. I slip out the front door and around the house to approach the woodcutters from the river side, slipping unnoticed into the work routine as if I'd been there all along.

Some of the men are preparing to start the engine. Others are prying the table saw into position so the belt will track evenly on the pulleys. While the early dawn has been damp and grey, the fields and river are now tinted a deep pink by a spectacular yet forlorn sunrise. There is a stiff chill that carries a ghost of winter as the men hustle around keeping themselves warm. A heavy coat of frost colours the table-saw grey like ashes.

Holding one hand over the engine's breather, choking its throttle, George begins to crank.

"Choke 'er, George, choke 'er," Danny shouts.

"Christ, she's choked ta death now," George snaps.

The old engine wheezes and snorts, coughs, and belches a *chunk-chunk-chunk* that jars the ground beneath the driving piston.

"Cough, ya black son-of-a-whore, cough!" George leaps back, crank in hand, as the engine gathers speed. The huge spoked wheels kicks into revolutions, the spokes becoming a grey blur as the engine sparks, falters, then gathers speed. The belt that runs to the saw jumps on the pulleys as the clutch is pushed in. The balance wheel hums and the circular blade adds a sharp metal note to the sounds of this crisp morning. We throw our coats to the ground, put on gloves and begin to hurry about, almost bumping into one another, as if we are being commanded by the machine not to waste its precious working minutes, but to hustle to its gait.

I take up a position near the end of the table, by the balance wheel. George works the table, Tom beside him next to the saw. With the old teapot, Danny pours gasoline into the carburetor; the strainer pail holds water for the cooling tank. That's the job for the youngest, the job that used to be mine, and I feel a little awkward now.

Four men carry the first log from the pile and slide it along the table. George and Tom tilt it to the snarling saw, and it's laid quickly into stove lengths, spraying the ground and my pantlegs with its driven sawdust.

"Can ya handle 'er?" Tom shouts.

"Yes, sir, I can handle this okay."

"Christ, yes, he can handle the job as well as a man," puts in George. "Watch how he sets himself ta throw. The boy's strong as an ox, Tom." The test has begun.

One Indian Summer

The saw snarls with ringing hunger as log after log is tilted into its rasping teeth. Sometimes the men have to hold back on large timbers, letting the engine rebuild speed. Sometimes they have to turn a huge block completely over, sawing into first one side then the other. Always I keep pace, throwing blocks, rebuilding the pile as quickly as I can, proving that I can be counted on as one of the men.

Blocks press more quickly against me, bigger and heavier to handle as the morning wears on. Under my flannel shirt I'm trembling with exhaustion, but I toss the wood as if all eyes are watching, trying to keep it smooth and easy, like the men. My knees are unsteady. When the dust clouds my eyes, I have to close them and throw blocks in darkness, sometimes cursing George and Charlie and the rest of the crew for this unforgivable test of manhood. And still the blocks keep coming, end on end they crowd the table in front of me, an endless blur. Shaking, I throw now with aching arms, praying for some vital part of the machinery to break, something to stop the whole operation for the day.

The woodpile grows into an oval dome beside the shed. I make a tier of big blocks behind me: a partition between myself and the main pile — a few less to throw. All the time, the steel saw rings and snarls, and the old engine labours through log after log. My arms are numb levers attached directly to my heart, driven only by my stubborn pride.

For Tom and the rest, this is more than a day's work. It's a social gathering. A day when the community will see what kind of firewood Tom has gathered, when Katie's best dinner will be compared to other meals served on woodcutting days at other farms, when jokes and gossip make the rounds. So-and-so has a cow that's with calf; another was late getting his hay in this year. They trade the news and laugh and swear. The work goes almost unnoticed.

I want to ask Tom for a break. If we were alone, he'd see my pain and my pride, and he'd find an excuse for a respite. But the men are watching, judging Tom's son as they judge his firewood and the meal his wife cooks up, and there can be no weakness in the Moars. Maybe Tom's being tested, too? I'll hold up my end; somehow, I'll hold up my end for both our sakes.

It's like when Tom and I are in church and I'm singing along with him because we share a hymn book, and my younger voice supports his rough song, the two of us in the back pew, the only ones there who are singing. And we're singing now, only the rest of the crew can't hear us. There is some strange harmony here, I think, in the rhythm of the woodcutting. Exhaustion blurs my eyes. "In the sweet by and bye, we shall meet on that beautiful shore." Tom's favourite hymn swells in my ears, and I can see pictures like those in Sunday school calendars, sun's rays golden around smiling crowds with outstretched arms. And I see Tom with his old felt hat in his hand, mopping his brow, introducing me to his father, his mother, men and women with Tom's features. They're proud of me, my family, my ancestors, and I'm strong as an ox and willing to show the world.

And the whining saw becomes a child crying, a screeching hurting protest against the constant pounding beats of the old black engines, and Cindy stands before me with her baby in her arms. "See, I knew ya could do this job as well as anyone can. Ya can make money workin' like that loadin' a truck. Ya wouldn't have ta go away ta get educated an' spend all that money neither." She smiles, and the baby, my baby, cries. I look for a vision of Amanda but she has no place in this day.

Between timbers, Tom wipes his handkerchief over his face. He could always hold his own, but today he seems older to me, and I see that he labours harder. He coughs and spits in the sawdust, then wipes the tears from his sore red eyes. This point is not worth winning, I think, but for Tom's sake I will keep on, keep on, keep on. He catches me watching him, and smiles faintly, gives me the nod I've been waiting for.

I signal Danny to turn the cog that shuts off the engine, but he ignores me. He tips the old teapot, filling the small tank on the carburetor with gasoline, and goes into the house.

My undershirt is soaked with sweat and glues itself to my back and chest. The hair beneath my cap is wet, my head itching, beads of sweat stinging in my eyes. Once in awhile sweat drops from the end of my nose and I can taste its salt on my lips. My own soul, I think, is pouring out in agony. There is no end.

And then, as if the old engine knows something the men themselves don't, it quits sparking and coasts gently to a stop.

"She's outta gas. Let's all take a break, boys."

The men sit on blocks in the lee of the woodpile, where the sun is warm, and roll cigarettes from the pouch of tobacco Tom passes around. The scents of tobacco smoke, sweat, sawdust and gasoline blend in a sweet perfume that drifts past me. I crave a cigarette myself, but think better of it in Tom's presence.

Too soon, Tom cranks the engine and the saw is ringing again. This time one of the other men takes over at the table, and I'm moved to the other side of the yard where I can help carry to the saw. The afternoon slips past and suddenly the pile is finished, the woodcutters gone. Our dooryard is a mountain range of maple blocks and miniature hills of sawdust scattered near.

The yellow September day is already beginning to fade into a damp charcoal evening when Tom and I walk in silence down to the river. Physically tired, we talk in monotones, the light conversation making deeper thoughts. A Canada jay hops before us on the pathway, screaming as it is spooked into flight, but the sounds of the driving engine and the saw still fill my ears.

We stop by silent agreement and watch the grey river move slowly past. Tom strikes a wooden match with his thumbnail and puts it to his pipe. He looks at me sideways from under his old felt hat as he gets it going, then pulls a package from his shirt pocket. Black Cat, tailor-mades. He passes me the pack.

"Have a cigarette, Steve," he says.

CHAPTER 22

My correspondence course arrived in the mail on the same day as Danny's first lesson in taxidermy. I will be studying authors, Joseph Conrad, T.S. Eliot, and Thomas Carlyle, and the course requires two essays a month for the next six months, with a final exam in the spring for my first university degree credit. I have written to the university bookstore in Fredericton for the books: *Heart of Darkness*, *The Waste Land*, and *Sartor Resartus*.

The Northwestern School of Taxidermy has sent Danny a small glossy booklet with an eagle's head encircled on the cover. It contains instructions, with sketches, on how to skin a bird. He has taken it to school with him.

Tom and I have spent the day splitting wood in the dooryard. It's been a breezy fall day, the wind's chill overpowering the sun so that we've worked with sweaters on to keep warm. By late afternoon we finish and Tom commences to wheelbarrow the split wood into the shed and tier it along the back wall. I carry in armfuls and when Danny comes from school he helps us, and we complete the first tier. Then Tom gets Danny to move his boxing equipment out of the woodshed and into the summer kitchen. While he's doing it, we sit on blocks to rest and have a smoke. Katie holds open the door and calls, "Supper'll soon be ready," and we go to the house, Tom walking ahead, stooped now and looking tired.

Howard has shot a deer and has brought us a roast, and through the long afternoon, whenever the back door opened, its roasting odours drifted into the yard. As Katie removes the roaster from the oven, and makes the gravy, Tom takes a swig of his brandy and sits in his place at the table waiting to be served. The kitchen is warm as we eat and there is an odour coming from the pot of spiced chow-chow that sets on the bread board covered with a dish towel.

After supper we sit at the table sipping tea, Tom reclining on the back legs of his chair, hands behind his head, smoking his pipe. Out the window, the remaining rays of a golden sunset touch on the tops of the tall juniper and birches that stand along the line fence that borders the potato field. With the potatoes taken from the ground, the field appears dry and warm, with small granite rocks scattered about. Runner tracks from the loaded sled twist among the bunches of snapping dry potato stocks that dapple the sand like tiny cocks of rotting hay.

"Why don't we burn the stocks tonight?" I ask, glancing across the table at Tom and nodding out the window.

"How's that?"

"The stocks, they'd burn now, wouldn't they?"

"Oh, hell, yes. They're dry as tinder," he nods. "And the radio does speak a rain tamara."

Danny is pretending to do his homework, his taxidermy lesson hidden in the pages of his reader. When he overhears us, he drops the book. "Oh, great! C'mon, let's go. Let's burn the stocks."

Then we get pitchforks from the barn and start toward the dark potato ground as Tom puts on his Ganzie and goes about the kitchen in search of matches.

Danny runs and gathers forkfuls, making a pile near the centre field, but when Tom comes, he beckons us to a spot near the line fence. "Over here. We'll burn over here — the trees'll break the wind."

In the brown hazy evening, the scattered stockpiles are tiny beaver lodges, so many alike having been carried to the rill side at digging time. Beaver lodges or forgotten piles of bunched hay, moulded black. This is a bonus crop, I think. A kind of license to burn, commemorating harvest's end.

And yet it seems like only yesterday that we put in the seeds here, soggy and freshly cut by Tom and wheelbarrowed to the field to be planted one sandal-track apart by Danny and his friends. How they cursed the gritty fertilizer stuck beneath their nails. Later in the summer, how I loathed the hot hours leading Prince by the bridle as Tom steered the cultivator, his mould boards half-covering the small plants. This, of course, was always done in the evening hours when the leaves pressed upward to catch the dew. At blossom time, the field was a jungle with a million bees. And then the frost turned the stocks a velvet brown, dulse-like as they curled and decayed. Digging time brought first the stalk-pulling and the hacking out of potatoes, limbless little men, the brand of which after generations Tom no longer knows.

And when we had grated them from the earth to the ring of iron diggers clanging on rocks and the diggers were used to rest upon with folded arms, the potatoes lay crowded, exposed to dry in the late September sun. Danny and his friends had come, half-dragging, half-swinging, the tiresome buckets, filling the sacks until they spilled over in the sand. We piled them on the drag sled, and as the horse nodded with digging hooves, the load of lumpy bags on the sled creaked towards the house. Danny had scrambled for a seat on the load but kept tumbling off with each nudge forward.

"Now, keep a bag for Aunt Edith," Katie told us as we emptied the sacks with a rumble into the chute that hangs from the cellar window.

"And here's two for the chicken supper," Tom said, throwing a couple of sacks on the ground behind the sled. Last year at the church supper, the minister praised our potatoes. "They're a good potato this year, Tom," he shouted across the hall. Danny and I were embarrassed when everyone looked toward our table. But Tom seemed proud, the labour of many hours being enjoyed by the town's people.

Now Tom lights a bunch of stocks at the leaf end and leans it against a rock. Invisible flame eats into the crisp leaves, catches into the limbs, and I ease a forkful of wind-dried stocks onto the fire. A rope of amber smoke curls into the air, sending sparks and bits of ash bellowing above the trees, making a glow that lights up the potato ground the way one would light up a single room in house.

We scuffle about carrying forkfuls to the fire as the flames leap with a rumble into the darkness. The brown smoke becomes a ceiling over the field, a perfume to be scented at other farms. The trees along the line fence become a wall of multi-coloured leaves, rusting and dropping the occasional leaf to the sand, and we hurry to keep the fire going.

Across the river, a screen door slams. Howard, still eating, stomps across the bridge with his lantern swinging and bobbing as he pulls on his coat.

"Hello fer a fog," he says "Hello fer a smell." He hurries to the nearest piles to help, lantern in one hand and fork in the other.

The growing flame can be seen at other farms, now, bringing folks to their windows as its light plays reflections against their wallpaper. With Howard to help, Tom stops carrying and stands by the fire. He reaches into his sweater for his flask of brandy. Then he lights his pipe, holding his hat beside the bowl to break the wind.

"One evening as the sun went down
A jungle fire was burning
Down the track came a hobo hikin'
An' he said, Boys, I'm not yearnin'. . ."

"Who wrote that one?" I ask.

"Oh, some old poet, God knows who. It was a song, I think. Yeh, it was an old song." Tom takes another drink, and then he coughs. "Oh, dear God, that's an awful cold surely. Consumption, I think, by the feel of it. I'm not long fer this world."

"Maybe you should go in out of the night air?"

"Oh, no, no, I'm alright."

"Are you sure?"

"Yes, Jesus, don't fuss!" he snaps. "Danny, bring that pile a weeds over there by the fence. The only way ta kill a mustard weed is burn 'er."

Tom finishes his brandy and throws the empty flask into the trees. His eyes are glassy in the firelight.

"Far away in sunny meadows
Where the golden sunset fell

There I strayed beneath the roses
Walkin' with a village gal
She was all I had ta love me
She was faithful, fond and true
And she wore beneath 'er bonnet
Amber tresses tied with blue."

"Who wrote that one?"

"I heard it somewhere. God knows where."

"It's a love poem. I thought all yours were the hobo kind."

Tom shrugs. "Lad, yer not goin' ta town much these nights. How ya makin' 'er with the little Reid girl?"

"That's over, I guess."

"Ah. I thought so."

"You did? How could you tell?"

"Ah, ya seemed a bit down in the mouth lately, that's all."

"Was it that obvious?"

"How's that?"

"Was it that plain to see?"

"No, but I noticed an' so did Katie. Growlin' about books en' lessons en' bein' hateful en' contrary with Danny. Since thrashin' day." He nods, and gazes out towards the dark river. "Why'd ya break 'er off?"

"I didn't do it. She did."

"Too high-toned fer ya?"

"No, she wasn't that way." I wonder how I can explain it so he'll understand. Danny and Howard throw the last of the stocks on the fire and wander slowly to the edge of the field. I hear a few words of their conversation: how to skin a bird.

"No?"

"No, she just had bigger plans. I wasn't included. Maybe I rushed her, I don't know." Tom listens, silent, and I find myself speaking the thought lurking in the back of my mind: "I guess we didn't have all that much in common anyway."

"Well, now, look at 'er this way. If she's not the right one yer better off knowin' first as last. The more time ya spend with 'er the harder 'tis ta leave. It's too bad, boy. A nice bit of a skirt, too, by the sounds of 'er."

"I was just really starting to know her. Boy, she took a chunk off me."

"How's that?"

"She was the right one, the one I wanted."

"Ah, hell, at yer age everyone's the right one. It's whoever ya happen ta meet first."

"I know others I don't care for."

"Yah, the one across the river, what's 'er name?"

"Cindy."

"She's everyone's girl. Don't ya get caught there!"

"Amanda is the only girl I ever wanted."

"Well, lad," says Tom, pausing to refill his pipe, "it's like the lad that kissed the cow. He said it was everyone fer his own fancy. But if I was you I'd look fer a good ol' country girl, one that can help ya and not just make a dress look pretty."

"I'm not looking any more now."

"Sure ya are. The right one'll come along. Yer young yet. Hell, I was well up in me forties when I met yer mother."

"I don't really care if I ever find anyone," I tell him. He shakes his head.

"See, it's like this. Ya gotta get a lady who'll love ya back. Wait fer that one, fer yer own kind that ya can be yourself with. Don't spend yer time chasin' a ghost."

"What do you mean? Chasing a ghost?"

"Every girl's great when they're new to ya, nicer than ya think. Till ya get ta know 'er. She could be pretty as a June colt but a hateful son-of-a-whore inside. Everyone has their faults. Maybe yer aimin' too high, lad."

"How could I settle for anything less, now?"

"I know she could sing an' play, but who knows? A high-toned thing like that'd keep a lad runnin' an' fallin', tryin' ta please 'er, wantin' everything she sees."

"Amanda had the right priorities, all right."

"How's that?"

"She wasn't like that."

"Still a ghost to ya. Steve, ya didn't know 'er that well. Hell, ya only went down three or four times. But I guess you could say she was one a the nice ones, an' you'll remember 'er that way whatever she was."

We stand in silence, staring into the heart of the dwindling fire. There's something I've wondered about Tom and wanted to ask, but we've never been able to talk this way before. Maybe it's the brandy. Far off in the night a dog howls, and I look into the darkness towards the sound. If I don't ask him now, I may never.

"So, what happened to you when you were my age? Someone leave you?"

Tom hesitates a moment.

"Well, sir, I had this girl over at the Wills' place. She was the wrong religion an' everything, but still I fell fer her. But she kept shyin' away like that, like a young heifer on the' tear but not quite ready ta stand. I never got that close. Well, I tried an' tried." His quiet laugh turns into a cough, and he spits into the fire. "I trucked 'er candy, helped Old Man Wills, sang to 'er, walked 'round with 'er, an' just like you I fell in love wit' 'er. But ya know, boys, I was only chasin' a ghost is all I was doin'."

"And then what?"

"She married a teacher lad, a delicate son-of-a-whore that had ta stand twice ta cast a shadow. She left with 'im an' I never saw 'er agin. So I know what yer feelin'. It bothered me fer years, ten years or more. I'd be goin' by 'er place, huntin' in the fall, an' I'd stop an' watch the smoke comin' from 'er chimney an' it seemed ta comfort me. But mind, I was only chasin' a ghost then."

"You got over it, though. Didn't you?"

"I met Katie. A nice sensible woman. An' I knew I had someone real who'd love me back. I give up that ghost."

"And you were happy?"

"Yes." He pauses, and for the first time turns to look straight at me. I meet his eyes for a moment but the expression in them is not one I recognize, and I drop my gaze to the fire.

"In a way, yes," he continues. "There's not much real happiness anyway. It's all in yer mind, if ya wanna be happy or not with someone. Now, Katie is a real good woman, moved in here an' stayed, an' helped me keep the farm goin' and beared me you lads, thank the Lord fer that."

I'm uncomfortable, hearing Tom talk about love and happiness, but somehow it helps me. I don't feel so desolate, so lost; still, I can see myself clinging to Amanda's memory.

"Oh, hell," Tom says briskly, "I don't know. Sometimes I think a man's better off without 'em, if ya ask me." And he changes the subject and mumbles about sage brush fires he built on the open plains when they were in the west, working on the harvest. He talks of jungle fires that burn for days unnoticed and of the smokeless hidden fires of highway men. He talks of the fires of hobos in shimshacks along the tracks, and I wonder why Tom ever came back here. "A man can be happy anywhere if he has the right woman." I've heard him say that many times.

Suddenly I realize that Danny and Howard have gone to the house. The stocks have all burned and now the fire is nothing more than a breathing dome of spark and ash, glowing when the breeze blows across it. We gather the forks, and as we walk from the field, I look back at the fire and there is one last straw blazing in the distance, filling the field with its odour. It is a lasting flame, I think, like the flame that burns for a long-lost love. Finally it twinkles in the distance and goes out.

CHAPTER 23

The second week of October: summer should be gone, but today is warm and we have to take off our sweaters as we work in the garden. We've spent the morning pulling beans, shaking sand from among the roots and placing them between two stakes, tying them top and bottom with binder twine. Then Tom wheelbarrows them to the barn and stands them on the thrashing floor for the winter. After lunch, we begin pulling carrots. These are like the roots of teeth and we pry them loose with the potato digger. Sometimes they break and have to be dug loose with bare hands. As I kneel, my jeans become caked with clay and the carrot tops collected between the drills leave green stains. As the sand on the carrots dries, Tom throws them into the wheelbarrow and takes them to the cellar.

It is almost sultry today, and through the afternoon a dog barks across the river while the occasional shot of a hunter repeats itself through the valley. Beneath the hill, in the alders, a partridge drums and Tom says, "That's the sign of a long, open fall."

When Danny comes home from school, he gathers rocks for his slingshot, then heads for the swamp. A little south breeze follows him down the river and rattles the dead corn stalks.

As I work, my thoughts are with my new correspondence course. I'm reading Conrad's *Heart of Darkness*. Conrad chose the river that winds within Africa to help him project a certain stream of consciousness, and the eventual deterioration of the human mind isolated from society. I'm giving thought to my first essay when a car rumbles on the gravel road. As it nears, it slows and the driver turns honking into our driveway. I glance over absently. A white convertible, with its top down. My mind is still on my essay and the carrots, and it is a moment before I realize what I have seen. The driver is a girl in red with long dark hair. Nick is with her, and another girl, probably Anna, his girlfriend from town. I can't accept what my eyes tell me, until the driver gets out and stretches her arms over her head, waving. Amanda.

"Steve! Hey, Steve! Is that you?"

My heart thumps, my legs grow weak, and I'm flooded with something between panic and lovesickness. Then embarrassment takes over. My T-shirt is damp and my dirty jeans have holes. My hands are caked with mud, and rivulets of sweat have streaked through the dirt on my cheeks. I pull my red hunting cap down over my matted hair as I cross the field to meet her.

I don't want her to see me this way.

I had not expected to see her again. As Tom puts it, I gave up that tantalizing ghost, though, I suppose, I kept in the back of my mind the shreds of a dream. A dream that I might meet her someday, somewhere, and show her a better side of me, impress her with my direction and scholarship. But here, coming out of the garden, looking like this, no. With some warning, I'd have crawled away to hide behind the row of corn stalks.

She leans on the fender like Marilyn Monroe, holding a cigarette fashionably in her long delicate fingers and blowing the smoke upward.

"Steve, how are you?" She smiles the same smile.

I try to wipe some of the dirt from my hands before greeting her, but when I extend my hand she passes it by.

"No, no," I say, "I'm too dirty, your coat."

She hugs me anyway, and the shield I've tried to put between us crumbles. My eyes close. I want to keep holding her, to kiss her, to tell her again how much I love her. But I wrench myself away.

"Amanda. So what brings you out this way?"

"We're just out driving. Nick wanted Anna to meet his folks; he showed us where you live." Over her shoulder, I see the other two climb out of the car and go hand in hand toward the river, waving back at us. "How's it going for you, Steve?"

"Not so bad. We're pulling the vegetables today," I say, showing my soiled hands. "It's the only way without the proper equipment. Hey, you look great. University must be treating you well."

"Tremendous. I'm really enjoying it. This is my first time home, Thanksgiving weekend and all."

"Yes, you've been away six weeks now."

"This is a nice place here, Steve," she says brightly, looking around.

"It's okay for a place, I guess. It's home. I was born there in the house, grew up here."

"Look at the size of that garden!"

"Tom's still planting for hard times." I take a deep breath. "Would you like to come inside and meet my folks?"

She follows me into the house. Katie is preparing supper. When she sees Amanda coming she wipes her hands on her apron and apologizes for her messy kitchen, for her old dress with the drooping hem. She's small beside Amanda's elegant height, I see, and nervous, unusually talkative.

"Pleased ta meet ya," she says, shaking hands. "Come in and set a spell. Could I get ya a cup a tea? Steve, take the girl's coat."

"No, really, Mrs. Moar, there really isn't time. I'm waiting for my friend who went across the river with Nick Long."

One Indian Summer

I lead her through the summer kitchen, crowded with hampers of cucumbers, green tomatoes, crabapples, a bag of pig grower, and Danny's boxing equipment. A horse pail steams on the range and there is a sickening smell from the small potatoes that are boiling for pig feed. Tom kneels on the floor, squinting into the stove as he stokes the fire with split kindling. He's wearing white cotton work gloves and his hat is pushed back from his sweaty forehead. His ragged grey sweater hangs open.

"Tom, I'd like you to meet a friend of mine from town. This is Amanda Reid."

"Hannah?"

"No. Amanda, Amanda Reid. The girl from town I told you about. Remember?"

"Oh, yes, oh, hell, yes. Well, well, well." He passes her his gloved hand. "God bless yer soul, how are ya anyway? Reid, eh? I worked with Reids in the woods, upriver, an' a Reid lad worked on the drive one spring but I don't mind his name."

"That's another Reid," I say.

"How do you do, Mr. Moar," Amanda interjects, smiling sweetly at Tom's effort to get up and greet her.

"Come 'way in fer a cuppa tea. Would ya stay fer a bite a supper?"

"She hasn't got time," I say quickly, steering her to the door.

As we cross the dooryard towards the river, the hens flock together and follow us, clucking and crowding around our feet. The cattle pastured on the flat have come to the bars and are bawling to get into the barn, to be fed and bedded for the night. The calves are shaggy now and long haired, and I can smell their warm breath as I shoo them away so I can lower the middle bar for Amanda to get through. On the other side, we step carefully among splatters of cow manure. We walk across the stubble field and then more pasture, silence stretching between us. I'm not sure what to say. I want to keep the conversation away from the question of our relationship, not to make more of her visit than what it is, to bring Anna and Nick.

"So how's your father?" I ask. "How's Mr. Reid?"

"Dad's fine. He keeps busy. He's president of the Rotary Club this year and he's got an office in the lodge, so that keeps him busy. And he's doing work for the Red Cross. But business is slow at the Inn."

"Have you met many people at university?"

"Oh, yes! Steve, I've met so many nice people, and the initiation was so much fun, there were so many great parties on Frosh Week."

"You must be happy you're there."

"What have you been up to yourself?"

"Not that much, really," I shrug. "Just helping Tom with the harvest. There's really nothing else to do around here. Oh, and I enrolled in a correspondence course — English."

"That's tremendous. It's better than wasting the year."

"How are your studies?"

"Going well. I'm really enjoying the music, and the city, too, as a matter of fact, and the people I've met. I'm rooming with a girl from Toronto, her father's a doctor. Sometimes a bunch of us go out to the theatre, or an opera."

"I see you're driving Gordon's car. Is he around these days?"

"No, he won't be home until Christmas. He left his car at our place for the fall. Poor Gord, he's such a nut, he's into tennis now. He writes every once in a while. I still think you'd like him, Steve."

"I might."

"When is it that you go to university? I've forgotten when you said you were going. Is it next year?"

"Well, I hope to," I tell her, "if things go well around here and I don't have to stay home to help Tom. He's not really able to farm alone anymore, but he won't stop. I suppose it's the only thing he has now, and he thinks there's no other way to live."

"So it looks like you'll be here for awhile at least?"

"Next year Danny will be old enough to help. He'll be staying home from school then."

"What a shame."

"But at least I'll be able to go. Hopefully it will be next year."

I want to reach out and take her hand, even pull her into my arms, but I know I must not. Once more, I fight my emotions. I have to accept the fact that our romance is over, and I'm wishing now that she hadn't come here.

When we reach the river, we meet Nick and Anna coming across, and together we walk up the hill. As we near the fence, the girls giggle and joke as they tip-toe around the splatters of cow manure.

Their visit seems to have lasted only a few minutes until they're in the car driving away. All of them wave as Amanda gives the horn a final honk, and the rumble of the car, with gravel stones hitting its bottom, can be heard for a long time.

Preoccupied, I go back to the garden, to where I had left the row of carrots. On my knees, I grub at the clay, reliving my embarrassment. Has anything changed? Did she come here to see me, to catch me looking like this? I doubt that. She has too much class. I think. But if only I could have been prepared. Maybe I could have asked her out, have spent the evening with her, Gordon being away.

But then I would have to relive the hurt, because I know it won't work. Certainly whatever opinion she has of me would have lessened by her visit here. She has seen my worst side, and Tom and Katie made bad impressions, seemed shabby and nervous, over-polite. And then there were the hens and the cattle and the splattered manure and the pig feed. Everything seemed to join in a conspiracy to work against me, stripping me of the ghost of a chance I might have had.

I hack fiercely at the carrots, flinging them away from the pile, out of the garden onto the sod land. When I see Tom coming with the wheelbarrow, I choke back this boiling unreasonable anger.

"The little one gone?" He stoops to throw carrots into the wheelbarrow.

"She's gone all right!"

"I thought she'd stay awhile."

"She had to go."

"Nice-lookin' little filly, eh?" Tom gives me a quick sideways look. "One of th' nice ones."

"One of the nice ones," I agree, laughing a little, bitterness and self-pity in my throat. "One of the nice ones, but that's my share of her."

"Oh?"

"I won't be seeing her again, that's settled now."

"Well, if ya ever wanna go see 'er any time, the car's yers fer the askin'." He clasps my shoulder, very briefly, then turns the gesture to a gentle cuff of his fist. "But don't chase a ghost. I wouldn't wanna girl like that meself."

"She's not interested in me anyway. She wants somebody with class."

"How's that?"

"She's not interested in a sand-grubbin' farmer like me." I throw the digger down on the heap of withered carrot tops, and swing to face Tom, frustration letting the compressed words come out like water from a faucet. "She's out of my class. She wants someone sophisticated, a town guy! With education! That's what girls like her want, I'd be no good to her!"

"Don't put yerself down like that. She's too high-toned, ya mean?"

"Not high-toned, just out of my class. I was ashamed. Look at us! Just stop and look at us! We haven't advanced ourselves very far, farmers is all we ever were and all we ever will be, farmers breeding more farmers. No one ever made a break to try to go anywhere or do anything with themselves. This whole damn place makes me sick. Sick! I'd like to get to hell out of here!"

Tom wipes his face with his handkerchief, his hands trembling. "Now hold 'er right there, young fella, ya don't know 'er all just yet. I never knew a woman ta want the kinda man yer talkin' about. Most of 'em wanna good strong man with a strong back and arms. A hard worker. By the liftin' Jesus, I'll bet a dollar to a doughnut she wants a workin' man an' not a readin' man."

"Tom, Tom, you're a hundred years behind the times. What you're saying may have been the case a hundred years ago. But not today. No woman like Amanda wants to marry a backwoods man."

"Whatta ya mean backwoods? We're livin' in a community here. We're not some camp in the backwoods."

"No girl wants to marry someone who digs in the mud for the roots of a carrot. Who in hell wants to get mixed up with someone like that?"

"Katie did, she came from the city."

"Today's woman wants someone strong in mind, not strong in body. We should have been living in town years ago. Katie would have been better off, too, she could have had friends and kept up with her music and education, and I might have had a chance with someone like Amanda."

"Katie's happy here."

"I haven't got a chance. A grubbin' farmer, that's all I am now. Amanda could see that today, if she didn't know already."

"Now you hold on a God damn minute. There's nothin' wrong with bein' a farmer. Damnation ta hell, yer readin' too Jesus many weird books, that's all's wrong with ya. *Heart of Darkness*, *The Waste Land*, Jesus Christ! I looked at yer books last night. A man would have to be a anti-biologist ta figure out what they mean, or some son-of-a-whore who swallowed a dictionary. And yer gettin' all soft an' crazy like a town lad."

"Those are good university books and that's why I'm studying them. I'm trying to improve my mind."

"It's Jesus trash if ya ask me. I don't think th' man knew 'imself what he was talkin' about, 'April is the cruellest month,' bullshit. I'd like ta see that lad around here in January, February."

"He wasn't talking about the weather."

"Read the Bible, that's what I read. Everything ya need is there. And ya'll see there's farmin' in there too. And get that other foolish stuff outta yer head."

Tom heaves an armful of carrots into the wheelbarrow and the load topples onto the ground. Groaning, he gets on his knees and jams the wheelbarrow legs into the ground to balance it, picks up the sideboards and slots them back into place. As he gathers the carrots, he starts to laugh quietly, talking more to himself than to me.

"Ha ha, that's a good one, boys, a woman not wantin' a workin' man. Good God. What's the world comin' to? Do ya think a decent woman's gonna marry some lazy son-of-a-whore who lays back with his head in a book? Not Jesus likely."

"That's the kind Amanda wants," I say. I'm suddenly tired of the argument. I just want it to end.

"Christ, if she thought anything of ya, she wouldn't mind if ya was farmin' a bit, she wouldn't mind seein' ya in work clothes with a bit a mud on ya. That's somethin' to yer credit, lad."

"Yes, and a great credit it is."

"Well, I can't see how ya can blame the farm fer losin' yer girl, is all I can say. A man has ta be 'imself in this world. Ya should be proud ta be seen in a garden. Nothing wrong with workin' in a garden. It's a good honest livin' and we're a lot better off here than a good many town folks who have ta go to a store fer everything. We never have and we never will. No sir, boys, there's no boughten vegetables fer this family."

"Yes, we've been here for generations and none of us will ever amount to anything for generations to come because of it."

"Lord be praised, listen to 'im. Listen to 'im, would ya, listen. He's eighteen years old an' he's tellin' us all how ta live."

"Sometimes, it might not hurt you to listen sometimes."

"Now lookit here, what are ya gonna do, let the farm grow up in alders? Move ta town, live in a box on the side of a street like a bunch a pigeons with not a blade a grass an' nothin' round ya fer a place? Them people don't have nothin' ta fall back on when hard times comes along. Hell, during the Depression, they were all on relief, livin' off the county. But we wasn't. By the liftin' Jesus, we wasn't. No goddamn way! We never took a cent, raised everything. This field here was planted fulla beans an' the flat was standin' to yer arse in wheat an' we shot a deer or two an' caught a few fish. No, sir, boys, ya can't tell me that horseshit. I've been around too long. I'm proud ta say there was no dole handed out ta this here family an' there won't be neither, not so long as I'm able ta put a seed in the ground."

"Well, I believe there's worse things than dole. There's nothing wrong with a helping hand if a person's resources are cut off. Too much pride's not a good thing, either. Everyone needs help sometimes."

"A helpin' hand is one thing, livin' off the county on relief is another."

"Well, I have my philosophy and you have yours. Let's leave it at that. Personally, I'd rather see a person in town, even if he needs assistance sometimes, than someone stuck out in the backwoods."

"I'm not talkin' about the backwoods, I'm talkin' about the farm here!"

"A small apartment in town beats forty acres in the back country. Living in town, you learn, get to know people, advance yourself socially." I notice Danny coming up from the river, slingshot in his back pocket and a dead yellowhammer swinging from one hand. "What will become of Danny in this place? A man can shrink to nothing in the country, fade away and turn foolish from going nowhere. Look at Howard."

"There's worse in town than poor Howard," Tom says, dropping his voice a little as Danny comes near.

"We're so far in the woods," I continue, "we don't see anyone or do anything. Damnit, I don't know how to act when I do meet people and I suppose I talk funny and don't even know it."

Danny catches my last words. "Yes, ya do talk funny," he says.

"You stay out of this!"

"Talk funny?" Tom presses.

"That's how I lost Amanda, not knowing how to act. I was afraid to be myself because I thought I was nobody. And when I tried to be someone else, like a town guy, I was phoney."

"Shoulda been yerself, lad, cowshit an' all."

"Hoo haa!" Danny roars, "be yerself, cowshit an' all!"

"Danny, you shut up. Keep out of this." I throw a sod at him and chase him from the garden.

"I'm goin', I'm goin'," he laughs.

"Now," Tom says sternly, turning me to meet his eyes, "how'd ya say ya lost 'er? Tell me the truth, straight now."

I take a deep breath and tell my father what I know, looking at the embarrassing truth as clearly as I can. "I hurried her, fell in love with her before I even knew her. See, in town, everybody knows everybody and they take their time on these things. A starving kid from the hills, that's what I was like," I admit. "It could have been anyone. Any girl at all, the first girl I met, just like you said. Thank God that Amanda's a decent person, that's all I can say. She could have had great fun with me if she'd wanted to."

"Well, maybe all us 'backwoods' people are crazy. Is that what yer sayin'? We could all be crazy an' I wouldn't know. I've been here a hundred years, isn't that right? Maybe we should sell 'er all an' move ta town ta find our sanity," Tom scoffs. He picks up the barrow shafts and wheels the heaping load toward the house, the iron wheel grinding in the sand and ringing as it bounces over the rocks. The wheelbarrow is on Tom's side too, I think, laughing at me.

"Buyin' everything in a store," Tom mumbles and shakes his head. "A piece a fish, a roast a beef, a carrot fer the table. Boys oh boys, I don't know where that lad gets his way a thinkin'. Readin' an' writin' too much. That's what's wrong." He turns to send a scowl back to me from under his battered hat. "An' he used ta be such a good one ta work."

I'm a disappointment to Tom. His oldest son, and I've betrayed him, betrayed my own flesh and blood. I'm suffused with guilt. Outside the family philosophy, I'm drifting on a separate course and grieving for the bond that's missing now, the link that won't seem to knit together again. Maybe I keep trying to be someone I can never really be, I think, but I have to keep trying and do what feels right for me. But I believe that Tom is right about one thing: a person has got to be himself first.

I shouldn't have argued with him. I should have kept my feelings inside. At least things would still be the same in his eyes. Now I'm afraid I've ruined that, and how could I have expected Tom to change? At his age? He's a land lover, like his father, and his father's father. Save for a few years in the war and a trip or two west, he has spent his life tied to this piece of land and that's all he knows. Yet, I know there's merit in what he says. Maybe the right course is somewhere in between, a bit of both? I must have taken after Katie, I think, a city girl transplanted and always slightly out of place. Maybe it's from her side that I get my strange ways of thinking.

When I come to the house, Katie has supper on the table. I wash up and sit down at the table across from Danny. He and Tom are already eating. Our argument is not mentioned again, nor is Amanda's visit.

CHAPTER 24

And then the wind is cold again and the elm leaves are swept across the dooryard to cling in the swamp grass. Some drift across the field and into the river, submerge and drift away. The apples that hang from top branches are mealy and soft: I knock them down with the clothesline pole and take them to the house for Tom. He likes them this way.

Save for the yellow swamp grass and the plowed land above the barn, the ground is faded and there are specks of frozen cow manure everywhere, the cattle having at last been brought in and stalled for the winter. By now, too, the days are short, the darkness overtakes us at suppertime, and the nights are clear. Frost whitens the fields and roofs and freezes ponds into plates that shatter when we step on them.

Tom says, "We could get a skid a snow any night now."

We put the last of the firewood into the shed and we bank the house with a wall of boards two feet high, the trough filled with sawdust. Then we cover it with boughs. With scraps of board we build a windbreak which extends from the outside kitchen to the woodshed and sheath the backhouse with old newspapers and bits of cardboard. While we work at this, Katie washes the storm windows and doors, ready to be put on.

On the hydro pole in front of the house, the church people have put up two posters. One advertises the chicken supper, the other the Doc Williams show with a picture of Doc bareheaded wearing dark-rimmed glasses. He looks like Buddy Holly, I think, but according to Tom he looks more like the "Raleigh man" than a western singer. Tom is a Jim Rodgers fan. But we can't go to the show anyway; we don't have the money.

My essay schedule leaves me few free evenings, in any case. Tom and Katie have given me the use of the dining room for studying and writing. With an extension cord, I've hung a light bulb over the centre of the table. I have my writing paper, my books, and Katie's old Remington typewriter. Dark and light imagery in *Heart of Darkness*: that's my essay now. In some ways, I think, Conrad favoured the dark side as he made use of the nights, the unknown, the evil, the impenetrable, and of course the river that flows out of that dark continent. I'm having trouble finding images of light; so far, there's only white tusks, and a few white men who exploited the elephants for their ivory.

As I write the outline, Tom comes into the room and pulls a chair from under the table. He spins it around and sits on it backward, folding his arms on its curved back. He smokes his pipe and talks about killing the pig, perhaps in the morning if Charlie will come. We're out of pig feed; besides, Tom is anxious to finish the fall's work so we can go to the woods to cut pulp. He wants to make a car payment ahead so we won't have to do it when the snow gets deep. I've been asking him to buy a chainsaw like the Lombard advertised in the newspaper, but he's afraid it will destroy the woods too quickly. So it looks as if I'll be using the bucksaw for awhile longer.

Tom is also worried about Prince, who has gone lame since the plowing. He rubs the horse with liniment and walks him to the brook night and morning.

"But walkin's hard on the ol' fella. He's favourin' the left front leg, looks like he's losing 'is weight." Tom picks up *The Waste Land* and flips through its pages. "A poor 'nough poet, this lad, if ya ask me," he sniffs. "His stuff don't even rhyme."

He calls Danny in and sends him across the river with a message for Charlie. "We'll be killing the pig in the morning."

At dawn, the sky is a steel grey, except in the east where a touch of yellow marks the sun's struggle below the horizon. As the dooryard lightens, the gables of the barn show against the sky, and the rooster crows. Tom starts a fire in the kitchen stove and sets the tea kettle on while I light the furnacette. Stove pipes creak as the fire struggles. Tom goes out to the outside kitchen to light the stove there, and the rooster crows again, this time closer to the house.

"Crow, ya son-of-a-whore, crow," Tom grumbles, feeding kindling into the stove and setting the boiler of water over the flame to heat for the pig scalding. He sets a crock of beans on the stove, then smokes his pipe by the stove and stirs molasses into his cup of tea while I'm bundling up to go out to the barn and feed the animals.

The dooryard is white with frost and slippery, and my footsteps make one long skidding track. At the barn I push forkfuls of hay through the feeding holes and listen at the dark stanchion for the grinding of teeth, feeling the warm regular breathing that mixes with the sweet scent of hay. The pig, unfed, grunts and frets in his pen. I turn away from his fat form towards the brightening rectangle of the open barn door. Outside, morning gathers strength. Across the barnyard, near the brook, Tom has built a crib of kindling beneath a drum of water. I light the handfuls of birchbark tucked among the wood, and return to the house.

Charlie has arrived. He sits in Tom's rocker with a cup of tea and a cigarette, his knives on the floor beside him, wrapped in canvas. Katie serves the hot beans, and I sit by the window where I can watch the fire in the barnyard leap against the grey morning.

One Indian Summer

After breakfast, we go to the different fires, Charlie and Tom, and Danny and I, and carry wood from the shed to build them up.

"Christ, ya got 'nough water ta scald four pigs," Charlie says. The men stand by the barnyard fire and sharpen the knives, spitting on stones and grinding in ever-smaller circles, checking the edges with their thumbs. Then they spit on the leather tops of their boots and slap their knives against them until they can shave the hair from the back of their hands. As the daylight grows, the air gets colder, and I tuck my hands into my pockets.

Charlie overturns the drag sled onto its runners and goes to the shed for boards to floor it over with, snapping at me as he passes, "Get the lead outta yer arse. Don't stand round with yer hands in yer pants."

"We'll have ta sew them pockets up," Tom agrees.

So they send me to George Cooper's to borrow his wire tighteners. I have to knock several times, then George comes to the door in his shirttail and flannel drawers.

"Ya burnt out?"

"I came to borrow your wire tighteners. We're killing the pig."

"Yeh, I'll lend ya me wire tighteners. But you boys wasn't much help the day I was tryin' ta thrash."

When I get back, Charlie grabs the tighteners from me, oils the wooden blocks and takes the kinks out of the rope. Tom checks the puncheon, which we haven't used since last fall. He finds the gam stick hanging on a spike by the pigpen and fixes the rope to the beam over the barn floor. Danny and I carry more wood and stoke the outside fire.

"Tom, I see ya got yer plowin' done," Charlie says, sweeping chaff from the floor where the pig will be dressed.

"Yeh, that ol' field above the barn is run out, but I'll try ta raise a disturbance on 'er come spring."

"That's it, plant 'er in April, hit or miss."

"She won't miss anything, too handy the road."

The water in the drum starts to dance and the steam obscures the fire. "She's ready, boys," Charlie shouts, and then he goes to the pen. I watch him scratch the pig's side so it stops grunting and leans against the gate, its white eyelashes drooping. "Nice little junk of a sow, too, ain't she?" He straightens up and thumbs the edge of his knife.

Tom lifts the small board gate and pushes the pig out into the yard. It sniffs around and eats the scraps of yellow grass, and Tom pours a dish of oats on the ground and goes to the house for his twenty-two.

"Yessir, a nice little junk of a sow."

"Can I shoot 'im?" Danny asks.

"No, young fella, ya might miss." Charlie turns to me, grinning. "But you could do it."

"I'm not doing it."

"It's no way ta kill a pig anyway. Shootin' 'em that way."

"How then?" Danny wants to know.

"Ya just stick 'em an' let 'em bleed. Makes good pork."

"Not around here," I say, feeling a little sick.

Charlie looks around for Tom. "Where'd he go fer that gun?"

"To the house. He'll be right out."

"Boys, we can't wait. Now, come 'ere an' I'll show ya how ta stick a pig! Quick, lads, we'll do 'er 'fore Tom comes out."

"Danny," I speak sharply, "go and see what's keeping Tom. I'm not killing it."

"Aw, bullshit, c'mere, gimme a hand. Here, hold me knife." Charlie loops a rope around the pig's front leg. "I'll show ya what ta do. Here, lad! I'll throw 'er and you stick 'er! I'll show ya where."

"Wait for Tom," I protest. "It's his last pig, he said so himself. Pork causes arthritis, he says."

"Last pig be damned. Tom'll always have a pig, ya know damn well."

"That's what he said, he said so himself."

"C'mon, stick 'er! We'll have 'er done 'fore Tom knows what's what."

"We'll wait for Tom. He'll shoot it."

"Then gimme that knife." Charlie's face reddens. But I know I can't let him bleed the plump little sow that's starting to wriggle beneath his hands. I stand taller and take a step back.

"I'm keeping the knife until Tom comes out," I tell him. Danny watches our faces and says nothing, perhaps a bit frightened. There's a thin silence, then Charlie lets the pig go and spits in disgust.

"Yer worse than ol' Tom, contrary, headstrong, always wantin' 'is pigs shot. Afraid of a little squeal! Christ, yer all gettin' soft! Hardly eat a good piece a pork any more." I march to the house to get Tom, Danny trotting beside me, and Charlie grumbles, words meant to be overheard. "Ol' Tom'll never be dead while that boy's breathin'. Walks like 'im, and that same jaw. Oh ho, the Moars do things their own way. That's their business, I guess."

I've never had much respect for Charlie. Now I can understand why Tom dislikes him. I once heard Tom say that Charlie had "a different face fer every day a the week." Still they have a civil relationship, and "in good coe" as Tom puts it. Maybe so many years in the country has done strange things to him, I think.

In the house, Tom opens drawers and upsets old tobacco cans of buttons and nails, searching for bullets for the twenty-two.

"Where in damnation would they go? There were three on the shelf the other day."

"I fired them," Danny confesses. "Howard and me, we fired 'em into a slab on the flat."

"Well, now, that's lovely, lovely altogether. And us with the water boilin', ready ta kill. Well, well, well, of all the god damned."

"Use the rifle," I suggest.

"Yes, make sure that pig is shot, Tom Moar," Katie says. "The poor animal needn't suffer. You know what Charlie's like."

Tom grabs the thirty-thirty, puts a handful of cartridges into his coat pocket, and lifts a bucket of scalding water from the stove in the outside kitchen. The sun glistens on the rifle's shiny barrel, cradled in Tom's free arm, and the hens crowd noisily around his feet as we go back across the barnyard. He kicks at the birds and they flap away toward the henhouse.

At the barn, Tom pours water into the puncheon and puts two cartridges into the magazine of the rifle, levering one into the firing chamber and easing the hammer down to half-cock.

"Here, Charlie," he says, passing the gun, "Shoot 'er!"

"What? Shoot a pig with the big rifle? Ya sure ya know what yer sayin' now, Tom? Yer pork'll be no good. A pig's gotta bleed!"

"Shoot 'er, by Jesus," insists Tom. "I won't have 'er squealin' an' upsettin' Katie!"

"Allright, allright! Whatever ya say, Tom. She's yer pig. You have ta eat the pork. I was just sayin', that's all."

The pig has its head down, eating the oats once more, quieter. Charlie takes aim, point blank, at the pig's head. I look off across the plowed field, noticing that the rifle crack is muffled, short, with no echo to disturb the cold morning air. The pig grunts, and I look back. It's still eating, having moved its head at the split second of the shot; Charlie missed. He swears, swings the lever to throw another shell into the chamber, and takes aim again.

"Now take yer time, Charlie, that's yer last bullet."

"I'll get ya this time, ya Norwegian christer," Charlie says, but he's laughing heartily as he tries to aim, staggering to keep his balance. I watch the rifle waver along the pig's jaw to its flank and unsteadily back, bracing myself for an explosion and for the gasping squeals of a neck wound.

"Give me that fuckin' gun!" I grab the rifle, point it, and shoot the pig between the eyes. It grunts once and drops to the ground.

"Got 'im!" Danny shouts and claps his hands.

"Well done," says Tom.

Charlie looks at me closely. "What's upsettin' ya, lad?"

"You're upsetting me."

"Here, gimme a hand. Grab 'er by the f'ard leg." I reach for a hoof. "No, not that leg, the f'ard leg, are ya deaf?"

I step back. "Do it yourself," I say. Charlie cuts the pig's throat and blood streams into a pool in the dust.

In the nearby stable the horse smells the fresh blood and snorts uneasily, jerking on its halter ropes. We carry water to fill the steaming puncheon, hurrying now, and drag the carcass onto the barn floor. The sickening smell of blood fills the back of my throat as we rope the dead pig and hoist it into the puncheon for the skin to scald. Then, the drag sled and boards making a work table, we pour on hot water and scrape the peeling skin. White bristle mat on the shed floor. And the tension fades. Charlie chuckles as he opens the animal and its entrails drop into a tub.

Tom points out a strip of lean running through the fat pork. "That's the day I went to town an' Katie fed the pig," he says.

"I must remember that one," Charlie says.

"There's enough pork an' beans here ta do us a while," Tom says, nodding at the stakes standing full of beans.

They finish butchering, and then Charlie is gone, and the white carcass hangs in the shadow of the beams, its belly pried open with a stick. The bristled water washes blood from the plank floor and the entrails are wheelbarrowed to a far corner of the field where ravens circle to feast. The doors remain open until twilight as the fire by the brook smoulders and burns itself out, its ashes swept away with the wind.

At dark, the air is clean and cold and lovely, and Tom takes a walk to the barn to close the big doors. He stands a moment in the yard, wiping his watery eyes and nose, his big square hands trembling a little. Then he coughs and spits, and shuts the door on the hanging pig.

"Whatta ya s'pose gets inta a man like that?" I'm hardly close enough to hear Tom's words, but, somehow, I don't think he's talking to me. "His pleasures are so few, he can't leave a thing like that alone."

His pipe glows in the darkness of the barnyard until Katie calls him in to supper.

CHAPTER 25

And now the winds are coming from the northeast as we've expected and there have been days of rain and ponds have accumulated everywhere. And a drifting low fog penetrates like ether, forcing the scent of decay into our souls. With the leaves down, the only colours are in the juniper that tower above the alders and sprinkle the bog with silent layers of orange needles. But the only real movement is at the swamp's edge, where the meadow grass dances among the cattails.

In the evening, I sit in the dining room working on an essay. I can hear the rain against the outside window and the fog is such that the window casts no light into the yard. Tom and Katie have spent the evening at the kitchen table, playing Auction 45 until around nine. Tom came in and said, "Lad, don't stay up all night, an' put a stick in 'fore ya come up" and they went to bed.

Danny heated up the outside kitchen and spent the afternoon and evening mounting a spruce partridge. He's received his shipment of taxidermy supplies and has borax, alum, burnt umber, potter's clay, plaster of Paris, glass eyes, wood wool and hay wire scattered on the table. Around ten, he brings in a sick-looking bird wrapped in white cotton and sets it on the stoves warming closet to dry, then goes up to bed. It is nearing midnight when a rap comes on the front door. I had put a case knife in the door's molding to secure it for the night and as I run to open it Charlie forces the door open and the knife is sent spinning across the floor, almost striking me.

"Come in, Charlie."
"Where's Tom?"
"In bed, hours ago."
"Gettum up."
"What for?"
"Ta drift fer salmon."
"But isn't this too bad a night?"
"No, it's the kinda night we want, no wardens."
"It's not a fit night to be on the river, that's why."
"For them, not for us," Charlie laughs. "This is not a bad night; hell, it's only October. I laid out worst nights overseas."

"You stayed out worst nights than this? I don't believe you."

"Yessir, lad, never doubt what I tell ya. Slept on top a dead German all night ta keep me outta the mud. Took me a week ta get the smell off me clothes. Tom did the same thing."

"I'll try to wake him."

In a few minutes, Tom is out of bed, dressed and ready to go. He puts on his long black raincoat, fastens its metal snaps, and boxes his felt hat so the rain will run off it. With no light, they go to the millshed to get the net and go to the river.

I put wood in the stove and light a cigarette off the coals, using a straw from the broom. The house is silent, with only the clock striking and a few ice pellets bouncing off the window, as I go back to write. But I am preoccupied now with the thought of the two men being on the river. It's not fear of their being caught by wardens. But their boat might capsize. I know, too, that neither of them can swim, and if Tom falls into the river, with his chest cold, he will no doubt get pneumonia. As I write, the hours slip past and later in the night it seems to rain harder and it is colder. When they finally return, I can tell they've been drinking. They are singing and laughing. They carry their fish into the summer kitchen and lay them on the floor so they look like one of those photographs of long ago that hangs in a fishing camp with details of a week-long fishing trip in the old days. They have fourteen salmon. They divide them, and Charlie puts his into a bran bag. Placing a potato in each corner, he takes a rope to fashion a kind of packsack and is gone, singing into the night.

In the morning, it is bright and sunny and warmer. Tom takes the fish to the brook, splits them open so they spread out like snowshoes, and throws the long strips of orange spawn into the field. Then we carry the fish into the shed and Tom places them in the barrel and sprinkles them with salt, weighing them down so they'll make their own pickle. Then he asks me to drive him into town so he can get his hunting license and some new winter clothes.

Tom seems irritable; he coughs and moans, and I have trouble driving to please him and to avoid the many ponds along the road. When we reach the paved highway, Tom falls asleep. As we drive into town, with the mud-splashed dirty car and Tom sitting asleep beside me, I am a trifle embarrassed. I park near the Delux and wake him. He is confused and wonders what we are doing downtown. He goes to the store as I sit in the car and read. When he returns, he has a new pair of gum rubbers tied together by the laces and thrown over his shoulder. He also shows me the new red and black patch jumper and the two pairs of two-piece wool underwear. We go into the hardware store, where he buys a skein of yarn for Katie, a hunting license, and a box of shells for his rifle. Then he goes to the liquor store and immediately wants to go home.

When we get home in the early afternoon Tom goes into the parlour and lies on the folding bed for a couple of hours. When he gets up, he puts on his new makinaw and his new gum rubbers and, taking his rifle with seven cartridges for good luck, goes out to hunt.

One Indian Summer

I do the evening's chores: water the cattle and horse, milk pitch down some hay from the scaffold for morning and carry in the night's wood. When Danny comes home from school, he has the mail and the Eaton's Christmas catalogue, which has a painting on its cover of a farmhouse not unlike ours, only with a windmill. The house is banked with snow, and some children are dragging a Christmas tree toward it as a group install a television antenna on the roof, taking down the windmill. Danny asks Katie for the Daisy air rifle which is featured in the gun section, but she says we can't afford to pay seven dollars for another gun. As dark approaches we stand around the dooryard and listen for rifle shots. We can recognize the sounds of the different rifles in the community. When it is dark and we haven't heard the thirty-thirty we go inside and wait, and when Tom comes in Danny runs to check his hands for blood stains. But he has seen no deer this night.

After supper, I look at the new television sets featured on the catalogue's back cover and try to visualize a movie on their oval screens. So far there is only one TV set in the community and it belongs to George Cooper. It's a Marconi with a seventeen-inch screen, and everyone who goes there in the evenings to watch it says the picture is snowflake clustered.

Danny has gone up twice and both times come home excited but disappointed. He says the TV characters don't measure up to the way we've imagined them from radio. He has seen Don Messer and His Islanders, Eve Arden as our Miss Brooks, and Guy Madison as Wild Bill Hickock. He likes westerns best but many of the actors have been changed from on the radio shows, which also takes something from them. Brace Beamer has been replaced by Clayton Moore as the Lone Ranger, and in *Gunsmoke*, William Conrad has been replaced by the taller James Arness as Matt Dillon. We are all going to Coopers on Friday evening to watch the boxing, as one of Tom's favourites, Sugar Ray Robinson, is fighting. If Tom enjoys that, we will try to convince him to cut pulp this winter to buy a TV.

But for now, I'm listening to the American stations on the radio from seven until nine in the evenings. A disc-jockey named Peter Tripp has a show called *The Curly Headed Kid in the Third Row*, which features the top-forty hits of that nation. These are not country songs but the new rock and roll hits by Buddy Holly, Chuck Berry and Elvis Presley. I wait to hear Elvis, but Danny prefers Buddy Holly. Tom says Elvis is a disgrace and sings like "someone running up a long stairs," and that Buddy Holly "whines like a calf in a wire fence." But he'll never get used to anything but his old Jim Rodgers songs.

While I'm listening to the hit parade, Nick and Cindy come in. They sit on the folding bed beside me and Cindy seems uneasy. I have not seen her since she was here pregnant in the summer. Tonight she is slim and she wears the same red sweater. Her hair is tied up in a pony tail. When Nick gets up to go to the Coopers to watch TV, Cindy stays.

Tom comes from the barn and sits in his rocking chair glancing over the newspaper, ignoring Cindy. Then he lights his pipe and immediately starts to cough. He goes outside and stands on the veranda coughing and spitting.

"Cindy, take off your coat and stay awhile. I'll make some tea."

"S'pose I should."

"Sure, relax, we'll have tea."

She takes her coat off and throws it over the banister. Her slim body seems to embarrass her; when she was here last, only three months ago, she was pregnant. She sits near me now and pinches my arm.

"So. How ya doin' anyway, Steve?" She flashes the same warm smile and has that look in her eye.

"Did you ever have your baby?"

"Yes. I mean, no. It was born dead."

"I'm sorry."

"It was only four months along."

"What happened?"

"I don't know, I just lost it."

"What was it?"

"A boy. I called it Steve after you. I guess it was never meant to be. I felt sa bad, I almost lost me mind. I had to see a psychiatrist, but I'm okay now. I'm just glad everything's over."

"I can well imagine."

"It just wasn't meant to be."

"How's the boyfriend, the lad from town?"

"Oh, Dale? That's all over, too, now an' I'm glad."

"You left him?"

"Well, we were kinda gettin' married there fer awhile, but when I lost me baby, he backed out."

"Nice guy."

"Took off the next day fer Ontario, I think. No one's heard of 'im since."

"What makes you think he's in Ontario?"

"I don't really know fer sure just where he is. He could be in hell fer all I care."

While Cindy's story is depressing, there seems to be a sense of relief that could follow her losing the baby or even the boyfriend. Certainly she seems a lot happier than when she was here last and had them both.

"How's your job? You're a waitress now, aren't you?"

"Not anymore. I got laid off when the baby started ta show. Boy, what an arsehole he was ta work for, no way I could please 'im once he found out where I was from. An' when he found out I was expectin', he was impossible. He made it sa hard fer me, I quit. I don't like waitressin' much, anyway."

"So what are your plans?"

"Well, I'm stayin' home fer the time bein', but I may go to Ontario meself in the spring. Ya can't get work around here with no education, especially after that baby racket."

"I've read where there's lots of work in Ontario for men at least, labour work on the Welland Canal."

"What are ya listening to on the radio? Why do ya have one ear in the radio that way?"

"It's Peter Tripp's top-forty rock and roll hits."

"I like Elvis meself, the way he moves. His song is on the jukebox at the Delux.

"Yes, I saw it there."

"They're dancing the jive at the Delux now. Ever jive?"

"No, I guess I never did."

"They say Elvis will be on television but they won't be showin' 'im from the waist down. Too many moves."

"Do you know all the steps of the jive?"

"Not all them, but I know a few. Come I'll show ya — ya have ta learn, Stevie."

She gets up and starts twisting and bobbing around the room, moving her hips and stomach, making gestures with her hands like she's strumming a guitar. Then she releases the elastic band that holds up her hair and lets it fall over her forehead, her head bobbing up and down, her lips puckered up to kiss someone.

When Tom comes in, Cindy doesn't see him and he has to step around her on his way to the kitchen. He glances at her and shakes his head in disgust as he talks to Katie.

"What in Christ is wrong with that one?"

"I dunno."

"Is she in some kind a fit? I thought that girl was expectin' a baby."

"Some kind of new dance, I guess." Katie keeps to her knitting.

"C'mon Stevie, let's do the jive, you an' me" Cindy grabs my hand and pulls me onto the floor. Then she moves around me, kicking up her feet, twisting and pulling me into her arms. We hold our hands high and twist under them, moving back and forth. "We could go ta town some night an' dance at the Delux, if ya really wanna learn."

"Yes, okay, I'd like to learn."

"Ya turn this way and then this way." She slows down her moves and exaggerates them for my benefit. "Ya'll know that much 'fore ya go doin' it in public."

"We can go down any night. I have the car when I want it."

Tom comes in and sits in the rocking chair to put a block into the furnacette. He watches as we dance again, now to the Buddy Holly song, "That'll Be The Day."

"What kind a Jesus dance was that, boys?" He says when the music stops.

"It's called the jive."

"The jazz?"

"No, the jive. It's a new dance around. They're all doing it in town."

"She don't look like much of a dance ta me. I never saw a man twist that way with a woman on the dance floor. Are ya sure she's a dance, boys?"

"That's what it is."

"Well, God be praised. What's the world comin' ta?"

Then we hear the train whistle and we all hurry to the window to watch the express go past. Its windows are a string of yellow beads moving across the farm and there are sparks dancing off the wheels. There are only one or two passengers visible in the coaches and the conductor is walking the isle.

"Not many on 'er now-a-days, is there?" Tom says. "One time ya couldn't get a seat."

"Everyone has a car, I suppose."

"Steve, would ya put me across the river an' bring the boat back fer Nick?" Cindy puts on her coat.

"Sure!" I go to the kitchen to get dressed.

Cindy goes outside and stands on the veranda smoking a cigarette, waiting for me.

"Where ya goin', lad, at this hour?"

"Just putting Cindy across the river."

"How's that?"

"I'm putting her across, bringing the boat back for Nick."

"No goddamn way are ya goin' across that river with her tanight!"

"I'm just putting her across."

"Yer not takin' that tramp home tanight, comin' over here an' movin' 'er arse around like that!"

"Why not, we're still friends."

"Now, ya know goddamn well what happens. Remember the last time." Tom's face grows pale and his eyes sparkle and he coughs and wipes his mouth with his handkerchief. "Be Jesus, she'll be blamin' ya fer another kid!"

"No, she won't. Hell, she's only . . ."

"Now just stay home, I tell ya, take off yer coat. Ya have ta stay away from that slut. Christ, she'll have ya in jail yet. 'Pon me soul ta God Almighty, what'll I do with that boy?"

"It's not like we're going to do anything. I'm just seein' her across."

"See 'er across all right. That girl comes across too goddamn easy fer 'er own good. I can put 'er across the river meself, goddamnit, if that's all she wants. I think she'd go with just about anyone. She smells like a whore from Tanawanda with that cheap perfume."

"The girl only wants to get home."

"Sure, sure, that's what you think. I bet if I put a little black in me hair and a new Ganzie, she'd go with me." Tom walks to the kitchen to get his coat. "She's the most unwanted sweetheart in this country."

One Indian Summer

I go outside and explain to Cindy that Tom is taking her over.

"Good God." He mumbles, lacing up his new gum rubbers. "Ya think a lad would learn 'is lesson after a while, wouldn't ya."

And then they are gone, down the pathway to the river, Tom's flashlight bobbing up and down with his footsteps.

CHAPTER 26

"You said you loved me once, anyway. I'm not letting you forget that."
"That was a long time ago. I almost forget."
"Were you pretending when you said it?"
"I was having a few drinks. I never pretend."
"Everyone pretends on Halloween."
"That's different."
"If you don't love me, why are we walking to the millshed?"
"We always go to the millshed when we're together."
"Which makes me wonder."
"There's nothing else to do, and you have cigarettes."
"Is that all I mean to you?"
"No, you mean more."
"How much more?"
"You're a good friend. We've been friends for a long time."
"A special friend?"
"Yes, you could say that."
"Still, we're only friends?"
"What do you want me to mean?"
"What you said once."
"I'm not sure, but it won't hurt anything to go there."
"Are you afraid of me?"
"Sort of — not likely."
"I hope your folks don't come home and catch you with me."
"They won't be back for over an hour. They're gone to church."
"Danny, too?"
"Yes, he's trying to impress."
"Your father don't seem impressed with you."
"I know."
"Does that bother you?"
"Not especially — sometimes."
"Will we hug, or will we smoke?"
"We'll do both."

"Cindy, I like you a lot, I've told you that many times."
"Yes, we are good friends."
"Friends." We go into the millshed and sit on the old car seat, and after we light cigarettes, I kiss her and hold her, rubbing her back and moving my hands down to her buttocks, pulling them close.
"You're moochin' with me, Steven Moar!"
"I know."
"Do you like it?"
"Oh, yes!"
"Let's do it, then?"
"What do you mean?"
"Let's make love."
"Oh, Stevie, I love you so much, I just can't help it."
"Now, you're getting serious again."
"I know, I just can't help it."
"Can't we just be friends, pretend for awhile and do the other?"
"And do what other?"
"Make love?"
"NO!" Cindy pushes me away, gets up and fixes her clothes. Her cheeks are flushed. "Nobody pretends with me! Not anymore. I've been hurt too many times already."
"But it could be real this time."
"No, it couldn't be real. The feelings ain't there, not for you!"
"I have feelings, too."
"So do I, but mine are different than yours. Yours are the wrong kind."
"Who knows the right kind? Is there such a thing?"
"Oh, there is such a thing. The kind you have for Amanda Reid would be nice."
"Yes, I have feelings for her. I love her very much. But where is she? She's hardly even real to me now. She's out of reach and she haunts me like a ghost."
"She was here with you the other day, an' ya went walkin' out here, an' I'll bet ya didn't do anything with her."
"No, we didn't do anything, just talked."
"Still, the feelings were there and still are."
"Yes, at least with me, they are."
"And with her?"
"If she had your feelings, we'd be madly in love."
"Life don't work that way. Not often."
"You're right about that."
"Could you feel that way about me and not want the other?"
"I don't know."
"Well, I only want them feelings and not the kind ya have fer me now."
"The other might come later."

"No, it has ta come first."
"How did you know Amanda was here?"
"Nick told me."
"I love her so much, I was afraid to try, afraid of losing her."
"Do ya think she's too high an' mighty ta make love to, ta fuck!"
"No, I just loved her in a different way."
"That's the feeling I'm talking about."
"I know what you're saying, but it has to be there. You can't invent it."
"Stevie, I have ta go. I wanna go home 'fore dark."

The mowing machine has been pushed into the shed and I sit on the iron seat and smoke and Cindy fixes her clothing. Then I give her a hug and kiss her on each cheek and then we walk to the river, and as I paddle across, she sings. When she gets out, she throws me a kiss and a cigarette for later.

It is cold and damp as I walk up the hill from the river. The fields are lifeless now, with only tiny chickadees flitting about the barnyard. In the dooryard, the elm and apple tree are black forks, and the house sits defensive, huddled behind its banking.

They have come from church and Danny walks about the yard humming "Abide with Me," the last hymn of the service. I melt some of Katie's preserving wax to make a candle, and we light the pumpkin and place it on the veranda railing. Its glow, and that of the lighted windows, is the only warmth that stands against the approaching darkness. I get an empty pail and call the hens into the barn and close the doors. Then I put the wheelbarrel into the woodshed and close the entry to the outdoor kitchen in preparation for the Halloween.

It is only dusk, but already the little ones are out. Near our lower line fence, they have dragged cedar fence rails and some barbed wire onto the road. Someone throws a flat piece of sandstone that curves in the sky and rattles off the steel roof of the barn, bringing Tom onto the veranda to shout at them. Someone whoops on the other side of the river. While we are having supper, they run around the house marking our windows with soap. Then they upset the back house and run into the swamp. Tom shouts again.

"Get, ya goddamn heathens." He throws a potato that carries to the edge to the alders. Danny rummages through the outside kitchen for old clothes to dress up in. It is cluttered now with boxing equipment, cream cans, bottles and taxidermy supplies; the frozen pig lies on the table, its legs pointing up. Danny puts on Tom's black raincoat and hauls a nylon stocking over his face, and we colour it black off the stovepipe. Then he dips some cattails into the oil can, and, lighting them for a torch, goes to Coopers for his treat.

After supper, Katie makes fudge as Tom sits in the parlour by the furnacette. He is wearing his white shirt from church and the flowered necktie with the wide striped police braces. He rocks and smokes and hollers to Katie, "Did the fudge get here yet, Mrs. Moar?"

There is a pounding on the front door and when I open it, Howard walks in. His face is blackened with stove polish and only the sockets of his eyes are white. He has turned his old grey winter coat inside out, and its dirty camel-coloured lining is ravelled. He has also reversed his hunting cap and its brown wool lining shows sweat stains and dirt. He carries a five-cell flashlight.

"Trick 'er treat," he says in a serious tone. Then laughs at himself, "Christ, yes, trick 'er treat, he says, and walks right in."

"How's she goin', Howard?" Tom says. "Set a spell an' tell us all ya know."

"Oh, there's no news, though," he says, taking off the cap and sitting on the folding bed. "Who stuffed the partridge?"

"Danny."

"Ha haaa, he looks like he came through a hurricane."

"What's all new over the river?"

"I'm working on the road now, I guess, fer a few days anyway. An' Charlie's cuttin' logs. Oh, yes, an' Charlie got a deer the other day, I guess."

"On the road, eh, how's that fer a job?"

"Oh, it goes in spits and starts."

"Whatta ya doin'?"

"Flaggin'."

"Well, how's the women treatin' ya, anyway?"

"Oh, the same."

"I guess the one across the river is back. There's a good woman fer ya now. She's one of the nice ones, by cripes."

"Naa, it'd be no use. She wouldn't go with me. She's after Steve here."

"She'll go with anyone."

"S'pose?"

"Sure. She likes you, I heard that somewhere."

"Oh, did ya hear that, though?"

"Yessir, I heard that somewhere." The fudge is soft and hot but Katie serves it anyway. We drink cold water to wash it down. "I'll pay that little one a visit later on tanight. I'll go trick 'er treatin' fer an excuse over. But how is the pork, Tom?"

"It's okay."

"But could ya eat it, though?"

"Yes, we're eatin' it."

As Howard gets up to go, he seems to be experiencing a new high. He puts his cap on backwards and his sand-coloured hair juts out from under it. "But that Cindy'd be a homely thing ta take out, wouldn't she?"

"Well, sir, she's one of the nice ones an' she's after you."

"Tom, that's a sin!" Katie says.

"Maybe I'll take er up ta Coopers ta watch the music box."

"That's it."

"Maybe I'll go over then an' try 'er a butt."

"Sure, try 'er a butt."

"Tom, stop that."

Tom appears pleased with himself that he has convinced Howard to go and see Cindy. Howard lights the flashlight and goes over the hill, nodding as he walks.

"Tom, you shouldn't have done that to poor Howard," Katie says. "He'll make a fool of himself."

"Comical duck, that Howard." Tom says.

Later in the night, I go outside to check the property, and the night is cold and still, the only sounds a dog barking, answered by a fox in the distance. The reflections of a fire across the river wink and blink against our buildings and make imaginative dancing figures on the walls, giving mysterious perspective to the hills. The houses appear copper, their windows blind and desolate and our picket-fenced garden artificial with the pumpkin still glowing on the veranda. The building burns and no one goes to fight the blaze, as if it were acceptable to burn even someone's hayshed on Halloween.

In the morning, when I go to the shed for kindling, there is one less grey barn on the landscape, its stone foundation smouldering against the frost. There is a sense of uneasiness at the night's loss.

Katie puts water on the stove to boil for tea, and I take the butcher knife and go to the outside kitchen to slice some bacon from the pig's rear quarter. Then Katie fries the bacon and makes toast over the stove's open cover. As she feeds the kindling into the stove door, the bacon curls in the bubbling pan of grease.

George Cooper comes in and stands by the table talking while we eat. During the night, someone took Howard's flashlight from him and he walked into the swamp and spent the night there. He got home at daybreak, according to George, "Blacker 'n the hubs a hell."

CHAPTER 27

The tar paper-sheathed horse stable door is propped open, and getting sprinkled with November rain. Tom has hung the lantern on a spike in an overhead beam, and its reflections light the dead grass in front of the door. Another shaft of light angles from the manure hole, making a square on the dooryard. Beside the barn, the drag sled leans on its edge, its wood runners smooth like the soles of moccasins. The stable is warm from the heat of the lantern, the sick horse. From the yard, we hear Prince pawing the plank floor, the short half-whinny. Sometimes he coughs and then gives a deep mocking chuckle, like his illness is all a bad joke. The attempted whinny is really a plea for help. We hear Tom talking to the horse and smell the horse liniment and wintergreen.

Tom coaxes Prince to eat oats, to drink lukewarm water from the horse pail. Sometimes he force-feeds by holding Prince's head and pouring saltpeter into his mouth from a Coke bottle. Prince hasn't eaten anything solid in a long time, and during this time Tom has made many trips to the barn. Sometimes he gets dressed in the night and goes, and I feel hopeless as I watch him crossing the dooryard to the barn, his pant legs making ghostly shadows in the lanterns glow.

I bundle up and follow him to the barn. Tom has the curry comb in one hand and the brush in the other, and is going over the horse's rump combing out the loose hair. "They'll be comin' round when they hear 'e's sick," he mumbles. "And I don't want 'em ta think we didn't look after 'im." He sticks the curry comb and brush together and lays them on a small cluttered shelf. Then he scrapes up what little manure there is on the floor and throws it out the manure hole. Nearby, Prince's harness hangs on three wooden pegs, the brass knobbed hames and the black studded bridle on another. In the adjacent empty stall, Danny's Union Calvary saddle hangs over a beam. There are brown cobwebs everywhere.

Tom sends Danny over to Charlie to come and look at the horse, and within an hour Charlie and Howard are here. They don't come to the house, but go first to the barn. Tom hurries out to meet them.

"He's got awful thin." Charlie says. "I'd say 'e's got the Black Water."

"The Black Water from not enough exercise," Howard adds.

"No, no. We exercised 'im," Tom says.

They untie Prince, and with Tom and Charlie pulling on the halter rope, lead him into the barnyard and over to the brook. The horse doesn't drink, but stands shivering. When they put him back into the stable, Tom scatters straw for bedding.

"Watch he don't get down on ya," Charlie says. "If he does ya'll have ta shoot 'im."

"If 'e's no better by mornin', I'm callin' the vet," Tom says.

"I can tell ya right now, she's the Black Water."

"Oh, yah, it'd be the Black Water," Howard agrees.

"Come way in an' see me shed a wood." Tom says.

We walk past the pigpen toward the house, and there are still blood stains on the grass where we killed the pig.

"Shootin' any pigs lately with the big gun?" Charlie asks, and both he and Howard laugh. "You can take a joke, can't ya, Tom?"

Tom ignores the joke but turns to Howard. "An' where'd in the name a God did ya get to Hall'eve night?"

"I got lost."

"Lost in sight a home?"

"In a Jesus bog hole."

"Why didn't ya falla yer back tracks, one's heels fo'rd behind ya?"

"I lost me light."

In the house, Charlie gives Katie a small bag of cranberries he has picked in the barrens. She makes tea and treats with a hot buttered corn cake. After they've eaten and drank tea and smoked, Charlie and Howard get up to go.

"Well, Tom, if'n ya need a hand with the ol' horse there, give us a holler. I'll shoot 'im fer ya if ya want. I know you Moars don't have much stomach fer that stuff."

"Thank ya, boys, but we'll manage."

After they've gone, Tom tries to get Jack McAfferty, the vet, on the telephone. He cranks one long ring for the central operator.

"Hello, Central."

"Hello, hello. Get me Jack McAfferty's, and all the rest of you shad-headed sons-a-whores, get off the line."

While Tom is talking to Jack, they have trouble with the noisy party line. But Jack agrees to come tomorrow to look at the horse.

"Ya'd think Jack was a doctor ta hear 'im talkin'," Tom says when he hangs up the receiver. "The big words he uses, oh, oh, oh, ya'd think he had more degrees than a thermometer."

Jack McAfferty is not a veterinarian. He's a farmer who prides himself in knowing horses. He does know many ailments and he knows a few remedies. He is also a good blacksmith and has made Prince's shoes. Tom seems more at ease, knowing he is coming.

In the evening, more men from the community come to the stable. They ask the same questions and make their own diagnosis — The Grinder, the Heaves, Black Water, Colic, Shoe Boil. Someone suggests it could be pneumonia.

It is late the following day when Jack McAfferty drives his pickup truck into the dooryard, scattering the hens. He walks to the barn, dressed in a long white coat and gloves. Danny and I stand in the rain listening as he looks at Prince.

"Goodness, Tom, he's all head and feet," Jack says. "Looks like he could be suffering from malnutrition."

"How's that?"

"He's lost a lot a weight. Is he eatin'?"

"No, he eats nothing."

Jack looks into Prince's eyes with a flashlight, then opens the jaws and looks at the back teeth.

"He's starvin', Tom. Look, his grinders are gone." Jack holds the old horse's mouth open.

"Good God, so they are."

"He's lost a lotta weight since I saw him last. He's likely dehydrated, too."

"How's that?"

"He's thin, wouldn't hold up a good set a harness."

"Oh yes, yes. He seemed ta weaken after harvest. I know yer right, He couldn't haul a sick whore off a piss-pot." Tom tries to cover any affection he has for Prince.

Jack turns and faces Tom, pushes the hat back on his head and as if everything said until now meant nothing, speaks dead serious.

"How old's the horse?"

"Every day a thirty."

"Well, Tom, ya best put 'im away. Put 'im out of 'is misery." Jack rolls down his sleeves and puts the flashlight in his black bag. I'd get Charlie ta do it."

"No, Christ, no! I'll do 'er meself. Brought 'im in ta the world an' I'll take 'im out, if it comes ta that. I'll do it tamarra. Come way in fer a cup a tea."

When Danny and I come into the house, Katie is in the kitchen crying. She rocks, humming to cover the sobbing and moving her silk handkerchief beneath her glasses. Jack finishes his tea and gets up to go.

"Well, Tom, let me know how it goes, if you decide to . . . ah, de-terminate."

"How's that?"

"Let me know if ya shoot 'im. Ga day ta ya both." He tips his hat at Katie. "But I'd get Charlie to do it."

"Well, sir, we'll see when morning comes."

"You're a reluctant man, Tom, a reluctant man," Jack says and is gone.

"Lord, be with us. What'll we do fer a horse an' it sa late in the fall," Katie filling the dishpan.

"I don't know. I was hopin' he'd last the winter."

"We'll get a new horse." Danny says. "A white one like Matt Dillon's. Prince was no good for a saddle."

"The hell with the saddle."

Tom paces to the window and then back to the stove, uneasy. "Charlie, good God, does he think I'd call him?" He seems annoyed at the vet, as if he had told him something he didn't already know or had faked the illness to annoy him. He looks out the window and talks. "Big feelin' lad, too, ain't he, the vet." He puts on his hat and jumper and goes back outside.

In the night, Danny comes into my bedroom wondering if Tom will buy a new horse, perhaps a colt that he could saddle train. I sleep restlessly and pray for Prince to be dead in the morning. I dream of Prince's death, wondering how we will manage without him. Certainly this will put an end to any chances we may have of getting a television. They are not dreams for sleeping sound, but rather for a night of thoughts from non-sleep. I have dreams of Prince, larger than life, hauling vegetables from the field and then hauling logs from back at the brook to the highway. Then there is a larger Prince still, hauling survivors from a train wreck, and another dream of him hauling the family in the sleigh on Christmas Eve, bells jingling on the harness. The horse gets bigger with the small hours of the night. He becomes a giant, carrying the farm, its whole existence, a giant with a human heart.

Across the hall, Tom and Katie are mumbling to each other, and Tom gets up several times to rub his chest with Sloan's Liniment. Its smell is strong through the house. Sometime in the night, I get dressed and go out into the dooryard and light a cigarette. I listen for Prince pawing in the barn, but there is silence, and I pray the old horse is dead. I go to bed, thinking it is over.

When I wake in the morning, it is still raining and foggy. Doors are slamming downstairs and there is the sound of a tractor on the top-hill. A moment passes and I realize what the day will bring. George Cooper and Tom come in the lane from the top-hill, George driving the tractor and Tom standing on its back hitch. I can see the mound of sand, red like an open cellar. It is beyond the pole fence near the woods.

When they come into the house, I do not ask the question but pretend it has already happened. I hurry breakfast and go to the barn and listen outside the stable door. There is silence. I open the door easy and peek in a narrow opening, and Prince is looking at me. He gives a deep chuckle and I close the door, both relieved and disappointed.

After George has gone, Tom comes out of the house cradling the thirty-thirty in the crook of his arm. He is wearing the long black raincoat and his hat is boxed to run off the rain, making him look like some kind of old plainsman.

"Why don't I go over and get Charlie to do it?" I say. "He wouldn't mind coming."

"No, Christ, no. I don't want that son-of-a-whore about the place. Not today. The man's got an axe ta grind here."

Tom unties the halter and leads the horse limping into the barnyard. Prince is shaggy black and no larger than an oversize pack mule. I think of the giant horse in my dreams. I think of Prince's place in our lives and how we've depended on a simple animal for so much of our livelihood. Now, his back is hollow and his ribs are visible, the teeth of a raker. Tom pulls on the rope and clucks his tongue to start him walking toward the top-hill.

This is a long walk, and I watch for Prince to drop on the way. But he seems to find new power as we go out the lane toward the top-hill which is the furthest field from the house. Tom has one hand on the halter and the other on the horse's mane. I am a few yards behind with the gun partially hidden under my coat. We slow to a crawl as we climb the hill near the railway and cross toward the fence bars. At times, Prince stops completely and Tom strokes the mane and pats his shoulder. This is a prearranged funeral, I think, with Prince-the-corpse walking with us, seeming to know where he is going and why, but wanting to go under his own strength.

As we pass through the open bars, Prince lifts his head as if to bolt. The old habit is remembered but the body doesn't respond. The bolt is little more than a gesture. As we near the mound, Tom talks to Prince and then he turns to me and says, "Whatta ya think?" He commences to cough, doubling over and letting go of the halter. Then he wipes his nose and eyes with his handkerchief. As I pass Tom the rifle, there is a strong smell of sickness around the horse. Sickness, and the new earth.

The day is warm for November, almost humid, and the fog that hangs over the river lodges in the shore grass and buckles the stems of wood breaks. Raindrops cling to fir needles and the tree trunks are greasy.

Tom is militant now, like a man with a mission. He looks at Prince not like an animal he has been working with for thirty years, but as a strange beast that stands in the way. He pushes his hat back and wipes his brow, and his hands tremble as he pushes the cartridges into the magazine and levers one into the firing chamber. I want to turn my head, hold my ears, and walk from the field, but I force myself to watch, as though I have to share this with Tom.

He puts the rifle to the horse's ear and the rifle barks short in the dampness, and there is no echo. The farm seems to shiver as the horse drops to his knees, blood spraying from his nose. The strong heart pumps hopelessly. Tom fires another shot and the old horse rolls into the hole, his feet in the air. Prince's shoes have been left on for good luck. There is a rank smell of blood and earth and I am vomiting on the grass. The pasture revolves around me and I clutch the grass and hold on.

Tom looks at me in bewilderment, like he has done some terrible thing. It is the first time I have seen this kind of uneasiness in his face. "It's all we could do! It's all we could do!" He walks away from the dying horse, mopping his brow, the rifle hanging under his arm. I follow along, and as we walk toward the house, Tom puts his hand on my shoulder. "Looks like the rain's about over," he says.

CHAPTER 28

My essay has been returned from the university with a note saying it has been written incoherently and lacks support from the text, especially in dealing with its light imagery. They have given me a C-, and suggest that I reread the book carefully and rewrite the essay. While I'm pleased to have the pass mark, I have now commenced to reread *Heart of Darkness*, and this time I'm making notes.

Since Prince died, Tom has had me take him to town to look for a horse, but so far he hasn't found one. I've had my eyes tested and am now wearing my new glasses whenever I read or write. I have also gotten some new clothes — a Harris Tweed sports jacket, gaberdine slacks and black penny loafers. Katie has knit me a turtleneck sweater of black yarn, and when I get dressed and put on my dark-rimmed glasses, Danny says I look like Buddy Holly. Tom thinks I am dressed well enough to be a preacher.

This morning, Tom has been up since half past five and has the fires going. In the front room, the furnacette is puffing like a small locomotive as it eats into the initial load of kindling, sending a glow blinking through the open damper onto the flowered linoleum. I add a block of maple and close the draft, silencing the stove and sending sparks creaking through upstairs pipes where I had warmed my clothes while dressing. On the kitchen range, the kettle simmers and there is a scent of beans burning as Tom scuffs about, preparing breakfast.

"I'll tend the barn," he says. "Keep an eye on the fires."

He puts one foot after the other upon a chair, drawing the laces tightly around his gum rubbers. Then he buttons his mackinaw, pulls the hem of a nylon stocking over his forehead and ears, and puts on his felt hat. Taking a flashlight from a cupboard drawer, he slaps it with his leather mitten until it blinks and stays lit. Then he goes out through the dark summer kitchen, its frozen floor cracking and snapping beneath his footsteps. As he crosses the dooryard, his bouncing light reveals the occasional frost flake descending through the chilly morning darkness.

I take the kettle from the stove and pour some water into the washstand. Then I use the dipper to add cold water from the pail until it is lukewarm, and wash my hands and face. I pour the rest of the hot water into the teapot, add a handful of bulk tea, and set it on the back of the stove. Then I go to the front room, remove Katie's knitting from the rocking chair, sit by the fire and have a smoke. Behind me the folding bed and the organ are like shadows in the dark parlour. The portraits in their oval frames stare fixedly — Tom's mother and father, Katie's mother and sister Edith, and the King and Queen taken in 1939. The only movement is in the clock on a shelf behind the stove, its gilded hand-painted scrolls framing a hinged door. Through the night, it banged on the half-hour like a restless spirit. Now, as dawn breaks, the pendulum swings contently behind the glass. But it rattles and begins to chime as Tom slams the doors as he comes in.

"That's a cold son-of-a-whore. Freeze the balls off a brass monkey." He sets down the feed bucket and scuffs his way in short jig-like steps toward the kitchen stove. "The river's fulla ice."

He huddles against the range, absorbing its radiant heat. Then he coughs and clears his throat, lifts a cover and spits into the fire, and wipes his face with his handkerchief. Then he pours tea into a mug, adds molasses for sweetener, and tests the hot brew with a slurrrp. His leather mittens are cupped around the mug, its handle outward. He tips the mug in his palms like someone drinking from a water bucket. "That tea'd float an axe." He mumbles setting down the mug to light his pipe. "Yes, sir, a cold son-of-a-whore."

I turn on the radio and while we are eating, Ernie Ford sings, "Sixteen Tons," and after that, fiddler Ward Allen plays the "Mary Ann's Reel." Then there is a weather forecast of light snow.

After breakfast Tom pours some Minard's White Liniment into a saucer and heats it on the stove. Then he rubs his throat and chest, working the hot liniment against his muscles beneath the underwear. He takes a piece of red flannel, heats it over the stove and pins it on the inside of his underwear against his chest. The smell is strong and sweet.

"Wouldn't a deer smell the liniment?"

"They'll smell me anyway unless I'm downwind," he says.

"Look, it's breaking day. I can see the barn."

"Yessir, we best be headin' back. Put lots on."

Tom helps me shoulder the packsack that contains the lunch, and then he picks up the '43 Mauser, works the bolt, and aims at the clock. For today, he has given me the thirty-thirty. With bullets rattling we slip out the front door into the frosty morning.

As we cross the top-hill, Tom whistles with each breath to cover his wheezing. Once we near the woods, even in this light, we can see the whole farm. The buildings around the dooryard are grey cubes against the frosted ground, and the smoke from our chimney streams straight up. "The sign of a storm." With the river bank leafless, we have a good view of the river with its moving, round plates of ice, the water high after the rain. At the edge of the woods is the frosted mound where we buried the horse.

But the woods are still dark and the rutted woods road is frozen into curving plates of brown ice, with the centre honeycombed and noisy. When we reach a small clearing, we take aim at a pine stub, holding our guns in firing position until the white beaded front sight finds itself into the V-rear.

"I can see the sights" Tom half-whispers. "Light 'nuff ta shoot."

"So I'll see you back there."

We separate. Tom goes to the north side of the brook and the better travelling, and I follow the frozen "gripping trails." As the daylight struggles to overtake the dawn there is a hollowness. As I near the brook, I come upon the ashes of last summer's lunch hole and remember Tom's superstition and the moose birds. But the brook is high, with the beaver pond froze over, and as I stop to have a smoke, the first snowflakes filter down, zigzagging among the trees and lodging upon the dead leaves and the roots. As it covers the frozen pond, it's like a giant goatskin tossed into the alders. There is a sudden dampness as snow clings to my coat. And using the rifle for a cane, I cross the brook on the dam and walk into the heavier woods.

Then, without making a sound, a small deer bobs onto the trail in front of me, stops and looks at me, its big ears spread like the open wings of a partridge. It stands, frozen as though to scorn me for trespassing.

I hold the sights steady on the animal's head, knowing a touch of the trigger will bring it down the way it dropped the pig and the horse. I hated the days that we killed those animals and I feel the sickness. The deer stares like the spirit of an ancestor that challenges me to keep with tradition. For Tom, killing a deer is a part of our livelihood, and while I cannot believe he enjoys killing, it seems necessary, like killing a pig or a dying horse. But now, for me, shooting a deer is for the pride it brings. I lower the gun and when I move my eyes from the animal, it vanishes in a cloud of snow. With the hammer at full-cock, I raise the gun and fire it twice in the direction the deer had run and I feel something between pride and disappointment.

A rattling cushion of dry leaves that only this morning would have made travelling noisy, has now dampened and my rubbers squeak in the new snow. I have a strong feeling of guilt for not shooting the deer and helping to support the family. I must not let Danny know what happened and I must not let Tom know how easy it would have been, and I know getting that deer would have made Tom's day complete. I push it out of my mind and I think of the boiling hole, with its bush tea, sandwiches and a cigarette lighted from a twig from the fire. I tuck the gun under my arm, and when I reach the spruce country I have already caught the scent of wood smoke.

Tom has built a fire beneath some low-limbed trees and is breaking sticks and feeding them into the fire beneath the boiling pail. "Ya made 'er, did ya." He says without looking up.

"Made 'er."

"A stepmother's breath, ain't she?"

"Yes, quite a storm."

"Good trackin' anyway."

"Yes, it is."

"Here, have a swig." He passes me a full pint of brandy. "It'll heat ya up. See any?"

"Yes, I saw one."

"Ya did!"

"Yes, a good-size deer."

"Was that you shootin'?"

"Yes, two shots."

"Was he runnin'?"

"Standing and then running."

"Did ya get 'im?"

"No, I missed."

"Ya missed?"

"Never touched it."

"Missed with that gun?"

"Yes, but it was running when I shot."

"Still, in that open woods, ya shoulda had 'im."

"Maybe it's my glasses. I don't know."

"Well, well, well, don't that beat all. I didn't think there was a deer in the country." Tom stands with his back to the fire, and the smoke seems to follow him. He rubs his eyes.

"Ya missed em, well, well, well."

"It was a long shot, too."

"I never missed anything with that gun in me life, but ya have ta know how ta shoot it. She's true as a hair."

"I don't blame the gun."

"If ya don't know how ta shoot, the best gun in the world is no good. Ya might as well be carryin' a barrel stave."

"I'm not a good shot and I don't want to learn."

"Why's that now?"

"I don't like guns all that much anyway."

"Ya used ta like 'em."

"I know."

"Well, well, an' me fighting sally bushes up to me arse, trying ta see one, an' you missing a deer down in that open woods. I'd like ta get me eye on the form of a deer, I'd wreck 'is wagon."

"Would you enjoy that, killing it?"

"No, no. Now, I don't enjoy killing. Not like Charlie, but the meat'd be nice. I see what yer coming at, do ya think I'd enjoy killing something?"

"I can't see how you would."

"No, no, I just want the meat."

"But Katie said not to bring home a deer, she wouldn't cook it."

"I know what she said. She's been sayin' that fer years. But ya can't listen to what a woman says. It's how they say it. That's the first thing ya should learn about handlin' women. She'll cook 'er all right if I take it home. Christ, I was brought up on deer meat an' moose meat. Durin' The Depression . . ."

"Let's not get into that again."

"Into what?"

"Hard times, The Depression, living off the land. That was twenty years ago."

"There's nothing wrong with it taday, either."

"Did you enjoy shooting the horse that day?"

"Not likely."

"I didn't enjoy shooting the pig. I hate killing anything."

"That's likely why ya missed yer deer this mornin'."

"I don't know about that."

"Ya did fire at 'im, didn't ya?"

"Oh, yes, I fired."

"Yes, I did hear the shots alright."

"They were just after the big white tail."

"Oh, never mind, it's no odds. Here, have another horn."

He passes me the flask and lights his pipe. He walks around the fire making gestures with the pipe in his hand. He drinks some more brandy and stumbles over the roots, almost knocking over the boiling pail. For a short time we are silent, with only the sounds of the fire, the tea simmering, and the snow filtering through the trees.

"*Winter kept us warm, covering*
Earth in forgetful snow"

"Whatta say, what's that now?"

"Just lines out of an old poem I read."

Then Tom speaks. "Well, sir, one fall I come back here on a day like this. Oh, it was an awful day, snowin' and rainin'. Down there be the upper landin', where the horseshoe is on the tree, I saw this here big shaggy ol' son-of-a-whore of a buck standin' there lookin' at me. That was before I got that rifle. I took aim with the Mauser an' I could hardly see 'im fer snow. When I fired, he went rollin' over the hill inta the brook."

"You got it."

"No, wait till I tell ya now, wait till I tell ya. He got up an' waded the brook an' 'e headed inta that big cedar swamp. Well, sir, I crossed the brook on a tree an' fallered 'im in, an' there was spots a blood here an' there. An' inta the swamp, an' I could hear 'im breathin' ahead a me an' I knew I musta hit 'im in the brisket. So I took a circle, an' Christ, sure a 'nuff there 'e was lookin' over a brush pile with that big hayrack a horns. I dropped 'im between the eyes, an' 'e never kicked."

"Was the meat any good?"

"No, couldn't eat et. Strong? Oh oh, tough as an ol' shoe. Later on that same fall I shot meself a dry doe, fat as a pig, an' tender?"

"You got two deer in one fall?"

"That was a great year fer deer, everyone in the country got one er two. Charlie shot four."

"How long do you want to hunt today?"

"Oh, I don't care a damn, I'd stay on till dark if I felt better." He takes another drink of brandy and I can see that he is feeling the affects of the alcohol. "We'll wander way out after a bit"

"Okay, I have an essay I should be working on."

"An' you have an essay ya should be workin' on."

He stands now with his back to the fire, rubbing his hands together behind his back. He looks off into the valley of the brook.

"Country's all gone ta hell, ya know that, Stevie? She's all gone ta hell."

"I know."

He picks up a burning twig and sucks its flame into his pipe, and the smoke is sweet like the ointment. He keeps his jaws clamped on the pipe, blowing the smoke through his nostrils. Then he takes a fit of coughing and doubles over to spit in the snow. I slap him on the back and he nods his approval.

"Oh, dear God. I'm in bad shape," he mumbles, then is silent. He tosses his tea into the fire and puts the mug in the packsack, and as he staggers about from the affects of the brandy, his face is long and pale. His new mackinaw, now steaming, hangs from his hunched back, his hat with the red handkerchief twisted around its band is dappled with spruce needles.

"Kick 'er out, Stevie. Let's get the hell outta this goddamn moose yard. It's not a fit day fer a dog ta be out anyway, an' ya have an essay ta write."

"We can hunt for awhile longer if you want to."

"Naa, it's no use. I'm gettin' too old fer this stuff anyway."

"Maybe we'll see something on the way out."

"Naa, odds againt it. Bobcats got 'em all. Bobcats an' poachers. The goddamn government don't look after anything. Me eyes are gettin' bad, too."

About four inches of snow have fallen and the greyness of the afternoon is fading as we walk along the road's centre for better travelling. There are clusters of fine top emerging through the snow, and the dead breaks are buckled and weighted down. Tom falls behind in places to look at the new growth and I stop to wait for him. When we approach landmarks, Straw Hill, the broken popple, and the bear den, he stops and tells a story, talking loud now like we are walking in the fields or around the barn. These are the same stories he has told me so many times I know them by heart. But I listen and ask him the "what year was that" or the "who was with you," and he forgets their endings and has to start again from their beginning. Sometimes he confuses one with the other and tells me fragments of two separate stories. Sometimes he mumbles bits of an ol' hobo song.

CHAPTER 29

It snowed almost a foot, but since then the days have been sunny with no wind, and snow has slid from the steel roof of the barn, making crusted mounds along under the eaves so we have to shovel to get the doors open. As if it were spring, the ground is baring under the trees and along the lee side of buildings. By now, the fields have been tracked by Danny and his friends as they play fox and geese, and there is a network of hand sled runner tracks on the dooryard. Near the millshed, they have built a snowman; there are strips of bare ground angled toward it, from where they rolled the grass-tangled loaves of snow. According to Tom, early snow is the sign of a long, open fall, and there will be plenty of bare ground before winter sets in. "It's the wrong kind a snow ta stay long," he says. "We'll have nice weather yet — Indian Summer."

Tom's health is worse and he coughs all the time. Sometimes he coughs until he is sick to his stomach. I have come upon him in the barn or the shed, stooped with his hands on his knees, coughing. I slap him between the shoulder blades and he nods approval, gagging and spitting into the chaff or sand. He has also suffered attacks of chest pain and he seldom lights his pipe. Katie thinks he has the Hong Kong flu and that others in the community are laid up just like him. "That east wind," she says, "is a lot to blame."

Tom thinks he can shake it and refuses to go to the doctor or have one come to the house. He spends most of his time in the parlour on the folding bed with a bucket beside him. With the wheezing in his chest, we can hear him breathing throughout the house. "It's pleurisy. I had it before. Don't fuss."

Katie gives him remedies that have always worked. She rubs his chest and back with the Sloan's Liniment and the Minard's White Liniment and puts the heated flannel on his chest. She also gives him regular spoonfuls of Paregoric. Her sister, Aunt Edith, has come from Fredericton to visit, and because of Tom's illness, has stayed a few days. We have not seen Edith for a long time. She looks like a cartoon of Katie; taller, older and with the same features exaggerated. She is very strict with us, a school teacher herself for thirty years.

With Tom laid up and a car payment due, I've been taking the bucksaw and axe and going back of the top-hill to what Tom calls "the var thicket" to cut pulp. Every day, I cut and carry a half-cord to the edge of the field, coming out at lunchtime to feed the animals. Danny helps on Saturdays. One day, Howard came and we cut almost a cord. Howard says sawing wood is how Rocky Marciano developed his strong arms. When Danny's with me he uses the saw.

Today, when I come from the woods for lunch, Tom is alert and craving chicken soup. I take the sleeper axe and a block from the woodshed, and while Katie and Aunt Edith are boiling the water in the outside kitchen, I go to the henhouse. The hens are loose, so I sprinkle a dish of oats on the floor, and when they flock together to eat, I pick a solid red pullet and carry it clucking to the yard. And holding its twisting neck across the block, drop the axe to sever its head. It flaps its wings against my leg and I hold its clammy feet as it twists for freedom, blood sprinkling over the snow. When it has been scalded and picked of its feathers, Katie and Edith clean it and put it on the stove to cook.

Tom hasn't eaten in two days, but when Katie carries the soup and vegetables to the parlour for him, he pushes the meal away, saying the smell sickens his stomach. He also complains about the firmness of the folding bed, so Danny and I help him up the stairs and into the hall bed. This bed is soft and the room is warmer, from the stovepipe going through from the furnacette. Until he sees a doctor, there is little more we can do to comfort him.

"Tom, I'll call the doctor to come," Aunt Edith says with a concerned look.

"No! I don't want no goddamn doctor, not tanight. I'm all right, I tell ya. I've been through worse. What does a doctor know?"

"The doctor would know what to do. What to give you for the pain."

"When I cut me foot with the axe up in the right away that summer, he gave me an enemy," Tom says. "An' when I crushed me thumb in the boxcar door, he just bandaged it over, broken bones an' all."

"Still, he's a doctor, he must know something."

"Yah, the son-of-a-whore'd put me in the 'ospital, that's all he'd do. Ta starve among strangers, no goddamn way. I'm stayin' in me own house. A man wants ta be home when 'e's sick, not in town among strangers, an' if ya don't like that ya can head 'er back fer Fredericton."

"Okay, okay," Edith says. "It's whatever ya think yourself."

"Steve! Where are ya?" Tom calls. "Come 'ere."

I go into the room.

"Stoke that son-of-a-whore of a stove down there, will ya? I'm cold. Throw a rug over the stove."

I go down and put a block in the furnacette, but already the house is hot and it is not a cold day.

Aunt Edith goes into the room to take Tom's temperature. "Here, Tom," she says, shaking down the thermometer. "Put this under your tongue."

"Sure thing."

After a few minutes, she pulls it out and holds it near the light. "Oh, my God! He's burnin' up."

"See that?" Tom says. "I'm gonna break that Jesus glass when I get me hands on it. Jesus, it's warm in this house, whatta ya burnin', Steve, axe handles?"

Katie has me go to the outside kitchen and get two salt gaspereau from the barrel. Then she takes some rags and wraps them around the bottoms of Tom's feet. "That'll draw out the fever," she says. "I'm going to pray for poor Tom tonight."

When Tom is sleeping, he raves on about the war, the railroad, and the farm. Sometimes he's chopping logs, shouting at the horses. "Feed that cow!" he says to me as I walk past his bed. "I can't do it anymore." Then he wakes and sits up, his eyes grey and glassy, the eyes of a sick man.

"Steve! Come 'ere. Come 'ere an' lissen ta me."

"I'm right here. I'm listening."

"Now, when I'm better, you an' me'll cut some logs, back of the brook. We'll make a landing. I saw this chance t'other day when we was huntin'."

"Okay, when you're better, we'll make a landing," I say.

"Steve, kick up the fire. This stairs is cold as a sheep yard."

"Yes, sir. I'll put another block in."

In the evening I go to the barn to feed the cows and hens and there is a stiff wind blowing and the hydro lines are humming mournfully. There is a dog barking across the river, and with the hollowness, it answers its own echo. When I finish, I go into the house and listen to the radio. In the weather forecast there is a storm warning: rain with high winds! A hurricane.

Katie and Aunt Edith are working in the kitchen. They have heard the storm warnings and they are cleaning the lamps and filling them with oil in case the power goes in the night. Katie appears uneasy, and she drops a lamp globe and it breaks and has to be swept up.

Before bedtime, I take the flashlight and go to the barn to check the doors to make sure they are buttoned. As I urinate in the snow, even though I am in the lee of the buildings, the wind is already such that I have to brace myself and back into it so as not to wet my trousers. When I come in, Katie and Edith are sitting at the kitchen table.

"Stevie, dear, ya best bring in plenty a wood." Katie says. "There's a hurricane coming an' we may get snow instead a rain."

"The radio spoke of rain and winds, that's all."

"Oh, how I worry about fires on a windy night. What would we ever do if the house caught fire, and Tom sick in bed."

"Try not to worry about it."

"Oh, God, spare us," she prays. "Bless us and save us."

"I'll bring in more wood. Don't worry. If anything happens, we have the car — we'll go to Cooper's."

We sit up late and try to keep the conversation away from Tom's illness and the storm. We talk about essay writing and books, and Edith reads the essay I've had returned and she gives me advice on how to improve it in the rewrite. But she and Katie eventually go to bed together in the spare bedroom across the hall from Tom. Danny, who has been reading lesson three of his taxidermy course, and seems oblivious to the seriousness of the situation, takes his book and goes to the lower room to sleep. Unable to sleep, I sit by Tom's bed and read, but I am unable to comprehend the works of Conrad so I read old western comic books.

Later in the night, I hear it raining and the wind rattles the windows. Everyone seems to be asleep, and Tom is wheezing and breathing in short puffs. When I put my hand on his forehead, it is burning with fever. He opens his eyes when he feels my hand but closes them again. Then there is a gust of wind and I can hear glass breaking downstairs. The lights go out. When I go down, the kitchen door has blown open, so I close it and put a knife through the casing. Then I light the lamp, put a stick in the stove and close the damper, and then carry the lighted lamp up to Tom's room.

The room smells of sickness, liniments, the oil lamp, and an unemptied chamber pot under the bed. I set the lamp on the bureau and turn it up so I can read. Tom is still lying on his back taking congested puffs of breath, his chest moving up and down. His face is pale and his jaws are sunken and his stubbled week-old beard is white, his white hair falls upon the pillow. His big square hands lay upon the covers, pale and claw-like. I wipe beads of sweat off his forehead with a damp cloth. When he opens his eyes this time, they are glassy; I am a complete stranger, and the room is strange to him.

"It's me," I say. "Steve."

"Who?"

"Steve."

"Whatta ya doing? What time is it? Oh! It's you, Steve." His mouth is dry, his lips sunken. "I thought ya was someone else. I musta been dreamin'."

"Are you feeling any better?"

"Oh, I s'pose. No, not much. Oh, some better." He coughs. "God bless ya, Steve, yer a great boy."

"Is your chest paining?"

"Oh, yes. I don't know, it's all through me this time. So weak. Weak as a sick dog. I'll not be long fer this world. Too much pain, can't breathe!"

"You'll have to see the doctor. Get a needle, a shot of penicillin."

"I guess yer right. We'll go in the mornin', you an' me. See what the ol' lad says."

"I could call him to come tonight!"

"No, no. I don't want 'im up here tanight."

"Okay," I say. "We'll go first thing in the morning, first thing."

"Is the power gone off?" he looks at the lamp.

"Yes, it's raining out."

Tom props himself up on his elbows, tosses away some of the covers and rolls to face me like he is going to get out of bed. There is a serious strain in his eyes, like a starving man begging for a meal. "Steve! Now you listen to what I'm saying, an' listen good. Do ya hear me?"

"I'm listening."

"When I'm dead an' gone, sell this place."

"Sell the farm?"

"Yes, sell 'er!"

"Why's that now?"

"Sell 'er, I tell ya. Sell 'er all ta Eagles. He's got the bundle an' he wants ta buy 'er."

"But where would we live?"

"Take Katie an' the boy an' go. Go ta Fredericton. There's nothin' fer ya here but hard work an' hard times."

"But we need this farm. We're farm people. We just can't walk away from a way of life, our roots."

"Sell 'er, I tell ya. I been thinkin' 'bout it. There's nothin' fer ya here, Steve. Not here there ain't. Get yer learnin' like ya always wanted. Be a scholar. Take the money an' go!"

"You could live for years yet. You'll be all right when you see the doctor."

"No, no, I'm not long fer this world. I'm prayin'."

"You were right about the farm. I'm a born and bred farmer. I'm no scholar. I'm a discontented farmer. A man has to be himself and work hard, that's all. I can't sell my stories, and the essays are poorly written."

"No odds, sell this son-of-a-whore of an ol' place, I tell ya!"

"I don't know if I could part with it."

"Sure ya could. I shoulda done it meself years ago when I met Katie, but I didn't have the education ta do anything, only hobo around."

"It would be taking an awful chance."

"Chance it, get a little place in the city fer you lads an' Katie. Go ta college. Forget all this ol' stuff I been tellin ya. This is no place fer a man ta better 'imself."

"Katie wouldn't leave this place."

"Sure she would. She'd move in a minute; she never liked it here. She stayed fer my sake an' yours." Tom lays back on the bed and motions for a drink of water. "Katie's at home in the city. Should a moved there with 'er years ago an' forgot this goddamn ol' place."

"You liked the farm, it was in your blood."

"Aah, bullshit. A man ken shake that if he wants ta. Katie shook the city fer me. She could play the piana as pretty as an angel when I met 'er. An' when she moved here, she never had one ta play. I could never afford ta get 'er someone 'ere ta fix the ol' organ even. Buyin' machinery, fixin' sheds. Couldn't afford a piana, imagine that?"

"Katie seems happy here."

"Naa, she's not happy, never was, I don't think. Now promise me ya'll do it. Sell 'er ta Eagles, he wants the fishin'. Now let's you an' me shake on this."

He passes me his big hand, damp with sweat. He holds onto my hand and keeps talking. "I'll be okay. Don't ya worry none."

"You'll be okay when you see the doctor in the morning."

"I'll be okay, Stevie."

"You better get some rest."

When Tom lays back upon the pillow, he groans from the pain, and I can see the ribs in his chest and his arms have gotten small. He looks like Lazarus from the Bible. I hold his hand like we are going to arm wrestle. He sits up again, holding my hand tightly, swaying the arms first his way and then mine.

"Now give me a hug 'fore ya go ta bed. I need a hug!"

I'm embarrassed by this and cannot bring myself to hug him. He has never given me a hug, his closest sign of affection a pat on the back or a tap on the arm, followed by the words "God bless ya, Steve, yer a great boy."

Katie and Aunt Edith overhear us and come into the room. "Is the power off?" Katie asks. "Oh, good Lord, it's an awful night, surely to the Lord. How are ya feelin', Tom?"

"I'm alright. Don't fuss."

They rub his chest with liniment and give him a spoonful of the Paregoric and Edith takes his temperature. Tom is asleep by the time she takes the thermometer from his mouth. Rolling it near the lamp, she whispers, "It's high — he's burning up." But they go into the spare room and I can hear them praying for Tom.

I sit by the lamp trying to read, and I have trouble trying to comprehend even the comic book story. At times he seems to sleep peacefully, but then there are the restless periods when he breathes hard, twists and turns and talks. And it's like he is a child again. "Oh, Father, don't do this to me . . . I can't lift anymore . . . Mother, tell him I can't, he'll lissen if you tell him . . . Yes, Father, I'll feed the oxen . . . I'm really a good boy, Father . . . Don't beat me if I can't lift it . . ." He recites. "Oh, why should the spirits of mortals be proud. Like a high flying cloud or a bird on the wing," then he seems to be in our own time frame. "Steve, feed that cow, you're a good boy ta work, strong as an ox . . . I'll feed the cow, I say."

Then he is quiet and seems to be resting peacefully. I put my feet on the bed, cover myself with a blanket and try to sleep. I listen to the wind and the rain rattling off the windows, and the creaking of the stove pipes, and I think about Tom's words "Sell 'er all." I wonder what measure of happiness he has found here. I wonder why he has changed his philosophy so suddenly, or had he always thought that way down deep. I think about him asking me to hug him and I wonder why he had never done that before. Would it have been considered a sign of weakness? Was he in his right mind now? Maybe he never asked for the same reason I couldn't hug him, embarrassment. I wanted to hug him, but couldn't. I wished he had asked me one more time. Was it loneliness or just a weakened old mind? I wonder about his relationship with Katie. Was he still in love with the girl on the next farm, himself? "A man can live anywhere if he has the right woman with him," he had said. A hundred questions go through my mind as I try to sleep, and all the time Tom is wheezing and coughing beside me. He swears when he starts to cough, like he's being attacked by some strange spirit that breaks his rest. It's a restless night for all of us.

In the morning, I am downstairs at daybreak to get the fires going and to get ready to take Tom to the doctor. He is sleeping, but I can hear him breathing from the kitchen. When the house is warm, Katie and Aunt Edith come down.

"Poor Tom had a restless night," Edith says.

"I only wish he would eat something to build up his strength," Katie says.

"I'm taking him to the doctor," I say. " He told me in the night that he would go this morning."

"Oh, thank God. My prayers are answered. He's decided to go then," Katie says. "He'd do it for you, Steve. Thank the Lord."

"That's an awful dose on his chest. I hope it's not consumption." Edith says. "The doctor will likely put him in the hospital."

"Oh, I hope not. That's an awful place," Katie says.

When it is daylight, we look out the window at the storm damage. There is no snow and the brown dooryard has ponds of water, ruffled now by the wind. The apple tree has broken, and its stump is splintered into a spear, the tree pitched forward, its trunk up in the air. There is paper, clothing and shattered glass scattered, the windows having blown out of the summer kitchen. In the field, there are sheets of tin from the roof of the barn, and there are several dead hens in the barnyard. The door blowing off the henhouse spooked the hens out into the night. When I look back of the top-hill to the woods, much of it lies flat, lodged like a field of oats.

For breakfast we have beans, bread and molasses, and tea with molasses. Katie and Edith prepare for me to take Tom to the doctor, laying out his new fleece-lined underwear, the new mackinaw and hat. I get dressed and bring the car around to the front door. It has stopped raining and the morning is mild.

When I go up to the room to dress Tom, there is dead silence in the room. Tom is lying peacefully, staring at the ceiling, his hands folded upon the covers. He is not wheezing, coughing, or mumbling, and when I feel his forehead, it is cool and clammy. I put my ear to his chest and there is no heartbeat, no rattling inside. Suddenly I feel hollow and empty and everything inside me is turning over and I have a throbbing headache because I realize that Tom is dead.

Aunt Edith comes up the stairs just as I am going down to tell them. "I think Tom is dead!" I say. "He hasn't moved!"

"Oh, my goodness! No! He can't be! We were just talking."

"There's no life in him, he's dead!"

Edith goes into Tom's room and is back out in a few seconds. "Oh, my God, what'll we do! Poor Tom's passed away."

She goes downstairs and tells Katie and I can hear them crying in the kitchen. When I come down, Katie and Edith are standing by the range, weeping. Danny stands looking out at the field, wiping his eyes and nose. Katie gives me a hug and I hug Danny. It's the hug I never gave Tom.

"Poor Tom is out of his misery," Katie says. "At his rest."

"He's in the next world," Edith says. "That's all we can hope for. God willing, we'll see him there."

"Listen! Listen, please! I think I hear Tom breathing!" Katie says. "Steve, go up and check him. I think he's still alive!"

When I go up to Tom's room, Edith comes with me. Katie and Danny are too nervous to go up where the dead man is. I listen at Tom's chest again, but there is silence. I close his eyes and Edith ties a necktie around his head and under his chin to keep his mouth closed.

"Tom's getting cold now, Father's getting cold."

"Poor Tom was a reluctant man," Edith says.

Edith phones George Cooper, who comes right over. Then she phones the doctor and Mr. Brooks, the minister. They also arrive within an hour, and the doctor signs the death certificate. "It was a combination of pneumonia and heart trouble, by the sounds of it."

Mr. Brooks has prayers in the kitchen, then he helps me feed the cattle and the hens. He stays most of the day talking to Katie and Edith. He talks to Danny about hunting and fishing and taxidermy work, and he talks to me about essays and short stories and the university degrees he has earned.

Later in the morning Katie and I go to town to make funeral arrangements. I go from the undertakers to the lumber company's office, and pick up an advance on the pulpwood to help pay for the funeral. Then I take Katie to a ladies wear shop and she buys a new dress. On the way home, I circle the block and drive past the Elm Inn. It was just something I felt like doing. Even now, in spite of my home problems, I have an urge to be with Amanda, and for an instant when I see her house, a warmth comes over, but this is immediately followed by hollowness.

In the afternoon, the undertakers arrive in their long black '57 Chev. They don't take the remains to town, instead they lay out Tom in the bedroom where he died. When they've finished, Mr. Brooks and I give them a hand to carry the coffin downstairs and into the parlour. While we're doing this, Katie and Aunt Edith stay in the dining room. Edith is reading passages from the Bible. The undertakers place some flowers around the room and light the pink bowl lamp, and that same smell is in the room as when Henry Cains was waked. When they open the cover, Tom is lying in the pleated satin, resting peacefully. His skin looks like plastic, with a shirt and new tie, and his grey hair combed neatly. I have never seen Tom look this distinguished. It's a good-looking remains, but it's not Tom. They hang a plastic wreath by the front door and leave.

The funeral was a large one, with people coming from around the river to fill the church. The weather held fine, as Tom had predicted. After the service, we stand by the grave as the grey casket is lowered into the ground. The November day with its thin sunshine fades to ashes and then dust as the young minister reads the old words and makes a cross on the cover. Katie and Aunt Edith cry, and Danny and I are dry eyed. I think of the words Tom used to say when he gave me one of his tests of manhood. "Can ya handle 'er?" In a way, I suppose, this is another test; the last one given me by Tom. When the minister finishes reading, he shakes hands with the family. When he shakes my hand, he says the same words Tom had said so many times. "God bless you, Steve."

CHAPTER 30

The mornings have been bitter cold. The drifting chunks of ice have frozen into a solid plate, making the river a field of craters separated by the zigzagging windrows of white shale. The bare fields have also frozen, and the trees on the horizon are a mixture of greys and blacks, the faded sky making the scattered pine appear as sentinels in a fog. The wind is raw and penetrating, and there is no warmth from the sun. It's the old bonfire season.

When I was Danny's age, on Saturdays I would build bonfires at the highest point on the top-hill, and send signals to Howard across the river. He would answer with a fire of his own. It was an outdoor game that broke the dullness. And the fires kept us warm as we dragged Christmas trees from the woods to our respective fields and stacked them to sell. Howard still does it.

Katie, Aunt Edith and Danny have gone to town in Sam Eagles' car to do the business with the lawyers. Mr. Eagles has bargained for the farm and it could probably be in his name by now, but it won't be his in my mind until after we are gone. Sam has agreed to stay with us for a few days to help us sell the machinery and personal things. When we get to Fredericton, we will be moving in with Aunt Edith until we can find a place. I will be enrolling at the university, my old dream and Tom's dying wish.

Since the funeral, Katie has gone through the closets and sorted out Tom's clothes. She has put them in flour sacks, for me to bring to the garden to burn.

I empty the sacks onto the frozen ground and sprinkle them with kerosene. The fire burns freely for awhile, then it smoulders. I use a pitchfork to lift and turn the remnants of wool underwear, still scented from the liniments. With each piece of clothing emerges a partially sunken memory, like I'm burning old experiences. As the clothes burn, big flakes of ash drift into the breeze, settling down in the adjacent fields.

Before I finish, Cindy comes up the hill, and when she sees me, comes to the garden. She is dressed in a black pea jacket and a red scarf, with her blonde hair tucked under a stocking leg cap. Her nose and cheeks are red from the cold but she looks lovely. She's made the first crossing of the season. Now she stands with her hands in her pockets, kicking tiny particles into the fire.

"Wanna cigarette?" she asks.

"Yes, please."

"So, whenna ya leaving?"

"In a few days. Katie wants to go before winter sets in."

"Will ya come back sometime?"

"We'll be back once in awhile. Mr. Eagles says we can use the place whenever we want to."

"It's not gonna be the same without ya around, ya know that?"

"It won't be the same for me, either."

"So, why are ya goin' then?"

"It's a dream I've had. Maybe I'm making a mistake. I don't know."

"How can ya base real life on a dream like that?"

"I know it's a risk. But Tom said I should chance it. He thought it was best for me."

"You're strange, do ya know that?"

"I know."

"But I still love you."

"I know."

"An' I really hate ta see ya go."

"You can come to visit."

"It'd be no use. Even when we lived close, I couldn't reach ya. You have your ideas, I have mine."

"Still, we can be friends."

"Friends."

"You're very beautiful and very lovely, don't lower your standards."

"Well, good luck with yer schoolin' an' don't settle fer anything less than yer dream. Keep the spirit."

"That's about all I'll have when I leave here."

I walk with Cindy to the shore, and as we pass the millshed I pull her against me and kiss her on the cheek. "You're moochin' again," she says. At the edge of the ice surface, she gives me a brief hug and turns quickly to follow the slanted bushes across. She does not turn around again, and when she gets across, she runs up the hill.

When I come back, the meat man has arrived to buy the cattle. He has a three-ton Chev truck with sideboards backed against the hill so we can lead the cows and calves onto the back. When this is done, he pays me and is gone, the barn empty. I am glad that this could be done while Katie is away.

Then I go into the house and put some wood in the stove. The house is in a vacuum now with pockets of electricity waiting to be ignited by a single glance. The old radio hunches in the front room, and suddenly we are crowded around it, listening to the fights. When I go into the dining room, it is full of thrashing crews, woodcutters, and the minister with all the politeness and good manners he brought with him. In the parlour, the old portraits stare as if to scorn me for not staying. And there is a greater vacuum still that pulls me upstairs, and Tom is there in the bed, thin and haggard, telling me to "Sell 'er all an' get ta hell outta this goddamn ol' place." The words echo in the empty stairs, and I wonder if Tom was of sound mind when he said them.

But everything here is from the past, memories and not dreams. "A farm is no good without the right people," Tom used to say. " A man can live anywhere with the right loved ones." The strongest memories are of the people: Tom, Katie, Danny, and even Amanda Reid or Cindy were part of it, and even they are magnified already by the passing of time.

I bundle up and go to the top-hill and then to the woods. I have brought Tom's rifle to justify my being here. I walk past the mound where we buried the horse, and I feel a vanishing part of us, a bonded struggle to cling to a passing way of life. When a moose bird flits across the field and becomes a grey speck in the alders, I think of Tom and our many days in the woods. "Old woodsmen's spirits" he called them. Maybe this one is Tom.

But the farm seems naked, the life gone from its buildings and fields. It's like a replica of the old place, without a spirit or a sun. The buildings across the river are also weak and sagging, stripped to the season's bareness.

It is late afternoon when Sam Eagles drives his loaded station wagon into the dooryard. When Katie gets out she is clutching a new bank book, the first one she has ever owned. Immediately Mr. Eagles goes to the phone and calls someone in Maine, informing them of the sale. Then we start going through things, setting up tables and benches, extending long planks around the yard to display things on. The machinery is left in the sheds. Mr. Eagles has told us the Americans will buy it all.

In the evening, Howard and Nick come over to help, and we carry the grindstone from behind the binder shed and set it in the dooryard. Then we carry hoes, diggers, rakes, churns and other items from the woodshed. Danny's Union Calvary saddle is brought out of the horsestable and hung on the fence bars.

"Ol' Tom'd roll over in 'is grave if 'e knew ya was sellin' all 'is stuff," Howard says.

"Yes, I suppose he would," I say.

"Oh, ah, when are ya leaving, Steve? I mean, when are ya leaving us, anyway?" Howard asks in a serious tone.

"I don't know. It's up to Katie."

"But will ya be back? I mean, will ya be comin' back, though?"

"Sure, we'll be back, Howard."

After all the cupboards and closets have been cleaned out and their contents placed upon the tables in the yard, the furniture is tagged with pieces of tape and priced. In the morning, we make a fire in the summer kitchen and prepare to use it as an office. The linoleum-covered table and long plank bench serve as desk and chair. By midday, word of the sale has gotten around and people of the community and beyond gather in the yard and house to pick up things.

For the next two days, I sit in the outside kitchen with the money box as Sam Eagles brings people to pay for things. Most items go for small sums of money.

One Indian Summer

The woodcutter and engine are purchased by a neighbour for fifty dollars. The mowing machine, raker and truck wagon go for small sums, much of which is to be paid for later, the neighbour not having the ready cash. The binder and the Moody thrasher go on the truck to Maine dealers. Many of the neighbours pick up small items for keepsakes. The old radio is purchased by Howard (who doesn't have the money either) for ten dollars. Old photographs and dishes go for bits of change.

Through all this, Katie walks about the yard chatting with neighbours, her long grey winter coat open, her black dress visible. She shows no signs of loneliness. When she comes to the old handmade patch quilt folded on a table with a tag of ten dollars pinned to it, she picks it up and carries it across the yard and puts in the trunk of the car, which is already loaded. I have put the canoe racks on the car's roof so we can tie our luggage to them.

By the afternoon of the second day, the weather has become very cold and people are huddling in the yard, their winter coats and scarves wrapped tightly. The men collect the last piece of chain or harness from the tables, but the Union Calvary saddle stays so Danny gives it to Nick. By early evening everyone is gone except Sam Eagles and the antique dealers from Maine who will be leaving first thing in the morning.

As we load the last of our things and prepare to leave, the car is setting so low on its rear wheels, it looks like the springs are broken. As Danny and I take our last look around the yard, Katie and Aunt Edith are already in the front seat, the car now facing the highway. They are talking constantly, about trivial things which seem to cover their feelings.

I feel shallow-rooted already, as though I'm going to float away with the penetrating wind that stings my eyes now, making them blur. It would be so much easier to turn and let the teeth of the wind hold us so we don't go anywhere, I think. And the farm seems to cling, as nothing but good is remembered, the way time and its magic does to a thing. But a power comes over me, one stronger than emotions. It's like the voice that spoke inside me on the night of the fight at David Cain's dance, the voice I couldn't control.

Danny gets into the car and sits in the back, surrounding himself with cardboard boxes. He does not seem to understand the gravity of this trip. Maybe he understands it better. All along, I had thought he wouldn't be dragged from the farm by wild horses. But now, he jokes about leaving to become a city slicker, until I start the car and drive onto the highway. Then we are all quiet. Katie and Aunt Edith never glance back and Danny hunches low, reading a *Kid Colt Outlaw* comic book. As the dust boils up in a cloud behind the car, I glance into the rearview mirror and I can still see the farm growing smaller as we distance ourselves from it. It huddles behind us, a jumble of grey buildings bonded around a windswept dooryard, left to return to the wilderness.